EVIL
AT ITS
EASE

"the horror of finding evil seated,
all at its ease, where she had
only dreamed of good."

Henry James, The Golden Bowl

JAMES E. COYLE

Outskirts Press, Inc.
Denver, Colorado

Outskirts Press, Inc.
http://www.outskirtspress.com

ISBN: 978-1-4327-4767-1

Outskirts Press and the "OP" logo are trademarks belonging to Outskirts Press, Inc.

PRINTED IN THE UNITED STATES OF AMERICA

INTRODUCTION
WRITING MY FIRST DETECTIVE NOVEL

Jim Coyle, the author of *Evil at Its Ease*, sent comments about writing his first novel in several letters to his long time friend, Don Knies in 1986. This introduction is in the author's own words, as excerpted from those comments.

I started with a lot of nervousness and hesitation not knowing whether I could handle dialogue or description but I've surprised myself and feel at ease with both. My main fear was that I would just plug in and ride the verbal factor. So I've been very careful. I spent almost two years reading over 150 detective novels and plotting my own. At first I had no idea how to do it. 200 to 250 printed pages is the standard and that means 270 to 340 typed double-spaced pages. So I was very careful with my plot. I made sure I knew where I was going and had enough detail.

Most important is putting in the time. For my college papers I just zipped through them and handed them in. It's very satisfying now to work and re-work something. Coming up with an image then polishing it is very exciting. What's really fantastic is creating your own characters and settings and then trying to give them life. Although it's not great literature, you do get to express some of your own vision of the world and feel part of a creative process. It also makes me wonder how a truly complex and great novel ever gets written.

My production speed is accelerating now that I'm gaining skill and confidence. Three to nine double spaced pages is a good day's work. And working with a word processor makes a tremendous difference. At first I wasn't sure I could work this way since I wrote all my papers longhand. But I've truly been astounded at how helpful it is. Everything is neat and clear from the start. Then revision and adding and deleting are not so laborious. Getting published, of course is a long shot. But I'm going to keep at it. My detective is named Walker and will continue into the next book.

My title is "Evil at Its Ease" and is from a quote from The Golden Bowl (my favorite novel): "the horror of finding evil seated, all at its ease, where she had only dreamed of good."

These are the Muses I invoked:

Clio to set my story in its proper place in the flow of time.

Thalia for the light touch and to amuse the reader.

Melpomene for the darker, tragic side of my story.

Erato so that love could also find its place.

Kaliope chief among Muses, so that she would grant the successful completion of my work.

NOTE TO THE READER

We—Jim's wife, Jeannie Coyle, and friends, John Bacialli, Don Knies and Bob Shea—decided to publish his novel in the spring of 2009. Jim's death in November of 2008 left us devastated. We had always felt his detective novels were stunningly original and it gave us great pleasure to read them. It seemed fitting to publish them as a tribute to his memory and also to give us a project to walk in his life again.

We thought the years together would last forever; not remembering we are perishable, impermanent domains. In company with the other, we were more than we are now. Are we diminished? Yes!...No! We remain bolstered by memories and by the words in this novel.

ONE

I had been warned he was dangerous.

At 9:20 a.m. I finally saw him. Terry Rose. Age, about forty. The Paul Bunyan of the Bay Area. A real monster. Hulk Hogan would think twice before shaking hands with him.

He came out of his apartment building and crossed the courtyard wearing a blue pinstripe suit coat without a shirt. Bare-chested, blue jeans and cowboy boots. Corn silk blond hair, neatly combed. Pale skin, with no trace of a tan, drawn tight over a hammered steel face.

He reached the curb just across from me and stopped. The occasional cars going by only blocked my view of him from the waist down. He was about six feet ten inches tall, an even seven feet with the boots, and weighed about two hundred and ninety pounds. Goliath incarnate. Kept looking down the hill on Sacramento, waiting for something.

I had a very good view of him across the sixty feet between us. I put on sunglasses and spread open the Chronicle so he wouldn't notice me watching.

On closer inspection I realized his blue pinstripe suit coat was actually a soft leather jacket, dyed blue, with thin white stitching forming the vertical lines. It was obviously custom made and meant, considering the bare chest, as a parody of a business suit. Very expensive. His brown leather cowboy boots also looked handmade. Mexican in design. Mucho pesos.

A gold amulet completed his fashion accessories. Fastened tightly at the base of that incredibly thick neck, a crudely shaped peace symbol. Craftsman's art. Power to the people. A tender memory of his Hippie days, no doubt. Displaying the world's need for love. It looked solid and must have weighed a pound. About five thousand dollars for the taking. If anybody cared to try.

His neatly combed blond hair also wasn't quite what it first seemed. On the left side, halfway back, just behind the ear, a single braid. Hanging like a thin knotted rope on the layer of smooth corn silk hair.

He was a pure phenomenon of nature. Not a weight lifter's body, where everything's been pumped and squeezed into shape, but an unadulterated child of nature. Thick bones and muscles, hands so big I thought he was wearing two baseball gloves. Shoulders twice the width of an ordinary man and a collar bone beneath them so thick, it spread across his torso like the wooden yoke on an ox. Maybe he was part ox. But I wouldn't want to suggest it to him. Maybe nature got confused and thought it was growing a tree instead of a man.

The only visible physical quirks, besides his huge size, were his mouth and eyes. On that hardened face nature put a mouth, delicate and sensitive, almost feminine. The lips of a poet, like on Byron or Shelley in one of those fanciful nineteenth century romantic paintings. Out of tune with the rest of him. Somehow disturbing in their delicacy, set in the middle of so much rugged masculine grandeur.

And his eyes. Pale. I couldn't quite make out their color. But even at this distance something vaguely reptilian about them.

Reptilian in their unblinking watchfulness. But also like a big cat. Watching everything. Watching nothing in particular. Confident that he was the only danger in his surroundings.

All in all I was sure we had a lot in common and would soon be fast friends. Getting along fabulously. Sharing our interests in literature. And history. Reading Beowulf together and discussing the legacy of the Yalta Conference.

Then I saw what he was waiting for. A cherry red 1955 Thunderbird convertible, top already down, pulled up. It looked like it must have when it was first driven out of the showroom thirty years ago. Flawless. Red upholstery, spotless whitewalls and gleaming chrome. Its sleek lines accentuated on the front side by nine slanted chrome gills preceding a small V with the number 8 set snugly inside its notch and, near the tail end, the word Thunderbird. Its frisky red finish, recently waxed and polished, glowed in the soft morning light, clearly reflecting the outline of my old black Mercedes and the Fairmont Hotel.

A garage attendant in white coveralls hopped out. He approached Terry in a casual manner, all smiles, and began talking in a rapid staccato voice which I couldn't quite make out. Leading Terry around the car, pointing out the fine points of his recent handiwork.

Terry followed him with a satisfied look of pleasure, his delicate lips forming a partial smile. His movements were both precise and graceful in a way you seldom see in really huge men. The simple relaxed economy of effort visible in hulking animals. Nature's special provision for her large predators. Like the giant bear that looks clumsy and cumbersome until you see it coming at you. Surprised, maybe too late, that anything that size could move so swiftly and effortlessly.

Another surprise was Terry's easy manner with the attendant. A minute before he had waited statue-like, impervious to his surroundings. Now he was loose and attentive, even friendly.

Now he reminded me of a big cat. A lion. Proud, regal and aloof. Also curious and maybe even playful like a kitten. Made me want to get out a ball of yarn and roll it over to him. But, as any trainer will tell you, a big cat is always dangerous. If I were to be his lion tamer I'd better keep the chair and whip handy.

When the inspection tour was finished Terry removed his wallet and handed the attendant several bills which produced a big smile and several more staccato phrases. Then he turned and trotted off down Sacramento leaving Terry with the car.

Now came the part I was waiting for. How to fit almost seven feet and three hundred pounds of driver into a three feet high sports car. But then maybe he wouldn't even drive it. Just pick it up, put it under his arm, and walk off with it.

But, like that final piece of the puzzle that never looks like it will fit that one last open space, the puzzle was solved. He walked around to the driver's side and slid in. A perfect snug fit. At least from the waist down. The shoulders were another problem. His left shoulder and arm extended outside the car and his head protruded above the top level of the windshield. He would never fit with the top up. It must be his fair weather car. He sat there for a minute and several passers-by eyed him circumspectly. Then he started up, turned right, and went down the hill on Mason.

My job was to tail him. Client and case as yet unknown. A personal favor to my sister, who had phoned and asked that I follow one, Terry Rose, who might lead me to one, Michael Sherwin. Long time friends and supposed business partners whose whereabouts and behavior were a mystery for the last eighteen years.

Until Terry Rose was seen by my unmet client in Monterey two days ago, like a past nightmare come back to haunt her. He was searching for his old friend, Michael, who had recently disappeared. Again.

My sister stressed that it was important to her that I help this woman. A woman well worth helping, she assured me, not without a trace of female conspiracy, as I would discover when I met her. Descriptions of Terry and Michael had been passed along with the warning to be careful, that Terry Rose was dangerous. Today I was to take potluck. Tomorrow I would meet my client in Monterey.

The fog had already burned off and it was a beautiful San Francisco morning. I followed at a safe distance as he headed downhill towards the Bay, his huge bulk filling the small car. A muscular Pillsbury Dough Boy overflowing his red muffin pan.

Apparently he had reverted to his indifferent mode, and I had no trouble tailing him. Traffic was light and the red convertible stood out from blocks away.

Like the large predator he was he took no notice of his surroundings. Not until he felt some instinctual urge would he come alert. Hunger, or its human equivalent, greed, would do it. Or if he sensed an intruder entering his territory. But this morning he was all at his ease. He wasn't suspicious or looking for a tail, and he kept his head and concentration straight ahead. He drew all the attention as pedestrians and other drivers stared at him in his shiny red T-Bird.

I followed him down Mason, around a cable car jammed with tourists at Jackson, and then across Union to the slopes of Telegraph Hill. Near the top of the hill he turned left onto Montgomery which dead ends about six hundred feet further on, just below Coit Tower.

I hesitated for a second before making the turn. There was no traffic at this time of the morning and I didn't want Terry to spot me hovering about in the middle of the street with nowhere to hide. Then I remembered there were two restaurants at the end of the street, so I took a chance and made the turn.

Here, on its dead end stretch, Montgomery is divided into an upper and a lower level. The northbound side we were on is the lower. It goes to the end where there's a restaurant and a turn-around, then comes back southbound on a higher level about fifteen feet above the other roadway. A concrete retaining wall and a row of trees separates the two levels except at each end.

Terry was parked, about a block short of the street's end, at a small apartment building. He had honked his horn once and was watching the front door of the building as I drove past.

At the dead end I pulled into a parking slot in front of Julius' Castle, a restaurant with a great Bay view that wasn't open yet. Off in the distance I could see the Tiburon ferry coming in past Angel Island.

After making sure Terry couldn't see me I carefully backed out and slowly started up the higher level. Just above Terry's car I stopped in front of the Shadows restaurant, also not yet open, and got out, careful not to slam the car door.

I peered cautiously over the edge or the retaining wall and saw Terry, ten feet below, still stuffed into his little car, drumming his fingers on the opposite seat back.

Between the building he was waiting at and the next one to the left was an open space about forty feet across, filled with bushes and trees. Here was the top of the Filbert Steps that climbed up the steep gardened hillside, past wooden houses and quaint walkways, from the Embarcadero below. Through and over a palm tree I could see part of the Oakland Bay Bridge, some of the Bay and Mt. Diablo towering over the East Bay hills in the distance.

Terry hit his horn again and its sharp blare made me jump. He kept watching the apartment building's front door impatiently.

The building looked familiar. It was off white, four stories, in Moderne style and had two relief murals carved in its sides. Also a large frosted glass mural over its entrance.

It was the building used in the movie Dark Passage. Where Bogart hid out in Lauren Bacall's apartment.

The door opened and out came a tall black woman. Slender and well over six feet tall in her high heels, she was a perfect match for Terry. In her late twenties she was both beautiful and exotic. An African queen with creamy milk chocolate colored skin. High cheekbones on an elongated oval face set with large dark eyes, eye-shadowed blue, and full rich lips, painted pink. She had shoulder length straightened hair with a single braid on her left side that matched Terry's.

Beauty and the beast. Or rather two beauties. Like Terry she also wore a navy blue pinstriped suit coat over her bare chest, buttoned discreetly enough to reveal only part of what lie beneath. Her tailored suit coat, however, was cloth and went with her matching slacks. She carried no purse and had a large butter yellow scarf, loosely tied at her throat and draped down her back, that completed her outfit. They made quite a pair.

She walked quickly over to Terry and got into the car just filling the small remaining space. A heavier woman wouldn't have made it.

She reached over and began stroking Terry's chest with her

long graceful fingers. Terry didn't move or say anything. Just watched. She leaned over and kissed him. Long and slow. Then pulled back and smiled confidently.

Finally Terry moved. He reached across and pulled her door shut. "Clementine. One of these days you're going to keep me waiting too long."

She almost cackled. "Can't ever wait too long for a fine woman, Sugar. Don't you know that?"

I got back to my car just as I heard the engine start. By the time they made the turnaround and passed me I was slunk down in my seat out of sight.

I almost lost them. There's only one way off the east side of Telegraph hill and it involves a maze of dead end streets. A little luck, a flash of red and that long yellow scarf kept them in view until they reached flat ground and turned off Vallejo onto the Embarcadero.

The Embarcadero is a wide commercial thoroughfare that skirts what's left of the town's working piers. I followed them south under the Bay Bridge down to a couple of navy ships. There were three of them, tied up alongside two piers, all very large, and unrecognizable. Some kind of modern support ships probably. No guns or other obvious functions visible. The new electronic navy.

Terry pulled across the oncoming lanes of traffic and parked against a chain link fence in front of the piers. I found an inconspicuous spot across the road and watched.

It was just after ten and there was light pedestrian traffic, mainly a few dozen swabbies in clean white middies milling around the pier entrance. Terry stayed in the car and Clementine got out.

She passed in front of the car and continued along the chain link fence about thirty yards toward a group of six sailors standing near the gate. One of them was holding a large shopping bag and they seemed to be waiting for her.

The catcalls began as soon as the other random sailors spotted her. About thirty of them quickly formed a line pressed against the other side of the fence. The fastest minds in the navy strained themselves in making suggestions and offering her encouragement.

She didn't disappoint them. Her walk was pure theater and she gave a great performance. She had the kind of body and composure that transformed a simple walk into a strut. Inviting their inspection, denying their access. Hips swaying, arms swinging, eyes straight ahead, smiling wide, tossing her yellow scarf back over her shoulder, she strutted her stuff.

I could hear the hoots and whistles over the sounds of the passing traffic. Terry sat immobile through it all.

When she reached the group near the gate they formed a small circle around her and she disappeared from view.

The sailors hanging on the fence went quiet and were as fascinated and engrossed as I was. It seemed as if we were all watching an outdoor magic show in bright sunlight. I half expected her to disappear. After a minute or two the circle opened revealing Clementine once more.

She was laughing, holding a yellow teddy bear, two feet high, under her left arm and examining a large yellow lace parasol. She opened the parasol, twirled it over her shoulder, and did a little cakewalk, all the while laughing and joking with the six sailors.

At her display a cheer went up from the men on the other side of the fence.

Then suddenly everyone went quiet and seemed almost to

come to attention. From the changed attitude I thought the admiral had arrived. Then I saw him. Terry had left the car and was on the prowl. Like all spectators at a magic show we had been caught off guard. Watching the magician's assistant, we had forgotten the magician.

Where Clementine had strutted with awareness of her own special gifts, Terry stalked with a tiger's fierce sense of his own power. Thick heavy packs of bunched muscle alternately stretched and contracted propelling his huge mass forward. Effortlessly. With long fluid strides he followed Clementine's path along the fence, taking no notice of the men standing there. As he passed, each sailor instinctively let go the fence and stood back.

When he reached the group of six sailors they did not form around him but backed off a little. Submissively. Only Clementine was relaxed, continuing her little prance, spinning her yellow lace parasol.

Terry spoke to one of the sailors, moving in closer, and I thought he dropped something into the open shopping bag. A few more exchanges and Terry turned facing the line of sailors along the fence. He looked calm and impassive. Like a lion selecting his prey from the herd. We seemed transported to the savannahs of Africa, the row of men like African impalas. Absolutely still. Prepared to bolt if they sensed danger.

Still impassive, Terry raised his huge left arm, extended comically out from his side, crooked down at the elbow. A grin spread across his broad face. Clementine gamboled up, handed the teddy bear to Terry and passed her right arm through his left. Then they began a promenade back to the car. Clementine twirling her parasol, Terry holding the teddy bear up for inspection in his bear-like right hand. Both grinning and saluting the line along the fence.

Another cheer went up as the sailors rushed against the fence once more, applauding the performance.

Their behavior left me wondering. Wondering if the yellow scarf that so carefully matched the yellow parasol and the yellow teddy bear were a color code. A signal. Wondering if the little yellow bear had a heart of gold or a heart filled with something else.

I continued my Cook's tour of San Francisco with my amiable guides, Terry and Clementine. Our next stop was out in the Mission District. They pulled up in front of a Mexican bar on Twenty-second Street just off Valencia. I watched from a safe distance down the street. Their performance this time was much less spectacular. Probably because there was no audience.

Again Terry waited in the T-Bird. Clementine went into the bar and came out a few minutes later carrying a brown paper bag spotted with grease. It looked like an order of tamales and tacos to go. But she put it carefully in the trunk of the car.

Well, that's one way to keep your fingers from getting greasy. Maybe they were part of the city's social welfare program. The Welcome-Wagon. Greeting lonely sailors new to our town. Or Meals-On-Wheels. Taking hot lunches to senior citizens.

Our next call was more promising. The Fillmore. What's left of San Francisco's small black enclave right in the center of town. Many of the urban black poor have been gentrified out of the Fillmore in recent years. Forced to seek cheaper housing out by Candlestick Park or over in Oakland as their old neighborhood is re-fashioned by an invasion of Yuppies. But there's still some of the old street life left.

Terry turned off Fillmore onto Haight and parked. I waited around the corner but kept a clear view.

A liquor store, a bar and a check cashing service all in a row. Also a good assortment of derelicts, hangers-on, hangers-around and general all-purpose street hustlers. Also the unfortunate unemployed. I felt sure such an appreciative audience would bring out the best in my new friends.

Terry was parked at the very corner, about twenty yards from the bar. Clementine hopped out and swished and swayed her sexy way past a ragged line of admirers. Their need to keep a wary eye fixed on Terry seemed to break their concentration and allowed Clementine to make it safely into the bar.

This time she was strictly business. No side remarks or teasing like with the sailors. Maybe the sight of so many of her own disadvantaged brethren reflected unpleasantly on her own well-groomed luxury. Maybe her social conscience was touched. Maybe those really were tamales and tacos in the trunk of the car. Maybe the Giants would win the pennant this year.

She was gone about five minutes. Terry remained impassive. I figured he'd have to move soon. His car fit so tight on him it must have interfered with his circulation. Several of the dozen men holding up the wall of the building exchanged drinks from a paper bag, always keeping one eye on the bright red T-Bird and its overgrown occupant.

The door of the bar opened again and Clementine came lunging out, struggling to maintain her balance atop her high heels. Apparently everything had not gone well inside.

After righting herself she smoothed the hang of her stylish suit coat, tossed her butter yellow scarf over her right shoulder and walked disdainfully past her admirers back to the car. An erotic milk chocolate candy dream that would never be real to the coveting eyes that ogled her passing.

Terry didn't move when she got in. His eyes were open but his vision was fixed straight ahead like an angel on Judgment Day. Clementine leaned her left arm across his oversized shoulders and whispered a few words. They resembled two cooing love birds. Then Terry got out. As he rounded the back of the car and headed for the bar I could see he was smiling.

The Haight Street regulars parted like the Red Sea to let him pass. Once he was inside the bar they re-formed along the wall and a buzz of excitement and several brown bags passed down the line. A few grouped around the bar's window trying to see the show.

A minute after Terry entered, a handful of customers came scurrying out. They formed a second expectant group along the curb. A few stray pedestrians also gathered, wondering what was attracting so much attention. They didn't have long to wait.

Even across the street I could hear the sounds of shattering glass and splintering wood. Then three more men came flying out the door. One after another. Their trajectories interrupted by the side of a battered pickup truck. Each seemed to land in one piece and they were definitely not customers. Big, rough looking men. If they had been bodyguards, they were going to need outplacement counseling and new job training therapy.

Then we all heard it. That sharp and yet resonant sound that only a large caliber handgun makes. Along the wall backs straightened and eyeballs rotated and clicked. Like a parade of old military men.

The men in front of the window made a hasty retreat to the curb as the bar doors banged open. Out came Terry Rose.

He was still smiling and he was also carrying something. In his left hand he carried a thick barreled revolver. In his right he carried a one hundred and eighty pound man. He had the man's leather jacket bunched up in his giant fist and held him, entirely off the ground, not quite at arm's length. The dangling man didn't even break Terry's stride as he headed toward Clementine.

By now everyone was gawking. Traffic was stopped in the middle of the street, including a bus. I had to get out of my car so I could follow the action along with the rest of the day's sports fans.

Terry brought the man over for Clementine's inspection, like a cat dangling a mouse. Fortunately, this mouse seemed pretty much alive, although his right arm hung at that awkward angle that only broken bones can make. Otherwise he seemed all right. Limply dangling, too terrified to even kick his feet. Terrified of Terry, now that his gun had been taken away. If he had taken a more careful look at Terry he never would have tried to fire it, but would have waited for the tranquilizer gun.

When Clementine had smiled her approval of Terry's catch of the day, Terry took the man over to the corner. He lifted the lid from a trash container and stuffed the dangling man inside, rear end first. He then broke open the cylinder of the revolver and dropped the bullets in after him. On his way over to his car he gave the gun to a bleary-eyed drunk. Then he got in and they drove off. I followed, leaving the street-side crowd to sort out what had happened.

I followed them past our starting place on Nob Hill and down California through the financial district. I had been warned, through my sister, that he was dangerous. Now I had the proof. It seemed he was an equal opportunity employer, but, whatever his business, it wouldn't be listed with The Better Business Bureau. Possibly loan-sharking or gambling, but more likely drugs.

Whatever the source, today seemed to be collection day.

They were a well-suited pair, Terry and Clementine. Nothing subtle about them. They seemed to like standing out, performing. The bigger the audience the better the performance.

It took a lot of nerve to do what they just did, if that teddy bear and that food-to-go contained what I thought it did. A lot of nerve or a lot of crazy to risk being caught while they went through their routine, while they played to their audience. Assuming their activities were illegal. Then again, who would suspect such public exhibitions. Part cunning and part crazy. A dangerous combination.

Their destination was Sydney Walton Square, just off the financial district, on Jackson and Front. After parking I followed them down Front on foot and into the block of greenery, through the ivy covered Tony Bennett arch which commemorates the importance to the city of his song, "I Left My Heart In San Francisco." The arch also commemorates that there's as much hayseed in this sophisticated town as in Omaha or Des Moines.

I trailed behind through the noon crowd, which found unexpected entertainment watching Terry and Clementine stroll across the square. Under the trees and past the numerous small grassy mounds that looked like an undulating green sea, afloat with shipwrecked office workers. Past the business district's speedy bike messengers, staking their claim to their usual hillocks, relaxing and smoking their noontime joints. Through the aroma of barbecued baby-back ribs wafting over from the MacArthur Park restaurant.

They sat down on a stone bench alongside the base of the stairs leading up to a walkway crossing over Jackson.

In summer San Francisco is frequently fog-bound, and, on a

sunny afternoon, the office workers scurry out of their warrens like salamanders seeking a warm rock. Today the steps of the stairway served as their warm rocks.

I picked my way up the steps through a dozen office lizards to the first open platform and found a vacant spot along the metal rail. I was about eight feet above Terry and Clementine, inconspicuous in the lunch time crowd.

They had barely sat down when a man in a three piece business suit walked up to them. His clothes might have been Brooks Brothers but that desired look was wasted on him. His wrinkled white shirt billowed sloppily between his pants and vest and a smear of black ink stained his left cuff. The back flap of his collar was crooked and his shoes were scuffed at their tips. Cigarette ashes clung to the front of his coat and his pants needed pressing. He was about forty, and nervously stubbed out a recently lit cigarette as he approached.

He stopped in front of them and remained standing. "Terry, Clementine. I like your suit Clem. Got good taste. It's just like mine."

He laughed appreciatively at his own social dexterity. A wounded laugh. Less laugh than a creepy, embarrassing sound of saliva and air sucked through his teeth. A noise so excruciatingly awkward he insisted on making it several more times.

He was the kind of sad little creep you felt pity for at first. Trying so hard to be sure of himself, trying to be a real grownup man. But, after five minutes with him, the pity would turn to disgust and hostility. Terry and Clementine seemed to have already passed their five minute mark. They ignored his comment and just stared at him.

This made him, if possible, even more awkward. He reached

for his shirt pocket and withdrew a pack of True cigarettes. He was obviously a man who thought for himself and sought that brand name identification that best expressed his inner essence. And True cigarettes were his inner essence from the desperate way he fumbled getting at the pack. After a few seconds he stood there sucking on his cigarette, his yellow stained fingers color coordinated with his yellow stained teeth.

True, a low tar smoke. Yes sir, nobody was going to get him hooked on one of those cancer causing high tar brands. He sucked the smoke down deeply into his lungs, seeking its promised relief. After a few deep drags he seemed to find it. His charisma level rose from repulsive to merely disgusting.

I could hear every word clearly. I was fifth in a row along the railing. The others were eating their lunches and enjoying the sun, oblivious to the conversation just beneath us. Terry and Clementine had their backs to me so I wasn't worried about them. And the other guy in the suit, facing in my direction, was too nervous to notice anything. He needed all his will power to keep his saliva from rolling down his chin. It was certain that their conversation would not be very revealing in such a public place but maybe I'd learn something about Michael Sherwin, the man I was supposed to find.

Finally, Terry spoke.

"Listen, Herbie. I don't plan to sit here all afternoon."

Herbie quivered apprehensively. He tossed his cigarette and fumbled lighting another, having managed to smoke one down in only five or six drags. His yellow fingers were shaking as he puffed on the new one.

Terry stretched out his long heavily muscled legs and waited. I imagined he was smiling.

"Don't you have something for me, Herbie boy?" he said, dragging out the sound of his last two words.

"Uuuhh. Not yet."

He glanced anxiously at Terry. Herbie boy seemed to be nearing a state of panic. His right hand reached reflexively for his left shirt pocket and its pack of cigarettes, unaware that it already held one.

He pulled his hand back too late. "Goddammit!" he yelled. Ashes tumbled down his shirt front from the lit cigarette and caught under his coat. "Shit! Chrissakes!" He did a little dance as he opened his coat and brushed the ashes away. A few sun worshippers looked up for a minute and then quickly turned back to their own business. He found a small hole burned in his vest, tried to rub it away, and finally re-buttoned his coat.

A voice so quiet and controlled that at first I didn't realize it was Terry's said, "are you trying to fuck with me?"

Herbie boy stopped as if paralyzed. Not a trace of movement. Not even breathing. Even the sweat along his hairline seemed to freeze. He stared as if he had just heard his own death sentence. He dropped his cigarette and started forward a step, his palms up, almost pleading.

At this gesture Terry pulled back his legs and sat upright. Herbie halted after one step, reconsidered and lit another cigarette.

"Hey! Hey, Terry. You know me. You know I'd never do that." He looked at Clementine, appealing for support. "Clem. You tell him. You tell him I'd never do that." His voice had a desperate hysterical edge to it. "I'll have it for you tonight. I'll get it for you tonight. Tonight, okay? Okay?"

Terry leaned back and stretched out his legs again and Herbie boy let out an audible sigh of relief. The sound of spit and air sucking through his teeth signaled the return of his social charms.

He was eager to move on to other topics. "Have you found Michael yet?" he asked. When Terry didn't answer he said, "I bet he's back up at the ranch by now."

Terry ignored his remark and said, "you just make sure you've got something for me tonight."

Then he and Clementine stood up and walked away, back toward their car. A hundred pairs of eyes followed their progress out of the park. Two of those most concerned belonged to the man in the crumpled three piece suit. Herbie boy. I don't think he took a breath until they were completely out of sight.

Since he knew about Michael and had mentioned a ranch where he might be, I figured I could get more out of Herbie than Terry. So I let the big fellow go. The one that got away. At least for now.

I turned my attention to my new friend and guide who was sitting dejectedly on the bench, smoking another cigarette. Whither he goes I go. After a few minutes he headed out of the park, west along Jackson, and I followed.

TWO

He led me straight to a porno arcade on Broadway near Kearny. Midway between Finocchio's female impersonators and the Condor, the club Carol Doda made famous with three thousand dollars worth of implanted silicone. The sign over the door he entered read: Talk To A Naked Woman For A Dollar.

I wondered if the high pressures of business had brought him here. Or maybe it was his recent meeting with Terry Rose. The humiliation he had felt. The need now to reassure himself that he was still a man. His way to be a man, with a naked woman, for a dollar a minute. A little noonday pick-me-up before heading back to the office.

The first room was painted a garish iridescent red and sold pornographic magazines and video tapes. Just a few customers, no sight of Herbie.

I went down a darkened narrow hallway with cracked plasterboard walls into a large open room. Two red bulbs provided the only illumination and cast an eerie glow over the place. Along the far wall were a half dozen cubicles, each with its own door. Three of the doors were open and three were closed. The room had an unpleasant musty smell of bad air and disinfectant.

A muffled shuffle of feet caught my attention. In the far darkened corner sat an old Chinese man. He must have been close to eighty, sitting on a wooden bench, indifferent to his sordid surroundings. At his feet was a large bucket filled with dirty water, a mop and a gallon jug of Lysol. Also a tray covered with dirty rags and sponges. He had the unenviable chore of cleaning out the cubicles after each patron left. He sat there motionless, seemingly unseeing, and as resolved to his task as Hermes at the entrance to Hades.

I crossed over to the three closed doors. I felt like a contestant on "Let's Make A Deal" about to guess behind which door was the prize. I gave the Chinese gentleman another look but he was no Monty Hall.

Behind door number one I could hear a rough gravelly voice that sounded like a drill sergeant barking orders to a new recruit.

Behind door number two was a prolonged whine that either meant sexual ecstasy or he was strangling a parrot. Maybe both. I quickly decided not to try door number two.

That left door number three. Did it conceal the prize of my dreams or would Monty Hall suddenly appear and lure me away with a large offer of cash?

The faint vibration of the cheap plywood door panel and the odor of cigarette smoke provided my answer. No wonder he came here, I thought. It allowed him to smoke during the physical act of love. No annoying partner complaining about falling ashes. Two simultaneous acts. More physical and mental agility than I had given him credit for.

My humor was turning sour and a nauseous sensation was creeping through my gut. I decided to leave him in his sad little world until he was finished.

I went through door number four and partially closed it, waiting for his exit. Inside was a cheap metal folding chair and a small counter. On the counter was an old black phone beside a slot. Above the slot was a sign: Insert money here, one dollar for one minute. On the other side of the counter was a large metal sheet.

Since Herbie was taking his time, I thought I'd find out what the attraction was. I inserted a dollar bill in the slot and the metal sheet lifted into the ceiling. Magic. Open sesame.

On the other side of a thick Plexiglas window was a young woman. She sat in her matching cubicle on a shabby vinyl love seat, under a glaring floodlight. Completely naked as advertised.

She was about twenty-five, pretty, with large, somewhat sloppy, breasts. A high thick tangled growth of black pubic hair stood out unreal under the harsh light. She had an unhealthy look about her as if she never got out in the sun. Except for too much make-up the only coloring in her face was a red puffiness around her nose. Her nostrils seemed permanently flared and were flanked by thin broken blood vessels. A cokehead by any other name would look the same. Maybe that accounted for that bored other-world look in her eyes. Or was it just the wonderful job she had?

The darkened booth and the bright light kept her from seeing her customer and I'm sure she preferred it that way.

I picked up the phone, careful not to get it too near my face, and said, "is this the San Francisco Public Library?"

She seemed to have heard that one before. She replied with a trace of irritation. "What do you want?" And when I didn't answer right away she followed impatiently with, "it's your money. You have to tell me what you want. What do you want me to do?"

"Could you get me a season's pass to the 49'ers games?" A look of confusion finally animated her bored expression just as the metal sheet descended. My minute was up.

It was just as well. I heard door number three open and saw Herbie leave the room trailing smoke behind him. As I followed him out the old Chinese man got up and started for the cubicle with his mop and bucket.

Herbie led me down Montgomery into the financial district. Past the massive bulk of the dark Bank of America building, known to some as the Darth Vader tower. After a few more blocks he entered another tall but less imposing structure, just north of Market, which served as local headquarters for another large California bank.

I stood right behind him on the elevator as he pushed the button for the twentieth floor.

I was glad now that I had not interrupted him during his little peepshow. I wanted information from him about Michael Sherwin and he would be more vulnerable to pressure here, surrounded by his fellow workers.

After observing what little character he seemed to have, I figured a little bullying combined with fear of exposure ought to do the trick. I would have to get him to betray Terry and maybe even himself. Which seemed possible, especially if he smelled a chance for safe and easy revenge and a secure and undetected method of escape. I would need a good con, something to impress a scared little weasel, and I thought I knew just what it would be.

At the twentieth floor the doors opened onto a large unobstructed area with about twenty desks or work stations, each with its own computer terminal. The lunch hour was over and everyone was busy typing away at their keyboards. Or, considering the new age of technology, not typing but entering data. At least the keyboards replaced the noise of twenty clacking typewriters with a faint clicking.

It was a busy place and nobody paid any attention to me. I stood near the elevator door for a second, studying the lay of the land, watching Herbie wind his way through the maze of desks. Hard as it was to believe, he seemed to be the boss in this little corner of the corporate world.

He stopped several times, passing out orders and asking questions in a loud intimidating manner I could hear across the room. He kept calling one woman "dear" with the patronizing air that the weak man mistakes for true concern. Minimal power seemed to corrupt his minimal personality absolutely.

He was the kind of boss who, in private, refers to his female workers as broads and sends his secretary out for cigarettes and coffee, confusing the women who work for him with both the woman who sits naked behind a Plexiglas shield and his own mother.

Otherwise, he was probably quite good at his job, despite the arrogant and condescending manners. He had put all his energy into his business image but was not up to the rest of life. A crippled form just beneath the corporate facade. The real down side of the man in the gray flannel suit. The kind of man who needed a suit and tie to keep his back straight. Well, it was going to be fun giving him back some of his own patronizing manner.

When he passed out of the maze of open work stations I started after him. Next came an area of junior executives, or middle-level managers as they're now called. About five of them, each with their own semi-private office, still out in the middle of the floor, but with six feet high glass partitions providing at least partial privacy.

He stopped only once here. I could see him sitting on the edge of a woman's desk, imitating that casual look he had seen on some television show but couldn't bring off. He was really turning on the old charm for her. Sucking spit and air through his teeth at a rapid rate, all the while approximating a grin and smoking his cigarette at the same time. If nothing else, he exhibited extraordinary hand to mouth coordination.

The woman was attractive, and pushed back as far from her desk and him as she could get in her small office. The faint outlines of a grimace marked her lovely face. Obviously, she had had practice in this kind of encounter before, but she still couldn't remove all the stress lines from her face. He probably mistook her pained expression of revulsion for a come-hither look.

She was literally saved by the bell when her phone rang. He slipped off the desk like a man with no bones and continued on with his busy work day. I'll bet he was the only person in the building who could sit down while he was standing up.

Along the outer wall of the floor were several enclosed offices. He passed his secretary, offering her a few words, and entered the corner, and largest, office. Probably told her he had just finished another power lunch and to hold all calls.

I walked over and read the title on his door: Herbert Trimbler, Group Manager, International Banking Division.

At least his secretary was alert. She noticed me right away and asked if she could help.

She was a young woman, about twenty-two, and rather pretty. I felt sympathy for her immediately.

"Would you tell Mr. Trimbler that Terry would like to see Herbie boy?"

"Pardon me?" she said, in a rising inflection that declared she heard the request but didn't know what to do with it.

"Just tell him those words. He'll know what they mean."

I could hear his phone ring twice inside his office and then heard her repeat my words. She set the phone down and made an inquisitive smirk.

"Go right in," she said.

I entered his office and closed the door behind me. It was about fifteen feet square with a row of floor-to-ceiling windows on two sides that only offered a view of some more office buildings. Trimbler was standing at the side of his desk with that same display I had seen earlier in the park, half fear and half pleading. When he saw me, relief, confusion and, finally, anger settled over him.

"Just who the hell do you think you are?" he demanded in his best tone of authority.

"I'm from the North Beach Community Council for a Better Environment. Would you care to make a contribution? To help clean up the filth along Broadway and other parts of North Beach."

"Fuck off, Jack. I'm busy."

But he eyed me suspiciously as he sat down in his big padded executive's chair, behind his large simulated wood desk, trying to intimidate me with the symbols of his authority. When I didn't budge he reached toward his phone.

"Do I have to call security and have you thrown out?"

Phase one, I thought. Bring down his house of cards and put him in the proper mood for betrayal.

"Actually I represent a young woman named Bunny."

He put his hand on the phone.

"After your special conversation with her today, she's fallen deeply in love with you and asked me to be her intermediary. She said no Plexiglas barrier could keep her from you."

"What the hell are you talking about? Are you on something?"

The names Terry and Herbie boy were bouncing around somewhere in that thick head of his. Finally they registered in his eyes like two lemons on a slot machine. Fear but not yet pleading entered into his manner. The pleading would soon follow.

"Why did you tell my secretary to say those names?"

"First things first," I said. "We'll get to that in a minute. First, about Bunny."

"Huh?" he said. Fear made him sharp as a tack.

"Bunny." I said. "She's really fallen for you. After watching that solitary love-making technique of yours this afternoon she's really hooked. Said she's never seen anything like it. Right hand, left hand, every which way. She thinks you're fabulous. Thought you might do even better with a partner."

The arch of his dark black eyebrows collapsed into a heavy squint. His mouth opened and his lower yellow teeth emerged.

It was the first time I'd seen him without a cigarette. An oversight he now remedied. He sucked on one a few times filling the room with smoke. Then he sank back into his chair like a man without a spine.

"But she can't see me in there. It's too dark."

If an idiot could blither, so could the Group Manager, International Banking Division. He was so insecure and yet so self-serving in his view of the world that only objects that could increase his position or threaten it made an impact on him. I had now become one of those objects.

He was pathetic and listless as I threatened his security with his secret. That was all he could focus on right now.

I had knocked down the false man he presented to the world.

Now I would have to give him some hope to stiffen his spine. Something equally as spurious that he could use for integrity to get him sitting upright and talking long enough for me to get some information.

"Forget that stuff about Bunny and your little love nest up on Broadway." I crossed over and stood beside him. "It will be just our little secret."

His eyes were still glossy but he was coming around to my sweet talk. For a second I considered putting my hand on his shoulder to brace him up but I thought better of it and sat down in a chair across the desk from him.

He managed to prop himself up on his elbows on the edge of his desk. I was offering him a way out and he knew it.

"I really want to talk about Terry and Michael," I said.

His eyes clouded with fear again and I thought he was going to slink back into his chair.

"You won't have to worry about Terry," I said. "Never again."

I rescued him from the embrace of his padded chair just in time. A creepy light actually came back into his eyes. He was all ears. I had captured his lack of imagination.

"Have you ever heard of Bruno Bacialli?" I began.

"Bruno who?"

"Bacialli. Bruno Bacialli. Listen asshole. His name is never even mentioned and you make me repeat it."

I paused a minute to let him squirm.

"Well, you'd better know it now because you'll never hear it again. I was given special permission to use it. Just this once."

His eyes opened like a small boy allowed a special privilege. "Okay. I've got it. I've got it."

"I'm giving you a onetime only opportunity to work for the Family."

I waited and watched his reaction. He reached for his cigarette, hand shaking, and gulped down some smoke.

"The Family? You mean....That Family!"

"I mean exactly that," I said, calmly and deliberately pronouncing each word. Lending them the force and threat he had come to expect from so many Mafia movies.

"We're taking Terry out," I said. "We're taking over his operation. And we're taking you out with him."

His eyes dilated into two dark holes. Sweat formed on his forehead and the rancid smell of fear permeated the room as his deodorant failed him. He almost managed to speak but slumped back into his leather executive chair. His spine, from long practice, seemed to fit any posture it was forced into. Except upright. That he couldn't manage. When he finally spoke, a high whine replaced any pretense of manhood.

"But why me? I'm, I'm not important." He almost groaned at the necessity of admitting it.

"You didn't let me finish. I said we're taking you out, unless...."

His spine stiffened just enough to get him back up to the edge of his chair. "Unless what?"

"Unless you cooperate. Unless you're smart enough to look out for your own interests."

He brightened considerably. Now I was speaking a language he could understand. Who else or what part of himself did he have to give up, sell out or betray? Made little difference to him at this point. Survival was his instinct. Later he could arrange the facts to provide a satisfying explanation.

A grinding guttural slur accompanied the gurgle of spit and wind sucking through his teeth. A moral cripple's attempt at a manly laugh. Letting me know he was my man, if not his own.

He opened a new pack of True cigarettes, lit a fresh one, and pulled his chair up to the desk. The chair back provided a vertical resting place for his own and helped strengthen his composure. A growing security transformed him back into the corporate business man, reasonably self-assured, and ready to make a deal.

"Just tell me what you want," he said. "I'm always willing to do business." A sly smile parted his lips, revealing intelligence and cunning hidden under all that moral decay. "Especially when there's something in it for me."

"We want the details of Terry's operation and all the players. And we want it now."

"I have to know what I get first."

His false whining confidence had returned and he needed a sharp reminder of who and what he really was.

I went quickly around the side of the desk and grabbed his tie in my right fist, just beneath the knot. A hard upward yank and he and his chair tumbled over as I dragged him across the carpet.

As he sprawled on the floor, I straddled his back, lifting his head, knee high. I shoved his face against the window. His chin clattered against the pane.

"That's twenty stories down there, Trimbler. And helping you make that first step is the nicest I'm ever going to be to you, if you jerk me around anymore."

Still straddling his back, I tightened my hold on his tie and pulled his hair with my other hand until his head came up and he could just see me out of the top of his bulging eyes, standing over him. His feet were still tangled in the chair and stale tobacco air was wheezing out of his throat, his face a red balloon ready to pop. He was about to pass out.

"Do you understand me?"

A nasal grunt signaled our new rapport. I let the tie and hair go and his face slid down the window to the floor. I went back to my chair and waited for our new and more honest relationship to begin.

It took nearly five minutes and a new cigarette before he was back in his chair, ready to try again.

"I ask, you answer," I said. "What is Terry's business?"

There was no hesitation this time. "Drugs."

"That's not enough answer." I started to get up.

"Wait a minute. I wasn't finished. I can still hardly breathe. He mainly deals high quality marijuana. Sinsemilla. But he's trying hard to move into cocaine and other drugs. Using his base and profits in sinsemilla to expand. Got a real bug up his ass about it lately. Really putting the blocks to me."

"Where do you fit in?"

"I'm one of his runners. A franchised distributor. A corporate candy man, so to speak." A little smirk crept across his face.

"More than that, aren't you? What are you supposed to have for Terry tonight?"

"How the hell do you know about that? Wait a minute, there's no reason to get up for chrissakes! Stay put. I'll tell you. I travel to Mexico and South America a lot for business. Terry's been using me to set up a connection. For a big buy he wants to make. Cocaine. Tonight I'm supposed to deliver the first shipment and introduce him to his new connection."

"Where does Terry get the marijuana?"

"He grows the shit. Not just marijuana, sinsemilla. The very best. Up to two thousand dollars a pound. More if it's in smaller lots."

"How does Michael Sherwin fit in?"

"You already know quite a lot," he said, and regretted it immediately. He waited nervously to see if I were going to bounce him off the window again. When I didn't move, he continued.

"Michael grows the stuff. It's his land and he's the expert. Terry's the muscle and the brains. He makes the deals and brings in the money. If you haven't met Terry yet, I offer a piece of advice. Don't get within ten feet of him. Not even with a gun."

"There are ways of overcoming all obstacles," I said. "Even very large ones."

He liked that. Helped boost his sagging confidence. He was getting used to his new master and needed less prompting. Looked like he was about to lick my hand. He went on.

"But Terry and Michael are more than business partners."

"You mean they're sisters?"

He frowned. "You mean gay? No way! They're old friends. They're each other's only friend. Michael's the only one with any influence over Terry and the only one who isn't afraid of him. In turn Terry shows him respect and even protects him."

"If they're so close, why is Michael missing?"

"I haven't figured that out yet. They're making good money and about to make a lot more. Moving into the big time. The big money."

His voice slowed to a dreamy pace. He almost lost himself in his daydream of big money and what it could get him. I kicked his desk and brought him out of it.

"I've only seen Michael once, so I don't know much about him. But he's a strange one. The total opposite of Terry."

"You told Terry you thought Michael was back at the ranch. Why? Terry doesn't seem to think so."

"You must be invisible," he said. "I never forget a face and I'm damn careful that nobody's listening when I talk to Terry. But I didn't see you. You must be good."

"You wouldn't have noticed Tony Bennett singing, "I Left My Heart In San Francisco," backed up by a twenty piece orchestra. I was there, remember?"

He coughed, fidgeted and lit another cigarette. Now he had two going.

"Well, maybe I was a little preoccupied today. Terry's been busting my ass about this new deal and I didn't have it ready for him. That's why I said Michael was back at the ranch. To get Terry off my back. I have no idea where Michael is."

That I could believe. "Where is this ranch?"

"It's not really a ranch," he answered. "It's mainly an orchard and a lot of woods. I've only been there once.

"They really grow pears there. Michael is very proud of his trees. They use the orchard as a legitimate front for the sinsemilla. They grow the plants right in the middle of an old, unused part of the orchard, and the pears are harvested at the same time as the marijuana.

"It's perfect camouflage, especially from the air. This will be their first really big crop. Probably the largest in the state, when it's harvested in September."

"Where is it?" I kicked the desk hard, making him jump.

"I'm not exactly sure." He hurried on, afraid I wouldn't believe him. "It's in Lake County, not far from Clear Lake." He was very nervous I wouldn't believe him. "I'm telling you the truth. I really don't know the exact location."

"Maybe you should think a little harder." I said it softly, with menace. Don Corleone would have been proud of me.

It almost popped out of him. "It's not far from Lakeport. Terry has his T-Bird serviced there. You could check at the garage, Herb's body shop and repair. I remember because it's my name. That's all I know. Honestly."

He sank back into his padded chair and watched me with blank eyes. Exhausted.

"We're almost through," I said, standing up. "What about Clementine?"

"That black bitch?" he muttered. "She's just Terry's private lay. Real uppity." Then his voice brightened and he stood up, leaning on the desk, smirking. "If you could get that cunt along with Terry, it would be just great." He pounded his desk with his fist. "Just great. Fantastic."

He was a nasty little jerk who couldn't get anything himself. I handed him my business card that read: Timothy Walker, Private Investigator and walked out of the room.

As I closed the door behind me I saw him standing there, examining the card. Confused. He had expected to read: Murder Incorporated.

Outside the door was the last thing I had expected. Terry Rose. Bigger than life, sitting on the edge of the secretary's desk, chatting away. She was laughing and obviously entertained by him.

His blond braid swung lightly past his left ear as he turned when I closed the door. He stood up and looked at me with big pale gray eyes. He seemed to look straight through me but I knew he had registered every detail. I just didn't matter to him...yet.

As I walked past him, all six feet two inches and two hundred and five pounds of me seemed small and frail. I looked at his eyes and then down a neck as thick as a tree trunk to a heavily muscled chest covered with thick blond hairs. They really stood out on his shirtless body, contrasting with his blue leather suit coat.

Behind me I heard the secretary say, "you can go in now, Mr. Rose."

Outside the building I saw Clementine in the red T-Bird, guarding it against unwanted meter maids. I didn't have time to get my car so I hailed a cab and waited for Terry.

He came out after a few minutes and I followed them up towards Fisherman's Wharf. When they parked, I got out of the cab and started after them. It was going to be a lot harder, now that Terry had seen me.

There were tourists everywhere and they provided good cover as I kept about a block behind them. Past the old sailing ship, Balclutha, and over to Pier 43 where, for a moment, I could only see Terry's head, bobbing above a sea of tourists waiting to take a cruise on the Bay.

When they emerged from the crowd they had picked up another member. A man about thirty, my size, wearing a white sweatshirt, jeans and jogging shoes.

The three of them made the turn at the Fisherman's Grotto and stopped in front of Alioto's at a sidewalk stand selling fresh cooked crab and shrimp cocktails. After a quick selection they continued on, each eating from their small cardboard container, walking and talking and attracting stares from the tourists. If they could count on him showing up every day, I'm sure the Gray Line Tours would put Terry on their list of famous San Francisco sights.

At Tarantino's they made the turn onto Jefferson. I waited a few seconds and then turned the corner after them, concealing myself behind a dozen Japanese loaded down with cameras and packages.

It was a bad choice. I should have picked a taller ethnic group. A bunch of big Swedes or a visiting college basketball team.

A little way down Jefferson, just past Tarantino's, stood Terry. He was leaning against the wooden railing, above the small fleet of fishing boats, and he was looking right at me as I turned the corner. About two dozen people were walking between us, but they were all too short to hide me.

I made a quick quarter turn left and crossed to the other side of Jefferson, but I thought he had recognized me. I made my way through the crowds of shoppers in front of a line of tacky tourist shops and crossed back over to Terry's side of the street about thirty yards past him. He was still facing the opposite direction, toward the corner I had turned when I first saw him. Clementine was talking to the other man and all looked well. Maybe he hadn't recognized me.

I leaned against the wooden railing, examining the fishing boats below, keeping Terry in sight out of the corner of my eye.

Terry had turned and was talking to the other man and Clementine. Nobody looked down my way. After another few minutes Clementine and the other man came towards me. Terry stayed behind, watching the water and boats indifferently, just like me.

She made an elegant stroll out of the short distance between us, like a model displaying the latest fashions on a Paris runway. Quite a few tourists paused to admire her. With each graceful step she alternately placed each foot across an imaginary straight line, providing just a slight bit of english to her stride, setting her hips on a soft erotic sway.

I had turned to appreciate her approach. She stopped right next to me, along the rail. The other man hung back about ten feet and Terry kept his original position.

"Do you see that rather large gentleman down there?" She pointed at Terry. "His name is Mr. Rose and he would like to speak with you." Her little speech finished, she smiled and waited for my reply.

She had precise diction, perfect white teeth and a flawless complexion. Dark almond eyes and a sexy asymmetric smile. Her buttoned, pinstriped jacket showed the full round inner curve of each breast and she smelled like exotic spices. Under her butter yellow scarf she wore a gold peace symbol similar to Terry's but much smaller. In her high heels she was two inches taller than I was.

Don't get near him, not within ten feet, not even with a gun, Trimbler had said. I decided I liked it fine where I was.

I smiled back at her. "Tell me, Sweet Pea, are you a down home Southern country girl or a big town Northern metropolitan lady?"

A slow-as-molasses plantation dialect answered, "why's hunnah chile," then slid off into her best university diction, "you will just never know." Then an abrupt, "are you coming?"

"No. A sea gull might steal my place at the rail."

Her lips curved into a cynical smile and she shouted back over her shoulder. "Donald. A little assistance here, please."

Donald was nicely tanned, muscular, and exactly my size. Clementine backed up as he trotted up and took her place. Terry was motionless in his spot down the rail.

"Now there's a lot of people around here and we don't want

a disturbance, do we?" he asked, reaching for my arm.

I brushed his hand away. "If we're going to dance, I've got to lead. I can't remember the steps otherwise." I extended my right hand.

He was confused for a second but then accepted it with his right hand. Immediately he tried a little game, squeezing with all his strength. I kept my hand limp, smiling at him. As he set himself for his final effort, I caught him off balance, giving a hard, sharp counterclockwise wrench to his wrist. His wrist didn't give but I nearly dislocated his right elbow and he winced with pain.

"You son-of-a-bitch!" he yelled and swung a wide left hook at my head.

I pulled back just enough, letting his swing pass, gathering force, and reached behind him as his left shoulder turned into me with the punch. My right hand caught his thick leather belt and I extended my left arm across his turning shoulders for leverage. I gave an upward heave with all my might, taking advantage of his own momentum, and pitched him over the wooden railing.

He landed with a loud splash just short of a fishing boat. A large crowd ran to the rail and watched him flounder about until he caught a net on the side of the boat.

I turned, looking for Clementine, but found Terry instead. Like that big bear in the woods that moves faster than you ever expected, he was now right in front of me. My eye level didn't quiet reach the bottom of his huge chin.

He looked down at me and I saw no movement in his eyes. Their unfocused gray irises seemed to float like pale pools, revealing nothing. Then those pouting, feminine lips curled into a dainty smile.

I almost didn't see him move. Suddenly, his great right hand enclosed my tightened left fist, lifting it above my head and further than it could go. As he extended his long right arm to the fullest extent of its upward reach, up over my head, my feet slipped off the ground and I went up with it. For a split second I dangled from my new height, held high for inspection in a giant's upraised hand, like the catch of the day, finally eye to eye with Terry Rose. His gray irises floated in place. Shark's eyes, unblinking in their watchfulness.

Then he jerked that monster hand that held me. The hot burning pain in my wrist registered a milli-second before I heard the bones crack.

It all seemed to happen in slow motion but it lasted only a few seconds. I was thrown back, too small to be bothered with, back on my own feet, on firm ground, leaning against the rail again. Terry and Clementine were disappearing through the crowd. Out for a casual stroll. They hadn't even waited for their friend in the water.

A crowd had watched in total silence. Over so quickly they hadn't realized it yet. A little disturbance in the smooth flow of a warm summer's afternoon. So abrupt it might not even have happened. But I could feel the hot flashes coming up my left arm from my wrist, which was bent down at a comic angle.

I hurried off, out of the crowd, before a cop could appear, and hailed the first cab I saw.

The cab dropped me at Children's Hospital out on California Street. Since I hadn't eaten all day, they set my wrist almost right away.

Sporting a brand new plaster cast on my left arm that kept my thumb and fingers free and stopped just below my elbow, I was home by nine, ready for bed.

The bizarre events of the day were behind me, but my shiny new cast was a vivid reminder that there were probably more serious problems ahead. I hoped my sister, Shirley, was right that the client I would meet in the morning would be worth the trouble.

At 3:00 a.m. the doorbell woke me. A uniformed cop waited politely while I dressed, then led me out to a squad car and drove me across Golden Gate Park into the Sunset District. To the end of Noriega, near the Great Highway and Ocean Beach. To an all night laundromat with two more squad cars, an ambulance and several other cars out front. The fog was in, heavy and wet, muting the flashing lights on the squad cars, lending an unreal atmosphere to the proceedings.

Through the window the harsh fluorescent lights and stark details of the laundromat's spartan decor contrasted sharply with the gray fog rolling down the street. I felt like I was looking into an Edward Hopper painting.

I hadn't been told yet what they wanted me for. My uncle, Matt, met me at the door. Homicide detective for over twenty years. He grunted at me and I nodded back. It was that time of the morning, coffee the order of the day, bleary eyes and sullen dispositions.

He took me down a row of washers and dryers to the back of the store. Along its wall were a line of large, heavy duty dryers at eye level. A group of five men were standing in front of one of them, blocking my view. Off to the side were two ambulance attendants. When they saw my uncle, one of them said, "do you want us to wait around, or what, lieutenant? This could take all day."

"You can go now," he answered. They grabbed their gear and scrambled out the door.

The five men parted to let us through. Matt stopped in front of the nearest dryer and said, "what do you make of this? Do you know him?"

It was Herbert Trimbler, inside the large dryer. Except for a pair of socks he was naked. He looked like a grotesque fetus. He had been bent like a horseshoe and stuffed inside. His head at the bottom of the drum, near the glass porthole, facing up and out. His mouth and eyes open, twisted with the unexpected, sudden agony of death.

Above and to the sides of his head were his legs, folded at the knees and curled down from above, against his chest, fetus-like. He looked like he was awaiting birth, but not into this world. His arms and his legs were at clumsy angles and looked broken. So was his neck, apparently, from the violent twist it made. His spine didn't look like it had made it intact either.

Oddest of all was that his buttocks, like his face, were pressed tight up against the round window, almost as if on purpose, providing an eye level view of his asshole.

He was a gruesome sight. He had tried for the big money, playing in a dirty game, and lost. My gut had that creeping feeling again and the sight of all those broken bones made my wrist throb.

"Do you know him?" Matt asked again.

"Herbert Trimbler," I answered. I met him for the first time yesterday afternoon. How did you know I knew him?"

He handed me a clear plastic evidence bag. "We found that sticking out of his ass." Inside was my business card. The one I had given him when I left his office.

"It looks like he was twisted into a pretzel just so we'd see your card sticking out of his ass. Like a greeting card. You know anyone with that kind of humor?"

I told him about Terry Rose. Showed him my own piece of his handiwork, covered by the plastic cast. Guaranteed him that Terry Rose was the man who did it. Mean enough and strong enough to break all those large bones in Trimbler's body. Crazy enough to leave my card as a warning. Shrewd enough to have a perfect alibi. Five or six people at least, swearing he was with them all night.

"We dragged you down here because we can't get him out of there. Rigor mortis set in and we'd have to use a saw. Or have to wait a couple of days until the rigor passes. So I called the coroner. Wants us to take out the whole dryer and bring it down to the morgue where he can disassemble it."

It pays to have relatives on the police force. I explained the drug-related motive for Trimbler's death, and, after some more questions and a warning to stay away from Terry Rose, I was taken home in a squad car.

It was just past five.

THREE

My old Mercedes was still parked downtown, so I got out my four year old Jeep Wagoneer, had an early breakfast at the Sugar Plum on California, and started down the coast at six, through dense fog, to meet my client in Monterey.

Although I moved out to San Francisco from New York only four years ago, I am as much native Californian as New Yorker. My credentials go back to 1849 when the first Walker sailed around Cape Horn and landed at the foot of Telegraph Hill during the gold rush. Now the state is thickly populated with us.

It was my father who reversed the journey as a young man and returned to the bright lights of New York, just before World War II began. When he and my mother died twelve years ago, my sister resettled to San Francisco, rejoining the rest of the family clan. It just took a little longer and a lot of pain before I followed, four years ago, just after my wife's death in New York.

Fate had intervened after her death, when my grandmother died and left me her house in San Francisco. And some money. Not enough to live on but enough to smooth out the bumps.

That's when I decided I needed the change and made the big move. After living in New York like a madman in a black pit after my wife's death. So I retraced the journey of my adventurous ancestor, except I did not round Cape Horn.

Warned by all my New York friends that California would

corrupt me, I bought both the Jeep and the Mercedes. Immediately. To annoy them. The symbols of the ultimate California degeneration of a born New Yorker: a Mercedes and a recreational vehicle. In New York I had been a somewhat successful actor. In California I was to become a detective. A great sea-change in my life, even though I came by air.

Right about now I figured Terry Rose had another sea-change in mind for me. Probably a quick trip by water through the rinse and spin cycles at some quiet, late night neighborhood laundromat. A frightening and brutal character, as I had discovered yesterday. Brutal in body and brutal in mind.

The case I had undertaken so lightheartedly yesterday was now pulsing out ominous warnings along with my heartbeat. And, like an ancient soothsayer, I began to see prophetic tokens all about me as I drove through the early morning fog. And I began to wonder just what my sister had gotten me into.

And the wonder turned to wonderment when seventy miles down the coast highway I drove out through the heavy curtain of fog and the magic show began.

Across forty miles of crescent shaped bay, it floated before me like a beautiful woman levitated by an unseen magician. The illusion was complete and I had the uneasy feeling that I was an unprepared spectator brought up to the stage by the master magician to verify his powers. After closer examination I still could not dispel the floating illusion.

I was just north of Santa Cruz when I was unsettled by this confusing apparition. In the distance a large, beautiful island with dark forested hills floated off the California coast. But I knew there could be no island there even as I stared at it through my bug-spattered windshield. After about ninety seconds of driving the floating image was gone, so I turned around and went back a short way, then turned around again.

Once more I saw it, an island that couldn't possibly be, shimmering in the bright sun of an ordinary California morning. It was about forty miles distant, drifting between a huge Pacific fogbank and the high coastal mountains, and there was a clear expanse of water on all sides of it. It had to be an island, an island that couldn't be.

The magic of the illusion began to wear off. Now I was the frustrated spectator who wanted the magician to reveal his trick.

I took out a map and measured my position in relation to the island. I was at the extreme northwestern end of forty mile long, crescent shaped, Monterey Bay, and I was looking straight down the chord of the long coastal crescent towards the Monterey Peninsula; but I saw an island, not a peninsula. I took out my binoculars and I could see water where the peninsula should have been connected to the land. It was an island.

Then it finally came to me and a smug smile spread across my face. I pierced the veil and dissolved the illusion; the hidden magician held no power over me. There was no island and I was looking at the Monterey Peninsula.

The expanse of water that seemed to separate it from the coast was the mouth of the shimmering Salinas Valley and I was peering down its flat hundred mile long throat that looked for all the world like the open sea.

The magician, finally revealed, was California, where land and sea and air are not always what they seem. I had driven this road many times but had never seen this particular act of California magic before.

The quintessential California experience. The illusion of

reality versus the reality of illusion.

I started up again and continued south. Within thirty minutes the huge fogbank moved in again and the land itself seemed an illusion. Soon I was driving through air so thick and wet I couldn't tell land from air and both seemed more like ocean. I turned on my wipers and drove slowly through fields of artichokes, barely making out the sign that proclaimed Castroville the "Artichoke Capital of the World." The smug feeling I had from solving the mystery of the floating island began to take on sinister overtones.

Detective work at best is only a temporary piercing of illusions, a brief focusing of unclear events and characters. It seemed that California had put on a special show to remind me to keep my wits sharp and my perspective clear in such a changing landscape.

The fog blew thick and straight at me. I put on the headlights and slowed down to about thirty. There was little traffic and I rolled down my side window and felt the chill, damp air.

Strawberries! Before I could even see them I smelled them. I peered into the swirling fog but saw nothing.

It was the end of June and the end of the strawberry season in this part of California. I knew that just off the road were trucks and packing crates and dozens of Mexican pickers moving through the fields, but try as I would I did not see them.

The strawberries' full rich odor hung on the wet air, smell without sight, a fragrance of a reality not yet perceived but palpably alluring.

It seemed the California magic show wasn't over yet. My "floating island" had mocked my certainty of what was securely real, disoriented and irritated me, and then left me with a wary eye to objects that seem perfectly clear in bright sunlight. And yet now my senses were excited and my perception sharpened by invisible strawberry fields! I began to feel that I was being both warned away and lured on.

The fog thinned a bit and I turned off my lights and wipers and accelerated to sixty. Suddenly, I was in a hurry. I sped past the dull and dreary buildings of Fort Ord and the drab sand dunes that flank them, an all too real blemish before the near perfection of the Monterey Peninsula. I took the Del Monte exit into Monterey too fast and forced the Jeep down to a safer speed, the fog hanging in the eucalyptus trees as I passed the Navy Postgraduate School.

Something about the sensuousness of those invisible strawberry fields made me nervous.

It was 9:15 as I drove out onto Monterey's Municipal Wharf for my 9:30 a.m. meeting, and I couldn't get that sensual smell of those invisible strawberry fields out of my mind. Palpably real, like the smell of those unseen strawberries, a sense of foreboding now hung on the cool salt air.

FOUR

The Wharf is actually a wooden pier jutting out just short of a half mile into the bay at the foot of the downtown area. It's a down-to-earth place with true atmosphere and working fishing boats. Nothing plastic or phony like the so-called Fisherman's Wharf just across the small boat harbor which is loaded with shops and draws all the tourists.

I drove about two thirds of the way down and parked at a partial barricade that said: AUTHORIZED VEHICLES ONLY BEYOND THIS POINT.

As I got out the smell of oil and diesel fumes faintly mixed with the sea air and my lingering mood of apprehension. The sight, smell and feel of the air greeted my senses with none of the ambiguity of my recent experiences. I took a deep breath and retreated from the brink of sensual overload.

I am a true California pilgrim. In love with the extreme contrasts of its landscapes. In spite of all its people, human civilization in California is fragile and tentative. Facing the setting sun, perched on the edge of a vast continent, it's completely exposed to the unquiet natural world surrounding it. And perpetually in danger of being overwhelmed. Either driven mad through overstimulation or lulled into an enervating "lotus land."

No wonder so many people out here are nervous. Someone once said that the trouble with California was that the scenery was so grand that the people couldn't hope to measure up to it and suffered by comparison.

Anyway, it's truly an unrivaled place, if you've got the sensibility to appreciate it. A real Garden of Eden, if you watch out for the serpent.

I was leaning against the railing looking down on the fishing boats tied up below, trying to spot a sea otter or at least a seal, when I first saw her.

She was walking back towards me from the end of the pier. Walking isn't really the right word. She seemed to glide, and I thought of my beautiful floating island. But she was no illusion. She had her eyes fixed on me and I knew she was my client, Mary Dugan.

She was elegantly outfitted in a black wool dress that looked like a St. John's knit, with a black felt hat topped with a marvelous white feather. The hat was set at a slightly rakish tilt that seemed to promise a sense of humor along with the sophistication that obviously went with it, and the feather hinted at adventure.

Even at the remaining fifty feet between us I could see the quickness of her eyes. My pulse raced as I straightened up and turned to face her. She moved with ease, radiating pride and sophistication, but not at all forbidding. Her left hand held a small white purse. Her figure was just this side of voluptuous and was accented by a white belt fastened firmly around her waist.

But what amazed me most was how she walked. She was wearing three inch white heels and yet she moved, almost floated, effortlessly across the rough boards of the pier, never looking down to make sure her heels didn't catch in the openings between the planks.

Obviously a woman who had met life head on and had succeeded. She took the last few steps separating us and extended her right hand.

"You're Timothy Walker," she said. It wasn't a question.

I made sure my mouth wasn't open and accepted her outstretched hand. Up close she was even more impressive. Only about five feet three inches tall, though the heels and the feather gave a sense of greater height, she was a mature woman in her late thirties. She did not try to hide it. There were no ambiguities here to confuse the senses.

She had lustrous, light red hair, falling loosely in a wide cascade just below the shoulders. She was not tanned but had beautiful Irish skin with a slight trace of freckles that contrasted with luminous green eyes. Her lips were rose colored and not quite full, with an easy, relaxed set to them.

She was smiling at me. She reminded me of Myrna Loy in a Thin Man movie. Urbane, sophisticated and elegant. I wished I were William Powell.

Reluctantly, I let go of her hand. "That's right," I answered. "What can I do for you?"

Her smile retreated slightly and a troubled look settled in her eyes, which were watching mine. "Your sister said you could help me. Let's walk back down the pier and I'll explain." We started past the barricade down toward the end of the pier.

"Shirley said I can trust you completely."

She said it like a statement of fact but took a slow, careful look at me to see if it were really true.

When she noticed the cast peeping out of the left sleeve of my jacket, she stopped walking.

"A memento of the help I've already given you," I explained.

She didn't understand. As I watched the questions form in her deep green eyes, I began to feel better about my broken wrist.

"I started a day early," I said. "Shirley said it was important, so I tried potluck and spent yesterday following Terry Rose."

"You didn't find Michael, did you?"

"No. No sign of Michael. Just that he's missing and Terry's looking for him. But I did get to observe Terry and a couple of his playmates."

She seemed to know what came next. She inhaled sharply, held it and took my left hand. Pulled back my sleeve, ran her hand up to the end of the cast, then back down and felt the thick plaster between my thumb and forefinger. Finally, she exhaled.

"Terry did this, didn't he? It's his special signature."

"That's right. Insisted on shaking my hand. Trouble was he shook the rest of me along with it."

She let go of my arm, and turned directly towards me. Her alert green eyes squinted up at me for a second, then relaxed.

There was a directness in her that startled me. Nothing coy or tentative like most beautiful women.

"I'm afraid I've already gotten you into a mess without giving you a chance to say no."

"Well, since I'm already in, why don't you fill me in on the details and what you want me to do."

"See that building down at the end of the pier? My problem started there over eighteen years ago, in December of 1966."

I looked at a large graying wooden structure that occupied most of the pier end. She didn't turn but faced me as if the building's reality needed no confirming for her.

"First a couple of facts. I have a daughter, Katherine, who will be eighteen soon. I have never been married and the last time I saw her father was on this pier. On the day before Christmas, 1966."

She gave no hint of embarrassment or apology but turned forward, and we started walking again.

"At the time, I was engaged to Michael Sherwin, my daughter's father. We were both seniors at Stanford and were home for the Christmas holidays. He was from a very wealthy family that he never felt part of, and we were always together, sharing everything. We were very close, or so I thought, and had just decided to get married after graduation, in the summer."

She paused at the thought of what had almost been, then continued.

"Well, Michael had always been troubled by his family. He had tremendous feelings of guilt. He could get very depressed and moody and had trouble talking with his parents. His family life had always been a mess but was even worse then. Because his brother and one of his three sisters had just died in separate accidents. After the accidents Michael felt his parents totally ignored him, so he was staying with his best friend, Terry Rose, and not at home."

As she talked we kept walking straight down the pier as if her past might be up ahead, instead of behind her.

"Michael set up a meeting, very formally, with his father. For the day before Christmas. Here on the pier. And on that morning I drove him to the place where I just met you. He was very nervous and planned to talk with his father about the accidents and tell him about our engagement. From the parking area I could see his father near the end of the pier waiting for him. Michael got out and started towards his father, and I drove off. That's the last time I ever saw him."

We had reached the end of the pier and were alongside the large, graying building which was used for processing fish. There were several men in rubber hip boots washing down the floors with hoses and pushing around large containers with wheels that were filled with freshly caught fish. The walkway made a loop around the building and we stopped midway, leaning against the railing facing each other.

She continued. "I never did find out why Michael disappeared. I tried for months, especially after I discovered I was pregnant. But he had literally vanished."

"And you want me to find him and bring him back after all this time," I said. I shouldn't have. She looked at me like maybe she couldn't trust me after all.

"Of course not! Any of those feelings for Michael are long gone. He never even knew I was pregnant, and I never told anyone that Michael was the father of my daughter, except Katherine when she was twelve. I was honest with her and she accepted my story without any anxiety. Over the last several years she's expressed a growing interest in her father and we've even considered hiring a detective to find him." She smiled at what she had just said.

I raised my eyebrows slightly to encourage her.

"Two weeks ago Katherine began receiving obscene, truly vile letters questioning who her father was and where he was. These letters, there were three of them, greatly disturbed both of us. Then last week Terry Rose showed up, asking me questions. He had disappeared with Michael and I hadn't seen him since. He said he and Michael have been together in business all these years, but Michael recently disappeared. Said he had to find him and thought he might have returned to Monterey.

"I was absolutely astounded. I had never liked Terry and he hadn't changed. I tried to question him, but he wouldn't talk, saying if I wanted to know anything I should help him find Michael. He didn't seem to believe I hadn't seen Michael and implied that he would show up. Then he left a business card with me and hinted that Michael had better contact him. On his way out he ran into Katherine and talked with her for a while."

She had been going at full speed and suddenly became aware of it. She began again, more composed.

"The night after Terry showed up Katherine didn't come home. I was frantic and kept thinking of those horrible letters. Finally, I realized that the card Terry had given me was missing. I remembered his address from it and the next day I found Katherine with him at his apartment on Nob Hill in San Francisco.

"That was two days ago, on Wednesday morning. Katherine was obviously much more disturbed by those letters than I had realized, and it seems Terry had told her he knew her father well and could help her find him."

I turned slightly, shifting my weight to my other foot, wondering if the daughter could be anything like her mother.

"How did he know Michael was her father?"

Her nostrils flared. "Terry is an animal and he has an animal's cunning. He knew us both years ago and, besides, Katherine bears some resemblance to Michael."

"Why does Terry Rose think he can find Michael through Katherine, since Michael doesn't even know he has a daughter?"

"That's what I asked him." She stopped. A flush of anger rose in her voice. "Actually, I was in a fit, screaming at him and threatening prosecution, since Katherine is underage." The anger in her voice faded to something more anxious and she continued almost in a whisper, "I finally calmed down when Katherine assured me nothing had happened. Then I brought her back to

Monterey and we agreed to hire a detective."

Her change of tone and intensity took me by surprise. She held her fears like rotten fruit that she was forced to offer me.

Hesitantly, I said, "don't you believe her?"

Her head jerked slightly. "Oh, yes, I believe her. It's not that! It's just that I had forgotten what fear can do to a person."

Her eyes narrowed determinedly, as if readying to give me a repugnant gift. She lowered her eyes and spoke quietly and slowly.

"You see," she stared at the cast on my broken wrist and started pushing the repellent subject towards me, "Terry is violent and dangerous, and just the thought of him with Katherine really frightened me."

After my experience yesterday, I didn't need to be convinced.

"Do you think he wrote the letters?"

Her voice grew stronger but had a carefully measured tone, as if she needed to describe the perilous situation I was now in.

"No. Terry is too direct to send letters. If you're going to help me you've got to understand him. He has a veneer of easy charm, but, as you've already found out, he's dangerously unpredictable. He's a frightening contradiction. That's what drew Michael to him. They were total opposites. It was as if Michael needed to expiate all his feelings of guilt by wallowing in the muck with Terry."

As she talked she kept pressing the palms of her hands together, then separating them. Over and over with just the faintest pressure. Not exactly a nervous gesture, more a quiet exercise, almost like someone praying.

As she described Terry Rose her entire body and manner had tightened. Like a lightly compressed spring, she was under pressure, waiting to see if I understood and would accept the description of evil she had placed between us.

My intuition was picking up her strange tone and began putting the pieces together. I wanted to help her and I wanted her to know I understood, so I began carefully.

"You're warning me that Terry is the dark, evil side of what you used to love in Michael, and that together they form almost a third personality, something like Heathcliff and Cathy in Wuthering Heights?"

Her lips opened and her eyes widened in silent answer.

"And that, when Michael disappeared with Terry, you became afraid of them both. And now you want me to find Michael, not for you, but to make sure he's safe for Katherine?"

All her constriction and tension disappeared. She stood straight up, facing me with a great smile brightening her face, the tip of her white feather fluttering in the breeze at my eye level.

"That's amazing," she said. "Shirley told me you used to be an actor and that you had an uncanny ability to read between the lines."

"I still need a few more lines to read between. For instance, how well did you know this Terry Rose?"

"He and Michael and I went to the same high school here in Monterey and we were also at Stanford together. I say together but I never really wanted to be with him. When I started dating Michael our sophomore year at Stanford, I also saw a lot of Terry. I used to argue with Michael about his being with us so often, but, where Terry was concerned, Michael was unwilling to listen.

"Oh, I admit I was often fascinated by Terry. He could be very charming when it suited him and he was very protective of

Michael. But then his veneer of charm would crack and violence and even cruelty would break out."

About a dozen twelve year old school kids and their teacher walked past and grouped across the pier from us. A couple of the boys even eyed Mary Dugan but turned away when she smiled at them.

The fog was burning off and it seemed incongruous to be talking so seriously to a beautiful woman in such a pleasant place about old problems. But there was a foreshadowing of something sinister that connected this now sunny day with the complications of the past. And it wasn't hidden in the receding fog bank.

"What scares you so much about Terry Rose? Did you ever see him hurt anyone?"

Her brows furrowed as she brought up the memories. "Mostly I just heard about them afterwards. His exploits were famous on campus and he was almost arrested several times. But it's not just Terry that scares me. It's what he and Michael became when they were together. Let me give you an example, to show what I mean.

"Once, during college, the three of us pulled into a gas station. I was driving. I had a 1966 Mustang, and Michael was in the front next to me and Terry was stuffed sideways into the tiny back seat and couldn't be seen clearly from the outside. A convertible pulled in next to us with four men in it. When they saw me they made a few obscene suggestions which I ignored.

"They didn't bother me, but I knew what would happen. First Michael got out and just stood there, holding the door open, like a chauffeur. The four men in the convertible stared contemptuously at Michael and Michael smiled at them."

She looked to see if I understood. I said, "they were playing off each other, Michael and Terry. They were used to it, almost as if they were doing a vaudeville routine."

She nodded. "That's what made it so frightening. Well, Terry uncoiled from the back seat like a hungry snake that had spotted its dinner. And for a second he just stood next to Michael, towering over my Mustang, staring at the four men.

"By this time the men in the convertible were fidgeting and whispering to each other. I think one in the back seat was urging the driver to pull away.

"But it was too late. This twisted little smile spread across those disturbing lips of Terry's as he walked over to their convertible, and with one hand he lifted the man, who had made the remarks, bodily from the front seat."

She stopped to take a slow breath. "It was simply horrible. Even though there were four of them it wasn't a fair fight. It was a beating and he enjoyed it. They only managed to hit him once. Within three or four minutes it was all over.

"The owner of the station called the police and when they got there they called an ambulance for three of the men. He had broken two of their arms, something that seemed to be a specialty of his, and cracked some ribs of the third man. And he was never even prosecuted. Supposedly because no one would believe he had started a fight with four men."

"I can believe it," I said. "I saw pretty much the same routine yesterday. What was Michael doing during all of this?"

"He just stood there watching, fascinated by it all. We had a lot of arguments about it later and I almost broke up with him. Michael was sensitive and even gentle when he was away from Terry and, despite his moodiness, he had an innocent sense of wonder and playfulness. That's what I liked about him.

"I used to blame Terry for the darker side of Michael that enjoyed watching the fight but later I realized that it wasn't just Terry. There was something wrong inside Michael that found expression through Terry.

"I was really very lucky that Michael ran away. It was the tough times I had afterwards raising Katherine all alone after my parents died that built my character. And since I feel that I was lucky to get out of my relationship with Michael, I'm very nervous about his potential influence on Katherine. Unless he's changed.

"Maybe I'm being much too grim. I'm usually not the somber or nervous type." And her eyes twinkled to prove it. "But having my old problems with Michael and Terry suddenly come back after all these years does not bring out my best side."

"You couldn't prove it by me," I said. "I can't even imagine what a better side of you would look like."

She almost blushed. Then she reached over and took my right hand and held it between hers, lightly, for just a few seconds, before letting go. She didn't say anything. Just looked straight up at me for the few seconds she held my hand. It was an exquisite pause.

"I really do appreciate your coming down here," she said. "And I'm sorry I didn't warn you more about Terry."

"That's okay. My sister said you warned he was dangerous. I just made a mistake in interpreting how dangerous. How do you know Shirley?"

"Oh, I've only met her twice. But I really like her. When I saw her Wednesday night I ended up pouring out all my troubles and she suggested you as the solution."

There was a certain ironic twinkle darting around in her green eyes as she smiled at me and I detected an elusive tone of feminine sharing and secrets.

We were interrupted by the school kids across from us, laughing and yelling. Their teacher had gotten a bin of fish parts from the plant and they were throwing them to about eight or ten large sea lions that quickly gathered and began thrashing and barking in the water below. We walked over to watch.

The kids were literally squealing with excitement. Each fish merely had a fillet removed from its sides and was otherwise intact. Some weighed over ten pounds and were eagerly fought over by the waiting sea lions.

"It all looks so innocent and appealing," Mary Dugan said, "but in a way its all my past problems recurring."

She turned away from the children and looked at me.

"I found out later from Michael's father that the day Michael disappeared they had a terrible fight here on the pier. Michael even hit his father. There was a group of children feeding fish to the sea lions that day, too. According to his father, Michael would have hit him again except that all the children nearby started screaming.

"A great white shark had come on the feeding sea lions and attacked two of them right in front of the children. Many of the children became hysterical. It made all the news broadcasts. The only time a great white was ever seen inside the harbor area. That's when Michael ran away, the day before Christmas."

Her face wore a subdued expression as she said, "some Christmas present, huh?"

Then she opened her purse and removed an old, worn envelope. She gave it to me.

"It's a note from Michael. The only time I ever heard from him, about two months after he disappeared. It's a quote, from

The Golden Bowl, by Henry James. Michael was an English major."

She was watching me intensely. I looked down at the fading envelope. It was postmarked February, 1967, in San Francisco. I looked over at the untroubled school kids, trying to imagine the connection between this happy scene and the ghastly occurrence here over eighteen years ago.

I looked back at Mary Dugan, beautiful and elegant in her stylish black wool outfit with her impish white feather on top. She was waiting as I opened the envelope. As I read the lines I felt a single bead of sweat run down my back like a spider coming down its web:

...the horror of finding evil seated,
all at its ease, where she had only
dreamed of good...

FIVE

As we walked back to my car the white wall of fog was waiting about ten miles off the coast. Waiting for the swelling afternoon sun to grow dim and dull, waiting to roll round again and cover the sun's crystal clarity with its muted blanket.

Satellite pictures sometimes show these summer fogs stretching a thousand miles out into the Pacific and two thousand miles along the coast, from southern Mexico to Oregon. And, all along this huge front, water and air, currents and temperatures, act out little local dramas. Opening and closing this huge curtain of fog, adding mystery and enchantment to an ordinary summer day.

But this summer day was not ordinary. The crystal clarity of its events was muted not by fog but the past, which, like the fog, promised to roll round again and obscure the present landscape.

While we walked back to my car we settled the terms of my employment and she showed me the three letters her daughter had received. Nothing remarkable. Just short, typed, obscene notes ranting about fornication and the corruption of impure blood in vivid, pornographic terms. Demented ravings combining the propagation of pure blood lines from ancient religious cults with the descriptive techniques of a modern X-Rated movie. Nothing unusual about that anymore. At least not in California.

She also gave me several photographs of Michael from their college days. He appeared slender and average height, somewhat handsome in a boyish manner. His eyes were alive and sensitive and his mouth had a humorous twist to it. Overall, he revealed an awkward, even diffident manner, as if he could never make things turn out right.

One of the pictures was disturbing. Michael stood facing forward with his arms at his sides. Standing just behind him, pressed flush up against him so that they seemed to form one figure, was the hulking form of Terry Rose.

The top of Michael's head just reached and fitted snugly under Terry's chin. Terry's huge arms and shoulders jutted out past Michael's slender frame so that, from the camera's angle, Michael seemed to almost fit inside Terry, like one of those primitive religious statues that has another, smaller figure inside the belly of the larger one. The picture was obviously meant to be funny. Michael was grinning and Terry's delicate lips formed a partial smile. But the effect was chilling.

We reached my car and I put the photos and the letters back in the envelope she had given me.

She had arranged for us to have lunch with Jonathan Sherwin, Michael's father, but first we were to stop off at the new Monterey Aquarium so I could meet her daughter, Katherine. She had a summer job there and we could catch her on her mid-morning break.

As I drove back off the pier Mary Dugan said, "I feel more relaxed now. Now that I've finally done something."

I glanced over at her. She was seated comfortably, half-turned towards me, holding her hat, triumphantly topped with its white feather.

"I'm glad to hear it," I said, "but I haven't fully recovered from that quote. It's quite a little stunner. The kind that pops your eyes open in the middle of the night and makes you look under your bed, wondering if you can trust your own mother. Have you ever figured out what he meant by it?"

"It's always reminded me of the shark attack on those sea lions. Everything peaceful and innocent, even idyllic, on the surface. Then this sinister form rises from below and destroys everything."

She moved her hand idly along the brim of her black hat, then up the spine of its white feather.

"I think that's why Michael sent the quote. To warn me that our relationship was also destroyed by something evil and dangerous rising to the surface in him."

She hesitated a second then said, "I used to think Michael specifically meant "my horror" at finally realizing he was evil."

I turned right into the flow of traffic on Lighthouse Avenue which takes you through the tunnel under the Monterey Presidio, which separates downtown Monterey from Cannery Row, where the new Aquarium is located.

"Finally? You make it sound like he always wanted you to believe that he was evil but you didn't."

"That's partially true," she said. "I told you Michael was moody and subject to depressions. He had tremendous feelings of guilt about his family."

"Guilt about what, what kind of guilt?"

She rolled up her window as we passed through the short tunnel under the Presidio. "His guilt took two totally opposite forms. He had a very unhappy relationship with his family and he swung back and forth between blaming them and blaming himself. Usually, he blamed himself."

"For what? Most young people have trouble getting along

with their parents."

We came out the other side of the tunnel and I turned off for Cannery Row.

"Oh, it wasn't just his parents. The few times I went over to his house it was really strange. Michael was treated by the whole family as if he were a guest, as if he didn't really belong there. Everyone was nice and civil but there was no feeling for him in that family."

"Did he ever have it out with his parents?"

She gave out a sharp laugh.

"No. Michael was totally non-confrontational. He was always running away from his problems. I think that's why he felt so guilty. He thought he had maybe done something terribly wrong and was guilty, but I think his guilt came from not standing up for himself. He always dramatized his problems with gothic overtones."

We entered the several block stretch of Cannery Row that has been developed for the tourists since the canneries closed. It's a typical tourist area without any real charm, except for the great views across the bay, and it's already overdeveloped, like most of the Monterey shoreline.

Monterey used to be a quaint working town set at the base of its magnificent peninsula, dependent on its fishing industries and a few tourists. Now there are too many tourists, and it's become a town that tries too hard to recapture its lost quaintness, but can't.

The real glory of the area is still its splendid, rugged coastline that starts just beyond Cannery Row in the town of Pacific Grove and curves south around the point and down into Carmel.

Just now I wasn't thinking of the splendid coastline up ahead but whether we could find a parking space anywhere near the Aquarium. And about what other kind of horror Michael could have been thinking of when he sent Mary Dugan that quote so many years ago.

I asked her. "You said you used to think Michael was referring to your horror. Have you changed your mind?"

She took a slow, deep breath. "Yes. I now think he was referring to his horror as well as mine."

She noticed my questioning expression.

"You see, Michael never really dealt seriously with any of his problems and I think something happened that day on the pier with his father that finally made them all too real for him. More real than he was prepared for or could tolerate.

"I think maybe he did realize there was true evil in him and he ran from it. And from me. But I never got anything from Michael's father to prove this, and now it's all so long ago. And yet it isn't, somehow. It's all coming back."

She said it with a tone of sadness, that the past was coming round again.

But, as if to prove that some things do happen just once, I found a parking space just down from the Aquarium. I pulled in and parked.

She looked over at me and said, "I hope you can help me put these old troubles to rest. I don't want to go through them again."

Then I told her what I had learned about Michael. About the marijuana and Terry's drive to move into cocaine. About Herbert Trimbler's broken body. Terry's punishment for betrayal and his bizarre warning to me to stay out of his business.

She shuddered. "My God! It's gotten worse than I ever imagined."

"Do you still want me to find Michael?" I asked.

"If it weren't for those horrible letters, I'd be tempted to say no. But that wouldn't work either. He's a mystery that's been left hidden too long. Katherine needs to know, even if it's bad. She's old enough and her troubles will only get worse until she's clear of this mess."

"One more unpleasant reminder of the past before we see your daughter. Do you have any idea who wrote those letters?"

We climbed out of the Jeep and walked over to the Aquarium.

"They were all postmarked in Salinas and I don't know anyone there." She parted her lips and let out a melancholy sigh. "But then I don't know anyone, anywhere, capable of writing such letters." A shadow seemed to cover her expression. "At least, I hope I don't."

SIX

The lady has pull it seems. She's on the Board of Directors of the Aquarium, so we sauntered right past the huge line waiting to get in.

Inside, the Aquarium was literally stuffed with people. The place has been a madhouse ever since it opened in 1984 and is now one of California's top tourist draws. It's set up to display the sea life and environment of the Monterey Bay area only, and its stellar display is a growing kelp forest in a forty feet deep tank with viewing levels on two different floors.

The immense crowd response to this new type of localized aquarium surprised everyone, and has necessitated the use of Ticketron to handle the ticket sales during the summer months.

We dodged our way through the crowd and made for one of the open air terraces that overlook Monterey Bay. We pushed through the door to the freedom of the relatively uncrowded terrace and waited next to an open tank that simulated the interaction of waves on a small tide pool. The rushing sound of the water as it churned through the rocks was a soothing counterpoint to the noise inside.

People kept coming up to see the tide pool exhibit so we crossed over to the outer railing and sat on a low stone wall. Two stories below us was the real ocean, rushing and slapping against the rocks and pilings at the base of the Aquarium.

EVIL AT ITS EASE

It was a relaxing setting as we sat, side by side, feeling the cool breezes and the warm sun, while we waited for her daughter.

"This is a great place," I said. "I made it down here once last winter when it wasn't nearly so crowded."

She locked her hands behind her head and tilted her face towards the sun.

"Yes. The crowds are too much for me in the summer, but I love to come here on a nasty winter day. Especially if it's raining."

I formed a vivid picture of her, all alone in the rain, wearing a trench coat and a wide-brimmed floppy hat. Something like Ingrid Bergman at the end of Casablanca.

She unlocked her hands and faced me. "Why are museums and aquariums always at their best in foul weather?"

Memories of all the peaceful times I spent moseying through museums with Janet on cold winter days back in New York rambled through my mind. I could practically feel the cold breath of my lost past on my neck. I almost shuddered.

"Back in New York my wife, Janet, and I loved museums on cold winter days. I think because the harsh weather outside helped create an enclosed, private world inside."

She was looking at me with a sympathetic sadness in her expression as if she knew what I was remembering. Then she said it. Softly. Just louder than the sound of the wind at my back.

"Shirley said your wife was murdered several years ago in New York."

She was attentive and beautiful, sensitive and receptive, sitting right next to me, almost touching, her eyes an open announcement of concern. But I couldn't quite push myself across the line.

"That's when I quit acting and moved out here." I looked at her self-consciously. "I'll tell you about it some day, when we have more time."

Her look of concern softened into a slight smile and she said, "I'd really like that."

I folded then unfolded my arms awkwardly. "Where did you meet Shirley?"

"In one of my restaurants."

"Restaurants? You're not the Burger King heiress by any chance?"

"Hardly. I own and run just two. One in Carmel, the other here in Monterey. I've been very successful at it. I was a fore-runner of the New California Cuisine. You know, fresh, local ingredients, carefully prepared and served in an elegant setting. Or," she grinned, "as some people complain, small portions at big prices and served in a room with too many plants."

"You should open a restaurant in San Francisco. Then I could have a regular place to hang out. Every private eye needs a hang-out. Like Peter Gunn at Mother's, the jazz club."

She started laughing. "Peter Gunn. Do you really remember that show? Monday nights, right? I had a real crush on Craig Stevens."

"Me too," I said. "Or maybe that was Lola Albright I had the crush on. Anyway, I need a place to take messages for me. Where I could store my extra bullets and be soothed after I get a severe beating. You could do the soothing. You could give me one of my extra bullets to bite on when you stroke my bruised brow."

"You'd better be careful," she said. "I'm going up to San Francisco tomorrow to scout locations for a new restaurant. Maybe I can even make it a jazz club."

Possibilities danced in my head like visions of sugarplums.

"Would you put your hat back on for me?" She had been holding it in her lap. "I love your hat. It reminds me of someone."

She raised the hat to her head, adjusted it slightly at an angle, cupped her cheeks with the palms of her hands and said, theatrically, "Whom do I remind you of?"

"Myrna Loy. No greater compliment can I, a humble private eye, offer than to compare you with Myrna Loy, who played Nora Charles in The Thin Man movies."

This time she did blush, and her blush deepened when a tall, red-haired girl came up, looked at me, then her, and said, "Mom. You're blushing."

The girl had an impish grin on her face. She removed her mother's hat and put it on her own head, glancing coyly at me.

"The only time my mother blushes is when I tickle her." She lowered her voice to the deepest level she could manage and then asked me in mock severity, "you haven't been tickling her, have you?"

I winked and gave her back her impish grin, linking us as co-conspirators.

"I just told her she reminded me of Myrna Loy."

I waited to see if the name meant anything to her.

"Myrna Loy?" She searched her memory. "Oh! The beautiful lady in those old detective movies." Her brow furrowed as she tried to remember something. "And does that mean you're what's-his-name? William Powell?"

She gave her mother a mischievous look as she backed up to get a better picture of me.

"No, you're much too big to be the Thin Man." Then she almost jumped forward in her eagerness to correct herself. "Wait! Wait! He wasn't really the Thin Man. I know! I know!" She smiled triumphantly. "The Thin Man merely referred to a character in the first movie of the series. I had that question in a game I played the other night," she confessed. "You know, Trivial Pursuit."

She put the hat back on her mother's head and adjusted it at just the right angle.

"I see what you mean. She does look like Myrna Loy. Especially with that hat on."

I liked her. She certainly wasn't a duplicate of her mother. She had the same red hair and beautiful complexion and the same glimmering eyes. But she was much taller, about five feet ten, and on the lanky side. High-spirited and full of energy, she was at that pivotal point where she would set the direction she would follow the rest of her life. It would be important to finally settle the mystery about her father.

She was talking to her mother, but loud enough so I could hear.

"Mom, I could only get a fifteen minute break. Linda didn't show up this morning and we're understaffed. I have to help feed the sea otters in just a few minutes."

She turned toward me and extended her hand, all serious now.

"Excuse me for not introducing myself. I'm Katherine Dugan. Just call me Katie, though. You must be Mr. Walker, the detective."

At the sound of the word she glanced furtively around the open terrace, as if the word "detective" conjured up dark shadows and secret meetings.

Then she returned to me and, almost unnoticed, she passed to me, as if it were all she had to offer, the fragile hopes of her youth. With determination in her eyes and just the slightest stammer in her voice, she offered her gift.

"I, I really want you to find my father. I never realized until recently how much I need to know about him. Is there anything I can do to help you?"

As I stood up and shook her outstretched hand, I could almost feel her teetering on that delicate balance between adolescence and maturity, between hope and fear. She had the same direct manner as her mother, and I wanted to help her make the same successful passage her mother seemed to have made so many years before.

"Can you think of any of your friends or anyone at school that might have written those letters to you? Anybody that has a grudge against you?"

My question startled her.

"Anyone at school?" She paused to consider the possibility. "No, I don't know anyone who dislikes me or hates me that much. Just the usual stuff. Minor arguments and disagreements."

Her tone was very sober now. "Okay. What did Terry Rose tell you in front of your house the day you went up to San Francisco to see him?"

"He told me he was a friend of my father's, his best friend, and that they were in business together."

"Did he say what kind of business?"

"No, he wouldn't say when I asked him. Then he said that my father had disappeared from their business about a week ago. And that since we both wanted to find him, maybe we could help each other."

She eyed her mother and gave a nervous laugh.

"He scared me. I had no intention of going to see him when he suggested it. But later that night I was very upset. I began to feel that I shouldn't be passive about finding my own father. So I just drove up to San Francisco and went to his apartment. I knew it was a mistake as soon as I started, but I felt I had to prove my worth by taking a risk."

She shifted her weight restlessly from one foot to the other.

"What happened when you got there?"

"He wasn't even surprised or happy to see me. He showed me a room where he said I could sleep. It had a bed and a television in it. Then he didn't pay any more attention to me. He frightened me, although he didn't threaten me or anything. I watched some TV, then went to bed. The next morning he said we should wait around. That my father was sure to show up. I began to feel that he was using me as a hostage even though I could have left. I was just about to call home to say I was coming back when my mother showed up."

She reached down and turned her mother's wrist to read the time on the small watch strapped there, then straightened up and looked nervously from her mother to me.

"I feel real bad not having more time, but I'm going to be in trouble if I don't leave right now." Her eyes took on a fixed intensity as she looked at me. "Is there any way I can help?"

In her eyes I saw both hope and uncertainty. I said, "just try to remember things that at first don't seem important. Anything that was a little unusual or didn't quite make sense. Either here in Monterey or when you were with Terry."

Her mother stood up and said to her, "you'd better go now. I'll see you at the restaurant about six."

Katie started across the terrace, then turned, saying, "I'll be there by five. I'm helping Roger with the desserts tonight." A little gleam came into her eyes as she said to me, "I'm learning the business. You should come too. I'll prepare your dessert myself."

Then she went through the doors and disappeared into the crowd. I hoped that the hard times ahead would forge her character, as they did her mother's, and not leave her emotionally crippled like so many others.

Mary Dugan stood there watching her daughter disappear into the crowded museum. Then she said, "how are you going to find out who wrote those letters?"

"I'm not going to try. At least not right now. Michael is the real problem and Terry is our main link to him. I'll use Terry to flush out Michael. Hopefully, we can clear up the whole mess then, including the letters. But right now I need more of a feel for Michael's background. Maybe we can get some help when we see his father."

She wore an uncertain expression. "I doubt it," she said. "There's something wrong about that family. They seem to lead secret lives in secret places." She paused, looking at me with a partial grimace. "Maybe I'm exaggerating. Maybe it's just my old fears coming round again to haunt me. But I keep thinking of that quote Michael sent me so long ago and I feel that, all these years, some hidden evil has been waiting to be born."

I wished I could have reassured her but somehow I was convinced she might be right. The entire day had an edgy feel about it.

I thought of the illusion of my floating island and the tangible smell of my unseen strawberry fields on the drive down and pictured the shattered innocence of the children's play when the shark attacked the sea lions. Illusion and reality, innocence and evil, past and present all seemed to be converging in the mystery of Michael's disappearance.

SEVEN

One half hour later, after driving about twenty miles south of Monterey, we turned off the coast highway at a brass sign that read: THE SHERWIN INSTITUTE.

We were about to meet the man who built it, Jonathan Sherwin, for lunch, to inquire into the mystery of his long missing son.

We stopped at a gate house where two armed guards used a telephone to confirm our appointment. Then we passed through two massive black iron gates.

The grounds were beautifully landscaped. Park-like. An English garden exploded by too much California space. Rugged yet beautiful. So beautiful, as a former acting teacher of mine would say, that you could almost weep.

Our surroundings were so manicured that I began to feel we had strayed onto the fairways of the Pebble Beach golf course. Especially when we crested the first hill and saw the stretch of coast, pockmarked with secluded coves and jagged, wave-beaten crags. Rimmed with cliffs and headlands, and covered with a velvety matting of dewy grass, all accented by the twisting forms of Monterey pines and cypresses.

The place conjured up images of a carefully reconstructed Garden of Eden. The kind of job God might have done, if he had had the money.

The road took a long slant down the ocean side of the hill

and then wound its way toward an impressive complex of modern buildings that hugged the edge of a large headland jutting into the sea.

The buildings were all of the same design, rough stone and unfinished wood, and blended perfectly with their natural setting.

We passed several clusters of separate luxurious cottages before we arrived at a series of long, one and two story structures that were obviously the administrative center for the Institute. There were many large windows with patios and terraces half-hidden behind sculptured shrubs that insured privacy.

The place reeked of moneyed seclusion. And it took big money to own several miles of coastline in this part of California.

I must have been gawking at all the grandeur when I noticed Mary Dugan grinning at me. Before I could make any excuses she said, "I'm just as amazed as you are. I've never been here before either. I thought it was a retreat house and would look austere, more like a monastery."

"Monastery! It looks more like a camp for millionaire boy scouts. What do you know about this guy, Jonathan Sherwin?"

"Not much, considering that he was almost my father-in-law. He built the Sherwin Institute in the late 1960's, supposedly to counter the growing Hippie movement. And there have been rumblings from the political left about the place ever since. Both Sherwin and the Institute, and especially its inflammatory radio station, KSOS, are favorite targets for this area's radical press.

"Sherwin frequently makes the news broadcasts and he has a lot of power and political influence. He's also on that crazy radio station of his, but I never listen.

"Except for setting up this meeting I haven't talked with him since that time just after Michael disappeared. And that conversation certainly didn't help me understand him. He didn't show any interest in Michael and he surely wasn't interested in me. Ever since then I've wondered if he wasn't the source of Michael's problems. Some human part of Jonathan Sherwin seems missing, and that makes him capable of almost anything.

"One thing I do know. He's a man of rigid composure. Absolute calm. Absolute control. But inside I think he's like a champagne bottle that's been shaken, then sealed with a cork."

The thought amused me. A bottle of Dom Perignon about to explode. "Do we tell him why we want to find Michael? That Katie's his daughter?"

"Yes. I want it all out now. I want to end the mystery, especially for Katie."

I saw the sign for visitor parking and followed its arrow around the side of what looked like the main building of the complex. There was a parking lot for about twenty cars. I pulled in. Obviously visitors were the exception. We were all alone.

Then I saw him. Another armed guard emerging from a small booth just to the side of the building's entrance. As we got out of the car he came over with a log book. I caught a glimpse of our names and the time we had entered the main gate.

He entered our new arrival time then escorted us to the door, opened it, directed us inside and returned to his booth without saying a word. Maybe they had cut out his tongue so he couldn't talk.

We found ourselves in an ample reception room about twenty feet square. Around the perimeter of the room were several easy chairs and a couple of couches. All very plush.

In the center was a large circular table with about eight cushioned chairs, table and chairs all hand carved out of beautiful black walnut. And they weren't antiques. They were hand carved in a modern fashion and that's rarer than antiques.

The center of the table was set with an array of sterling silver trays, each topped with its own fitted glass cover, revealing an assortment of fresh crisp vegetables and fruits. Nearby were lead crystal drinking glasses and a matching carafe filled with a clear liquid, probably water. There was also a small stack of fine china plates and some small serving tongs and forks. Heaven forbid you should use your fingers.

There was a polished brass plaque in front of the food display which Mary Dugan read.

"You can be assured of the absolute purity and integrity of the food on this table. All the vegetables and fruits were grown on the Institute's own farms and orchards without the use of any pesticides or chemicals. The drinking water has been collected from ancient glaciers in the interior of Greenland and has the purity God intended before man learned to pollute His world."

Then she looked over at me and opened her eyes and let out a low whistle. "It certainly ain't the salad bar at Jack-in-the-Box."

"Integrity of the food? Does that mean it won't lie to me if I ask it if it tastes good?"

She had wandered across the room. "Come here. Look at this!" I went across the thick green wool carpet making nary a sound.

There in front of us was a small cockpit-like area in the corner of the room. A padded reclining chair faced a television monitor. A sign on the arm of the chair said: Push This Button To Begin.

She pushed it and a small hidden motor started and thick black velvet curtains closed off the chair and screen from the rest of the room.

I found myself standing on the opposite side of the curtain from her. Then her hand reached out around the curtain's end and she said, "come on in."

I took her hand and she pulled me behind the curtain. I felt like a teenage boy in a game of Post Office, called into a dark room to deliver a kiss. It was pitch black. My eyes hadn't adjusted yet and I couldn't see.

I bumped into her and we both reached out to keep from falling. We held onto each other perhaps a few seconds longer than necessary. We regained our balance but she was still pressed up against me, not stiff and uncomfortable like most people would be, but loose and relaxed. I could feel the top of her hair brushing against my chin.

She said, "I guess you're really supposed to be sitting in the chair when you push the button. Would you like to try it?"

"No thanks. I like it where I am." I felt the swish of her long hair against my chest and knew she had turned her head towards me. "But I am glad you left your hat in the car. I'd be having real trouble with that feather about now."

The television monitor came on with breathtaking and inspirational aerial views of the Institute grounds. Now we could see quite well by the light of the screen. We heard, then saw the headset at the top of the chair. It was emitting a subdued but quite audible sound similar to the Sermonette at the end of a broadcast day.

I also saw that there was a little more space in our curtained nook than we were using. She noticed that I noticed and said with a smile, "I guess I had a little more room over here than I thought. Do you want to get the full effect and put the headset on?"

She still didn't move over. "I don't think I could take the full effect," I said.

The screen images continued as the camera lovingly covered every angle of the Institute grounds. We were watching a very expensive but insipid promotional tape.

Then she said, "well, I guess we can only stand here so long," and reached down and pressed the button marked Stop.

The music stopped, the screen flickered off, the little motor whirred and the curtains opened. Once again we were in the bright reception room.

I walked over to the center of the room, feeling a bit awkward with our new intimacy. She picked up on it.

"Listen. Two people can't share an inspired video experience like that and not be on a first name basis. You'll have to call me Molly now. Obviously our relationship isn't going to be on a strictly professional basis."

I especially liked her word "obviously."

"You're quite a surprise, you know. Most women flirt but won't be direct. You don't flirt but you're surely direct. Well, Molly it is."

She accepted my compliments straight out. She was a lot more at ease than I was. I walked over to the inside door.

"We'd better find out where everyone is."

I tried the handle on the thick wooden door. It was locked. I turned around to make a joke about being locked in together when I heard the bolt slide open on the other side.

I stepped back and a man of about thirty entered the room.

He was carefully groomed, wearing gray flannel slacks and a gray cashmere jacket buttoned once over a white wool turtleneck sweater. His face displayed no imperfections nor any signs of character. But, my goodness, was he ever handsome. Steel-blue eyes beneath a crop of corn-blond hair, blown dry and meticulously combed. He was an advertising man's delight, lean and trim and well over six feet tall. He seemed to belong in a champagne commercial.

He walked over to Molly, apologized for keeping us waiting, then shook both our hands, saying, "I'm Elliott Russell, Mr. Sherwin's executive assistant."

Executive assistant. His hands were perfectly manicured, like the grounds of the Institute, and he was wearing the appropriate smile for visitors. I took him for a Stanford Business School grad.

"Mr. Sherwin will be with you presently. In the mean time he asked me to give you a tour of the Institute. If there's anything I can do for you, be sure to ask."

We hadn't said anything so far. I looked at Molly and saw the faint outline of a smirk. I looked back at Elliott.

"Actually there is something you can do for us." He leaned ever so slightly forward, his manner all accommodating. I moved closer to Molly then said, "we'd like to see the warden. Tell him we're ready to play ball with the district attorney."

His jaw dropped open and out came a confused, "I beg your pardon?"

Then from Molly. "Your pardon! Oh, no! We beg our pardon. That's why we want to see the warden." I felt her tug at the back of my sleeve.

He was more confused than ever. Then his perfect composure broke and he actually grunted.

"Oh, I see. A little joke. Because you were locked in the room here."

His lack of personality was beginning to grow on me, so I offered him a way out. "Shall we begin the tour?"

He regained his composure and his polite smile came back in place. He opened the heavy wooden door and said, "this way, please."

He guided us through several buildings which showed what could be done with a lot of money and a need to create a lush but pure and ordered world.

All the while he assured us that Jonathan Sherwin, himself, was the very soul of the Institute, and that it perfectly mirrored his desire to purify the body and the soul.

The place was part revival church, part health club and part social watering hole. Except that the water was from thousand year old glaciers. No alcohol was allowed, he assured us, and the members took the purity of body and soul regime seriously.

There were lecture halls, a library, a multitude of sound-proofed meditation rooms, saunas and steam rooms, several indoor and outdoor swimming pools, and even a good-size movie theater, where only "suitable" films were shown.

All the facilities were rich and sumptuous. The members we saw along the way were also rich and sumptuous. Otherwise they seemed ordinary enough, although a large number of them were young, in their 20's and 30's, which surprised me.

Even the gymnasium and indoor jogging track were paneled in expensive tropical woods and had the air of a Victorian men's club. But this club also admitted women. As long as they were the right kind of women. There was a careful screening process he told us. To insure that the members had the correct attitude.

Also, I assumed, to insure that they had the correct bank accounts and proper investment portfolios. Only the very well-heeled were admitted to the Sherwin version of heaven.

When we got to the large dining room we were told that it was the very heart of the Institute.

It was an immense room that could seat several hundred people. The center of the room had a huge glass dome with stained glass panels and a spectacular crystal chandelier. Around the perimeter was a regular forest of plants and ferns with a large stage in front where speakers could harangue the diners while they ate.

Or, maybe it was like ancient Rome, California-style, and they watched a welfare recipient fight a lion while they consumed organically grown Brussels sprouts.

I was growing bored by all the displayed wealth when I heard Elliott say to Molly, "before you leave you must try our water. It's absolutely the purest water on earth. It fell in the form of snow on the Greenland ice cap thousands of years ago, before man polluted the earth."

He had a lump in his throat as he said it and I could imagine tears in his eyes. So I said, "why I couldn't possibly let Ms. Dugan drink your water. Not after the facts published this week in the Harvard Review of Medicine."

Molly was watching, waiting to see what the game would be.

He seemed truly offended. Obviously the glacier water was the very "blood" of the Institute.

"Why! What do you mean," he demanded.

"Don't you people keep up on the latest health information."

I really had him now. I had challenged the very essence of the Institute.

"On an expedition to the interior of Greenland this spring all the members of Harvard's anthropology department, after drinking the supposedly pure water from an ancient glacier, came down with Herpes Simplex number forty two."

He was anxiously listening.

"Oh yes. The entire party lost their hair and developed facial sores."

"But it couldn't possibly have been from the glacier water. That water came from God!" I saw Molly turn her head to keep from laughing. "It must have been something else," he insisted.

"No. They tested the glacier water thoroughly. It contained Eskimo urine."

He looked at me incredulously. He began to sputter when Molly burst out laughing. He looked at both of us, his face beet red. Everything in him wanted to yell at us. But he couldn't do it.

It took him just about a minute to regain his non-expressive expression. When it was securely in place he said, "I certainly hope you don't intend to speak to Mr. Sherwin in such a manner."

He walked over to a stand that held containers of his precious glacier water. Every room in the place had at least one of these stands, an up-scale version of the office water cooler.

As he poured the primal liquid his hand still shook with his repressed anger. He stood there for a second with his back to us, like a priest at an altar, imbibing the sacred substance. When he turned back to us the magic elixir had done its work. He wore a benign smile that seemed to say we were troubled children but he had forgiven us. I almost expected him to bless us.

I asked him, "by the way, where is Mr. Sherwin? He's rather late."

A slight frown clouded his beatific glow and a hint of nervousness returned.

"He phoned me as he was leaving his office in Monterey. He should have been here at 11:45. It's not like Mr. Sherwin to be late."

His eyes moved slowly around the beautiful room as if reassuring him of its perfection and his lips pursed as he tried to recall the imperfections of the world outside. A dull look of surprise crept over his face as he remembered its annoying problems.

"I'll bet he got caught in traffic."

His answer restored his sense of contentment as quickly as the glacier water had. His world was in perfect order again as he treated us to his best blank smile.

"I'll take you out to Mr. Sherwin's cottage now, where you'll have your luncheon meeting with him."

He led us over to a side door which he held open. Molly took my arm as we passed by him, rolled her eyes slightly, and said under her breath, "he must have left his personality in his other suit."

EIGHT

We walked away from the building, up a pebbled driveway, about a hundred yards to the very tip of the headland.

Behind us the Institute and its clusters of expensive cottages fanned out in an arc along its base.

In front of us was Jonathan Sherwin's palatial cottage, almost completely hidden in a dense thicket of Monterey cypress trees.

Twisted trunks and limbs ranged round the huge house like a grotesque but beautiful picket fence. Their foliage of dark-green, cord-like twigs was all at their tops, and the raw coastal winds had shaped them into broad flat canopies that leaned away from the wind, like exotic hairdos caught in a gale. Little else grew on the exposed promontory, and their density and wind resistance provided both an anchor and a shelter for the cottage secluded there.

The building and the trees were holding fast to the very edge of the cliffs with a four-hundred-foot plunge down to the surf. Only the inland side of the cottage, where we approached, had any open ground.

It was still a bright sunny day but we could see the endless wall of fog several miles out to sea, like an army waiting to advance. The breeze was light and the sun warm as we walked up to the front of the cottage.

I squinted out at the fog. It was only a few hundred feet deep but stretched forever, bright white, both up and down the coast and out to the far horizon. Settled snugly on the surface of the sea, waiting for the heat of the land to cool at day's end, so it could resume its march inland.

I was peering out and down onto its white roof, imagining myself in a plane high above the clouds. Or a traveler come to the edge of the world. Then we heard the car coming up the pebbled driveway.

It was a huge Packard limo, one of the Custom Super Clipper models. Either 1946 or 47, I guessed. Its great weight and size offset by its subtle, light yellow color. It was in perfect condition and a sight to see as it pulled up in front of us and stopped. The driver's door and both back doors opened simultaneously and three people got out.

They were all in a hurry. Something had definitely gone wrong. Obviously they had met more serious problems in the outside world than heavy traffic.

A tall, strikingly handsome man in his late fifties and a much plainer looking woman of about thirty came towards us with tension straining their faces.

But I was watching the driver. He stood anxiously off to the side of the huge car. He also was about thirty but he looked more like a bodyguard than a chauffeur. He was dressed like Elliott Russell, with an expensive jacket over a turtleneck sweater.

He looked like a well tailored line backer. About six-four, two hundred and twenty pounds. Prime USDA beef, wrapped in a college education, with proper social manners the only additives. Except this particular side of beef had been recently damaged.

He stood there rubbing several large bruises on his face which were rapidly growing purple. His nice jacket and sweater were

stained with blood from a deep cut above his left eye. The slight
bulge of a shoulder holster was visible beneath his left arm.

I finally realized he was more embarrassed than anxious. From
the looks of him he probably hadn't done his job right.

The tall handsome man didn't shake hands. He nodded to
Molly, then me.

"I'm Jonathan Sherwin. This is my daughter, Penelope. I hope
you'll excuse us for keeping you waiting. We've had some unpleasant business. And I'm afraid I'll have to keep you waiting a
few minutes more. Penelope will show you inside."

He was used to giving orders but he covered them with his
regal manner. Then he walked briskly over to a side door of the
cottage and disappeared inside.

The bodyguard shuffled over to us and Penelope introduced
him as Dryden. Then she shook our hands.

"I remember you from years ago," she said to Molly. "I remember your red hair and how pretty you are. From when Michael
brought you over to the house."

She gave this compliment like the plain girl who is always in
awe of glamour and beauty. Which, on closer inspection, was a
little strange.

She also had long red hair but it was pulled back severely and
knotted in a bun. Her skin was pale with no trace of make-up to
highlight it, but her face was quite striking and beautiful when
you took time to notice it. She wore a tweed skirt and jacket,
though expensive, more suited to a woman twice her age.

She almost seemed to be in disguise, to be purposely dressing
down, to be hiding herself. Maybe she was afraid of what she had
because all the right equipment was certainly there.

I could see the rounded curves beneath her heavy skirt and

jacket and realized that with her wide, full lips she was actually beautiful. Also sensual. A voluptuous, earth-mother in hiding. Or an exotic desert flower lying dormant, waiting for that rare heavy rain.

Molly gave me a quick glance that said she had also noticed. She acknowledged Penelope's compliment with a smile then said, "well, you've certainly grown up since I last saw you."

Then, with a look that said she wanted to see her reaction, "but you've gone a long way past pretty."

Suddenly Elliott chirped in with, "she sure has." Then he repeated "way past pretty" as if it were a chant or his private mantra.

Well, what do you know. Elliott's in love. But, from the indifference Penelope showed him, it was definitely an unrequited love.

Their compliments didn't set well with Penelope, but made her nervous, uncomfortable. Maybe she didn't want to know how grown-up she really was. Maybe she was like Peter Pan. I decided to rescue her so I asked the bodyguard what had happened to his face.

"When we left the office in Monterey some guy started bothering Mr. Sherwin. I had to stop him."

I suspected we were sharers of the same misfortune and I should have showed him sympathy, but I couldn't resist.

"Did you succeed?"

He shot a quick glance at my plaster cast and then gave me a lingering, hostile stare, trying to figure out if I was laughing at him.

"Well, we're here, aren't we?"

It seemed to be the best he could come up with as he eyed

me suspiciously.

Penelope took pity on his embarrassment and said, "it was Terry Rose." She looked at Molly who seemed to shiver. "You must remember him, don't you?"

Molly moved a step nearer to me. "Yes. I remember him. I remember him very well."

"Well, he came up to my father as we were getting into the car and said he wanted to talk about Michael. Father said he should make an appointment. But Terry didn't like that. He started to pull my father off to the side. That's when Dryden and Shadow got into it."

"Who's Shadow?" I said.

Elliott answered. "He's Mr. Sherwin's other bodyguard."

"He's my partner," Dryden said a little too loudly. He was still giving me his cold cautious stare.

"Shadow? Well isn't that cute. I bet you two are inseparable."

He didn't like me needling him but he couldn't do anything about it just now. He was out on a limb and had to saw it off to get back down. A little twitch of his facial muscles tried to pull the corners of his mouth into something like a smile.

"His real name is William Johnson. Shadow because he's black, I'm white. We're a team, in business, always together. We're the best."

He seemed to like explaining the logic of his macho-brotherhood to outsiders. I said, "your shadow is always with you but I don't see him. Where is he now?"

Penelope answered. "He's in the hospital in Monterey. Terry broke his arm." She looked sympathetically at Dryden, and I felt like hiding my cast inside my sleeve. "Then he hit Dryden and threw him out into the middle of the street. He threw him into the side of a passing car." I could see Dryden wince. "He was almost killed."

In a strange, distant tone Molly asked, "what did Terry do then?"

"He disappeared. A crowd had formed and he simply disappeared."

Dryden was aching to salvage his damaged pride. He said, "next time won't go so easy for Mr. Terry Rose." He patted the gun under his left shoulder. "Next time I'll be ready for him."

Molly seemed to be in a daze, held captive by her memories of the past. But Dryden's boast of future revenge brought her back to the present with a start. Her eyes focused intently on Dryden and her tone had a mocking quality when she spoke.

"I hope you're not one of those men who's not afraid of anybody. If you are, you'd better make an exception in this case."

"Stop. You're scaring me to death." He was almost sneering now. "There's no need to warn me. He just had the advantage because I was reluctant to get rough with Miss Sherwin present. Shadow and I can handle anybody. We know our business. And we don't need you sticking your nose in it."

Molly raised her right forefinger and lightly touched her nose with it. I couldn't tell what was coming but I knew I'd enjoy it.

"I'm not trying to warn you. I'm trying to save you."

His sneer stayed in place. Molly turned to me then looked back at Dryden. This was no game or laughing matter to her and she was clearly frustrated.

"You've been using your ears so long to hang your sunglasses on it's affected your hearing."

Dryden's sneer disappeared. She had his attention now.

"Now listen to me, you macho saphead! Before you can get

that gun out of its holster, Terry Rose will already have stomped you and be using your teeth to clean the bottom of his shoes!"

A nervous giggle came out of Penelope. Dryden was getting angry and about to say something but Elliott stopped him. We all just stood there, awkwardly, for a minute. I seemed to be the only one enjoying myself.

Finally Penelope broke the tension with, "I think I'd better take you inside now."

As we shuffled through the main entrance I said to Molly, "Sam Spade couldn't have said it better."

We passed through a small reception room and entered a large rectangular area that covered most of the left side of the cottage on the ground floor. It was about twenty-five feet across and stretched about sixty feet to the back of the house.

There were two large fireplaces, both along the inside wall. The first fireplace was the center piece for a comfortable living room area. Two plush couches, several plump easy chairs and a scattering of fur rugs and oversized cushions centered around it. About midway down the same wall a spiral staircase twisted its way up to the second floor.

The other fireplace was at the end of the inside wall about three-fourths of the way toward the back of the house. This fireplace, open on two sides, formed the corner of the inside wall which doglegged off to the right, revealing another rectangular area, open to the main room, and running along the back of the house. Both walls on the back and left side of the house were made entirely of huge clear panels of glass that ran ten feet high, from floor to ceiling.

Penelope led us to this back corner of the room where the two rectangles joined. It was a light-headed, dizzy experience. An incredible view, down the coast and out to sea, as the rocky cliffs plunged several hundred feet down to the sea just outside.

Then she said, "Elliott, you'd better help Dryden clean that cut. There's a first aid kit in the downstairs bathroom." They went off through a door that opened behind the spiral staircase.

She smiled cautiously and took us over to a beautifully set round dining table, hand carved out of goncalo alves, an exotic Brazilian wood, amber colored with dark, almost black, swirls and streaks.

The table was nestled in the corner of the two glass walls and had a view that would make an astronaut airsick. It could seat six but was only set for three, so Penelope wasn't to be included in our luncheon party. We all sat down in a little semicircle, facing the open sea.

I began to feel like Alice when she fell down the rabbit hole. I had entered a strange world where I was out of place. Everything in this world was recognizable but somehow distorted.

Here we were, sitting down to an ordinary meal at an ordinary table with an ordinary view. Except that the view was ordinary only if you were a sea gull and the table had only recently emerged from some Amazonian rain forest.

And by now I had a pretty good idea about how ordinary the meal and the man we were to share it with would be.

Too much money and too much time and too much rarefied imagination had gone into making his world just right. And I didn't like it.

Molly said, "do you know why we're here to see your father?"

Penelope fidgeted. "I, I just know it has something to do with Michael." I couldn't tell whether she was hiding something or just trying to be socially discreet. "That's all I know about it." Her tone tried to conceal a small flutter. "That's all he told me."

I asked, "do you know who I am, what I do?"

"Your name is Walker. You're a detective."

The word made her uneasy so I pushed it a little further. "I find out things." I thought I saw her pull back. "I look into secrets. Mysteries. I unravel them and try to make sense of them."

She had definitely pulled back into her chair, stiffly. Her eyes jumped around the room for a few seconds before settling again on Molly, then me. She breathed out sharply, relaxed, then gave me a small, slow smile. She seemed to have decided her secrets were safe from me.

"That sounds fascinating. It must be very rewarding work."

She was beginning a game, trying to turn the tables on me. "When did you last see your brother?"

Her game ended abruptly. "Why, I haven't seen him since he ran off, years ago."

"Were you very upset when he disappeared?"

"No. Not at all." The simplicity and finality of her answer annoyed me. "We weren't close at all. He was the oldest and I am the youngest."

"Was? Do you think Michael is dead?"

Molly became very still. Penelope looked confused, then said, "why, no. Of course not! I said 'was' because Michael hasn't been part of my life for such a long time."

"From what I hear he never was much a part of your life. Or part of the family. Can you tell me why?"

She looked accusingly at Molly. She started hesitantly, as if deciding how much to give me. Like a politician paying off the local cop.

"Michael was moody and distant. He was often unpleasant to be around. He was always suspicious."

"Suspicious of what? Was there something to be suspicious of in your family?"

Her blue eyes narrowed as she chose how to answer. "Don't be silly. I was just a young girl then. I was only thirteen."

She had decided on the offhand approach. To keep it superficial, as if relating yesterday's ordinary events.

"Michael was distrustful of everything. Of everybody. He was a very disturbed young man. He even hit my father."

"Why did he hit him?"

"It was an argument over drugs. Michael was using drugs all the time. They made him unbalanced."

I looked at Molly. She was shaking her head "no." Almost imperceptibly.

Penelope noticed. She said, "not only did Michael distrust everybody. No one could really trust Michael." Then she turned to Molly and gave her her best sly smile. "Isn't that so, Mary?"

"Yes Penelope. That did prove to be true." Molly looked Penelope over. Slowly. Deliberately. From toe to head. Then she gave her back her own sly smile. "Since then I've learned to carefully examine the way people look. Sometimes they try to actually disguise themselves. To appear to be something or somebody they're not. Can you imagine that?"

Penelope fidgeted uncomfortably. Her little game had turned against her.

"Did you know Terry Rose?" I asked. She looked at me, glad to be out from under Molly's scrutiny.

"I used to see him quite a bit. He was always with Michael. In fact, if Michael trusted anybody, it was Terry."

"What did you think of Terry? Did you get along with him?"

"Well, I was a lot younger than Terry. He was always doing tricks for me."

"Tricks?"

"They weren't really tricks. Things he would do to show how strong he was. He used to break walnuts in the crook of his arm and he bent quarters using just his thumb and forefinger. As a young girl I was very impressed."

I was impressed too.

Dryden and Elliott came into the room and crossed over to our table. Dryden had a bandage covering the cut above his left eye. He also had on a fresh turtleneck and a new jacket. There must be a bin of them somewhere. Standard uniform for service at the Institute.

Elliott stood beside Penelope, watching her with big calf eyes. Dryden stood off to the side watching me. I think he wanted to show me the quickest way down from the cliff.

Finally our host returned. He came from the back corner of the house. A long-legged stride along the back wall of windows. Easy mannered. Confident. Oblivious to our waiting or the precipitous drop just outside. Wearing a dark charcoal silk suit. Elegantly tailored to his long, slender shape. A crisp white shirt with buttoned cuffs. None of the new color shirts or ornamental jewelry for him. A dark maroon tie. Not too wide, not too narrow. Perfect. Polished in the old manner.

He must have been sixty. Or a shade under. Still had full, jet black hair. Probably was real. Probably had the same barber as Ronald Reagan. He was a handsome man. Reminded me of an ageless George Hamilton. But more sophisticated. More patrician.

As he reached the table his presence set everyone but Molly and me in motion. Dryden straightened up. Almost at attention, his eyes left me and followed his master. Even Elliott came out of the spell he was under with Penelope. He moved a step away from her. Alert. Waiting for any instructions.

Penelope stood up. Glad to see him. Maybe so she could get away from us. Quite a contrast. Her so plain, him so elegant.

"Father. You took so long. I've got to leave immediately. I'm almost late already."

A gentle chiding. Like a loving mother for her favorite son. He took her hands and smiled. The apple of her father's eye.

"I'm sorry, dear. I had to straighten out that problem we had. You run along now. I'll see to our guests."

She looked at Molly and me and said it was nice talking with us. Then she walked down the long room and out the door we came in. Not a glance at nor a kind word for Elliott. He looked dejected and his soulful eyes followed her out the door.

"Elliott," I said. "The successful suitor of Penelope must be able to string Ulysses' bow. And beware old cunning and wily Ulysses himself."

I might as well have said it in Greek from the uncomprehending look he gave me. But the words "suitor" and "Penelope" got through to him. He stood awkwardly waiting for any comment Sherwin might make. He seemed to act in all things as if he feared their consequences.

Sherwin ignored Elliott's embarrassment and said, "I won't need you until after lunch."

Elliott's expression brightened. He excused himself and

hustled out the door after his beloved Penelope.

When he was gone Sherwin turned to me and said, "he's no fool, you know." Then he told Dryden to wait in the small reception room.

Molly and I had remained seated. When we were alone, Sherwin sat down across from us with his back to the corner where the two walls of glass came together. I wondered if this were another imperious gesture. Turning his back on all that grandeur. Letting us have the view. Reminding us that it was his whenever he wanted it.

"We'll talk while we eat," he said. "I follow a strict regimen and I'm already an hour off schedule. I have my own chef and a special kitchen downstairs. I'm very particular about what I eat. You can either share my meal or my chef will make something to suit your own tastes."

I looked at Molly and she nodded. "We'll have whatever you're having."

"Good. You'll be better off for it." A Japanese waiter in a white coat suddenly appeared. "You can begin serving now." The waiter disappeared through a door next to the fireplace.

Sherwin took a drink of water from the glass in front of him. "Glacier water. The purest on earth."

Molly said, "Mr. Sherwin. Do you know where Michael is?"

The skin just beneath his left eye twitched. "It's that damn Terry Rose. Stirring up trouble, after all these years. No. I don't know where Michael is. And I don't want to know."

"Don't you care about your son?" she said.

"He's no son of mine." The same patch of skin jumped again. "Not anymore, he's not."

"The reason we're here," I said, "is that Mary Dugan's

daughter, Katherine, is also Michael's daughter."

His eyes were hard and calculating. "Don't take me for a fool. I figured that out when she was born. But what's that got to do with me? I don't need any grandchildren at this late date."

"And my daughter certainly doesn't need or want you as a grandfather." Molly was anxious to disown him as any potential family member.

Somehow Molly's outburst pleased him. He leaned back in his chair and smiled.

"Good. Now that we've got that cleared up, I'll do what I can to help you."

He was a tough old bird. An aging king protecting his dominion from unwanted intruders.

"Have you seen Michael since that time on the pier?" I asked.

He took a while to answer. Probably wondering how much I knew.

"No. I haven't seen Michael since that day."

"Would you tell us what you two argued about?"

The silent waiter reappeared and set a small salad and a basket of bread before each of us, then disappeared again.

Sherwin saw me examining the bread and said, "it's unleavened bread. The fermentation needed to make leavened bread is a corruption of man's potential purity."

Like Alice in the rabbit hole. Curiouser and curiouser.

I began to pick at my salad which was quite good. Sherwin seemed more interested in explaining what we were eating than in answering my question.

"The oil and vinegar comes from my own olive and apple orchards in the San Joaquin Valley. Most of the vegetables are grown in the Pajaro and Salinas Valleys. No pesticides or any other chemicals. Everything is carefully monitored. No additives. No impurities."

Molly gave me a light kick under the table but didn't say anything. She continued eating her salad. Content to let me joust with the Mad Hatter.

"About your argument with Michael," I said.

Reluctantly Sherwin's attention came back to the world of additives and impurities.

"Look around you, Mr. Walker." It was the first time he had acknowledged he knew who I was. "Do you like what you see? I mean the whole place, grounds and all."

"It's very beautiful. Almost perfect. Maybe too perfect."

"Nothing can be too perfect! Perfection of body and spirit, this place, have become my life's work. And I owe it all to my prodigal son."

He was as zealous as an Old Testament prophet. And probably just as tough and determined.

"I built this Institute after Michael disappeared. It's a monument standing against my son's wasted life. That's what we argued about that day on the pier. My son's wasted life."

"What had he done to waste his life?"

"Drugs! He had a weak personality! He wasn't strong enough to stand firmly against the blowing winds."

Molly jumped in again. "That isn't so. Michael might have had a weak personality but he wasn't using drugs. Not before he disappeared. Remember I was with him all the time then."

Sherwin looked at Molly as if she were a small child who had spoken out-of-place.

"There are many forms of corruption, my dear, and Michael

indulges most of them."

"How do you know what Michael indulges? I thought you said you haven't seen him."

He looked at me like I was another offending child.

"I haven't seen him. But I did keep track of him for a time."

He took another drink of his precious glacier water. Keeping us waiting. Reminding us who had the upper hand. When he was sure he had made his point he began again.

"I kept track of Michael for about a year after he disappeared." He answered my unvoiced question with, "through certain private resources I have available to me."

Then he spoke more to Molly than to me.

"Michael and Terry both vanished into that sinkhole of despair, San Francisco. More precisely into that area know as the Haight/Ashbury, that breeding ground of corruption."

He was pleased that he had our full attention. Was enjoying his own description of Michael's fall from grace.

"That was at the very beginning of 1967. The very beginning of the so-called Hippie movement that led to their so-called 'summer of love' later that same year."

He laughed. Coarsely. His mood was taking an ugly turn.

"Michael and Terry might have been the architects of the entire Hippie movement for all I know. They were certainly there at the beginning."

"How do you know all of this?" Molly asked.

"Let's just say that, though not precise, my information is accurate. For the first few months they were involved in all kinds of community activities. Real idealists. Trying to build a utopia."

He watched us with flaring eyes and a sardonic smile.

"This was just before the summer started and every freak in

the entire country who wasn't locked up slid into the area. Well, they gave up on their false utopia when the drugs took over. Drugs became their masters.

"Michael was admitted to a clinic once. Kicking and screaming, they told me. The result of a bad trip. And Terry was picked up by the police several times for suspected muggings. All drug related, but he was never prosecuted.

"They were quite a pair. Twin spirits. Real soul mates. Michael had turned twenty-one and, by the end of that summer, got his hands on a trust fund I had unwisely set up for him. He withdrew all the money. All I could find out was that he bought some land. After that Michael and Terry disappeared."

"How much money are we talking about?"

He had waited for me to ask. It was his way of putting me in my place.

"Oh, not so much. About $250,000."

"He could buy a lot of land with that amount. Especially back then."

"Depends where the land is," he said. Reminding us again how different his world was from ours.

"And you never found out where the land was?"

"No." Then he ended the discussion with a wave of his hand. "And by that time I didn't care anymore."

It was over. He had just dismissed us. I figured he was lying about not knowing the location of the land, but I knew we wouldn't get any more useful information out of him.

I was tired of him showing the whip hand. So, for my own amusement, I said, very politely, "you have been quite patient with us. But you really haven't been much help."

He hadn't expected to hear that. I had taken something away

that he felt he had given us, and he didn't like it.

"You see, we really need some current information that can help us find Michael now. Your information is outdated."

I felt Molly's foot tap against mine. She was eager to get in on this too.

"We felt that a man of your importance, with your resources," she began, "would know something worthwhile. Not just old gossip."

The patch of skin under his eye began dancing to an erratic beat.

I wanted to keep him off balance. Hoping we'd learn something. "We need information that can clear up this mess about the letters."

He was just about to terminate our meeting when I mentioned the letters.

"Letters? What letters?"

With perfect timing the silent waiter appeared with our main course.

Unobtrusively, he set a platter before each of us. An entire fish, head and all, some brown rice and snow peas. Sherwin's two eyes watched me, demanding an explanation. The topside eye of the fish also watched me, demanding nothing.

Some kind of a sea bass, I thought, that never swam in the open sea. Too much impurity, too many pollutants. Raised in a tank or a pond for sure.

When the waiter had left us I looked up at Sherwin and said, "A man may fish with the worm that hath eat of a king, and eat of the fish that hath fed of that worm."

"Not that fish. That fish never saw a worm in its life. Grown in tanks and fed a special diet." So much for Shakespeare. "Now what about these letters?"

First I turned to Molly. "Does your fish have a certain wall-eyed sadness about it?"

He was not amused. "The letters Walker! Don't play games with me. You might not like the way they turn out."

"I am not one of your silent house boys. We did not come here to serve you or make your life more pleasant."

He sat back in his chair, ignoring his food, scrutinizing us. Calm outside. Inside all agitation. Elegance and childish petulance. Maybe even dangerous rage. Like the bottle of Dom Perignon, shaken then sealed with a cork. About to explode.

"The letters, Mr. Sherwin, were written to her daughter, Katherine. Three of them. Vulgar, insane rantings about the whereabouts of Katherine's father. Rantings about corrupt blood. That's why I'm here. To find Michael and stop these letters."

His eyes had lost their focus and he was deathly still.

"Corrupt blood?"

He muttered it several times. Each time softer and less audible as if he were descending into some private subterranean world.

I tried to bring him out of it. "Do you know who might have written such letters? If the writer knows your son is Katherine's father, it might be someone who has a grudge against you. Or your family."

He gaped at me as if I were speaking some incomprehensible language. I didn't think he had heard me when he said, "do the letters mention Michael by name?" His tone was completely flat, with no inflection.

"No. Michael isn't mentioned. In fact the letters seem totally impersonal. Except that they were sent to Katherine. They seem like sermons from some fanatic religious cult."

Molly said, "have you ever been threatened by someone like this? Someone who's obviously crazy?"

She looked at me. Sherwin didn't seem to be listening, although his eyes were watching us.

"Then, again, maybe the writer doesn't even know about Michael," I said. "But a man of your position might have enemies. Might especially attract the lunatic fringe."

He still didn't speak. But he watched us. I decided on a little shock therapy.

"I understand that two of your other children were killed in accidents earlier the same year that Michael ran off."

His brows tightened. The alert predatory look came back into his expression. He had been off somewhere in a private world but he spoke to me as if he had just been interrupted.

"I didn't have much time to check you out, Walker. I like to be prepared for these little meetings. But I didn't have time for a complete run-down on you."

Molly and I exchanged confused glances. He didn't seem to be having the same conversation that we were.

"All that I really learned was that you moved to San Francisco from New York several years ago. That you're a private detective, not married. That you live in a house on Pacific Heights that a private detective couldn't afford. That you have relatives prominently placed on the San Francisco police department."

His eyes squinted at me like he was sighting me down the barrel of a gun.

"Anything you'd care to add to that?"

Though all his lights were on, I began to wonder if anyone was at home. Maybe my question about his two dead children was too much for him. But he didn't seem upset. He was alert again and his expression showed a curious interest in me. Like a spider that just noticed a fly caught in its web.

I ignored his question and kept to my own line. "I understand that Michael talked to you about the deaths of his brother and sister that day on the pier?"

"So you moved from New York to San Francisco?"

Point-counter-point. We were sitting there in the same place, across from each other. But, like parallel lines, we would never meet.

"Isn't that like moving from Sodom to Gomorrah?"

I kept to my opposite, parallel line.

"The reason I asked about the deaths of your two children is that trouble sometimes runs in families. Maybe that explains some of Michael's problems. These letters refer to corruption of the blood. Michael felt that way too. That he was corrupt. Evil. If there is, so to speak, bad blood in your family, someone else might be troubled enough to send these letters."

He didn't like my questions about his family. His internal agitation seemed to expand inside him as I spoke. Seemed to fill him up, building to an unbearable pressure. For a second I thought he would literally pop his cork. Like the Dom Perignon. Outwardly he was still calm. Like those few seconds of total quiet before you feel those first tremors. Before you feel the full force of the quake. Even the tic under his left eye stopped.

Then I noticed it. Realized what had bothered me since I first saw him. The skin and muscles on the right side of his face, under the right eye and all the way down to his jaw, were frozen. They had not moved since we started talking. The tic under the other eye had distracted my attention and I hadn't noticed.

He had had a stroke sometime. A mild one probably. And it

had left the right side of his face partially paralyzed.

His next sound confirmed it. A soft, almost guttural, slur. Like a wheel caught in the sand, spinning to find traction and free itself.

"Yooouurrrr." He didn't finish. His eyes darted between Molly and me. Fear that we had heard. Had seen and noticed. Betrayed. That he had given himself away. Out of control. His arm reached out for the glacier water. Shaking perceptibly. His eyes vigilant. Uneasy. He grabbed the water with both hands. Holding it steady. Raising it to his lips. Like a priest. Blood of Christ. He gulped. Closed his eyes. Drawing power from the sacred liquid. Calmer now. Control returning. He opened his eyes, setting the glass down with one hand. A nasty gleam about the eyes. The spinning wheel finally caught and freed.

"Walker? You're not one of those New York Jews who move out here and change their names, are you? Or worse. One of those New York Jew homosexuals?"

I got up and walked over to the window. The fog bank was blanketing the horizon but the coast was still clear and sunny.

I turned. Molly gave me a bright-eyed look and tapped the tip of her nose with her finger. The mad lord of all he surveyed was leaning back in his chair. Composed and in control again.

The crafty old bastard was enjoying himself. But something about the letters had momentarily broken down that patrician presence. If I were to get anymore useful information from him, I had to keep him off balance. I decided to jump over to his parallel line and see what I could stir up.

"Golly, Mr. Sherwin. I sure wish I could help you out. I'm not really a Jew, you see. But I dearly love my bagels and I do get a craving for Dr. Brown's Celery Tonic now and then. Could that count, do you think? And just the other day I was thinking about opening my Chanukah Club account. Only six more months, you know."

I crossed over and stood behind Molly, resting my hands on her shoulders. Sherwin stared as I continued to beam sincerity at him.

"I'll use the account to buy presents for my little schiksa here." I patted Molly's head proudly. "Isn't she one gorgeous goyishe gal?"

"There's nothing amusing about Jews," he said pedantically. "And play-acting can't disguise their invidious influences."

Invidious? Now there's a word you don't hear much. I sat back down in my chair, giving the impression of a dejected child.

"Play-acting? You're accusing me of acting? I assure you I've never acted in my life."

Molly gave my performance a wry smile of appreciation. I showed Sherwin a nervous, almost pleading expression.

"My God! What's happening to me!" I almost shouted.

My level of anxiety startled him. He was my front row audience, waiting for the next scene. I held eye contact with him and began with a quiver in my voice.

"You see, this isn't the first time this has happened to me."

He watched me, his interest growing stronger than his suspicions.

"Last week, after returning from the Safeway store, when I unpacked my grocery bag, I found...At first I refused to believe they were mine...Refused to believe I had bought them."

I stopped. Looked around furtively. Building his impatience. Drawing him in. Setting the hook.

"Found what?" he said too quickly, belying his matter-of-fact manner.

"Matzos," I confessed forlornly. "Matzos instead of Saltines. Gefilte fish instead of Mrs. Paul's."

Sherwin's agitation level began rising rapidly. Dripping sincerity, I looked at him. "I guess that's what you meant by invidious. I guess I didn't get out of New York in time."

The muscle under his left eye began its spastic dance again. The Dom Perignon needed just a little more shaking.

He expected respect and was used to giving advice. Nothing would anger him quicker than mocking his usual position.

So, I said, with a tone of full respect, "I need your advice. Do you think I have a chance? If I promise to go straight? If I promise to buy retail, never discount? If I eat Wonder Bread, instead of rye? If I give up my Chanukah Club account?"

Like the eye of a hurricane, the paralyzed patch on his face was calm, while all around it the storm was forming. Little strings of muscle tightened, giving his face a harsh, stretched appearance, anchored at the two hard lumps on each side of his clenched jaw. His eyes were two fixed points of disdain.

He shoved his chair back abruptly and stood up. Leaned forward, bracing himself against the table with the knuckles of both hands. His head rigid in the concave arch of his hunched shoulders. Fanatic eyes glowering down at us like an old-time preacher from the pulpit. The prophet Elijah in a silk suit and Italian leather shoes. The wrath of God was about to descend upon us. The God of the glacier water.

"Sarcasm and disrespect are the devil's ways. Hallmarks of the lost and soulless man who has given up hope. Hope of ever attaining the strength and purity of body and spirit that God intended for us."

A few stray drops of saliva landed in our direction. I suspected he would be foaming at the mouth before he was through.

"Puuurr...ity." This time the slurred speech did not embarrass him or diminish his zeal. "Puurrity is both man's task and his reee...ree...reward."

He was like an elegant time piece running down.

"But purity is not a gift," he continued. "That's why I founded this Institute. To keep back the black tide of a sick world. A world lost in cynicism and sensual and spiritual corruption. The lost way to God is through purity of spirit. And purity of spirit is achieved only when the body has been purified."

Obviously purity was the big word here. He had managed to say it four more times without slurring. He was coming down from his emotionally-charged high and was back in control. His eyes lost their heavenly glow and regained an earthly focus. He saw me smiling at him.

"Amen, Reverend," I said, folding my hands in a prayerful attitude.

He pushed himself back from the table to an upright position. Disrespect and sarcasm were all around him.

"You remind me of my son, Michael," he said calmly enough. "The same smartass manner. The same lack of character and commitment. You'd better straighten yourself out, if it's not too late already?"

"Is that what you told Michael when he came to see you the other day?"

"Who told you that?" he demanded.

"Are you finally ready to help us find your son? Stop preaching at us and give us some information we can use."

"Who told you that Michael was here?" he demanded again. We were back to our two parallel lines.

He had tried to keep his rage bottled up inside and seemed determined to be rid of us before anything broke through again.

He said, "you asked for my advice a minute ago. Now I'll give it to you. Little men should be more careful of big men."

Molly and I remained seated.

"Do you mean little in relation to height or little in relation to overall size?"

He was all calm and efficient again.

"I have a radio broadcast to prepare and you are both leaving. Right now." He gestured down the large room toward the door. "You can find your own way out."

"But we haven't touched our main course yet," I protested.

He didn't respond, but stood with stiff composure. We both got up from the table.

Finally he spoke. "You think you're insolent manner quite amusing, don't you?"

"Actually, what I think, Mr. Sherwin, is that you've known where Michael is all these years. And, although you might not have seen him before, you did see him recently. And I do find it amusing imagining your motives for not helping us. And also why such a big important man like yourself is so easily disturbed by such a little man like me."

With that we turned and left. Faithful guard dog that he was we found Dryden sitting behind the desk in the small reception room. He was reading a glossy magazine.

I asked him where Sherwin's radio station was located. He gruffly replied that the main studios were in Monterey but that Sherwin did most of his live broadcasts from a small basement studio just beneath us.

During the drive back to the main gate I asked Molly what she thought of Sherwin.

"There's something wrong with that whole damn family. And I wish I could keep me and Katie out of it. I wouldn't be surprised if Sherwin wrote those letters himself. Anyway, I still want you to find Michael. Katie needs to finally come to terms with him."

Setting her feathered hat in her lap, she turned sideways, facing me.

"But it's more important than ever that you make sure Michael is okay. That Michael is safe for Katie. She doesn't need to come to terms with a long lost father who turns out to be a psychopath."

I made the sharp curve at the top of the hill, where we had first seen the Institute, and its strange world disappeared in my rearview mirror.

She also had watched it vanish. "I'm glad we're away from that place. What made you so sure that Michael had gone there to see his father?"

"I wasn't so sure but it fit. Something brought Terry down here looking for Michael, made him accost Sherwin on the street today. And there was something in the air between Penelope and her father I didn't like. A family secret or disturbance they wanted to keep from outsiders. So I got Sherwin upset enough and off-balance enough that he proved my suspicion when I surprised him with it."

"Do you really think he's kept track of Michael all these years? Can he really be that cunning and that insensitive? To have watched Michael so long with apparently no trace of feeling? And for what purpose?"

"He's like an Old Testament prophet. He's fanatical and very righteous. Michael seems to have affronted him personally, or his beliefs, which probably amount to the same thing. And for his transgression Michael was cast out. Why Jonathan would want to keep track of his son is still a mystery, but I think we can rule out fatherly concern.

"Maybe Michael is a threat to Jonathan and the perfect world he's constructed. Maybe that was the basis of their fight on the pier so many years ago. One thing's certain. I shook him up when I mentioned those letters. And I wish I knew why."

"Well, the father certainly isn't going to solve our mystery for us," she said ruefully. "You'll have to find the son for that. Maybe I'll finally learn the meaning of that note he sent me. Maybe that's been the real mystery all along."

We reached the main gate and were stopped by the two guards. Jonathan Sherwin had built his own personal heaven on the California coast. A heaven where you were greeted at the gate not by St. Peter but two armed guards. It seemed appropriate after what we had experienced inside.

They logged our time at 1:47 and we turned left onto Highway 1, back toward Monterey.

NINE

"So, You've just come from the Inner Sanctum?"
A burst of small, thin wrinkles spread out from the corners of her eyes and mouth. Like a miniature sunset, warming the small room.

"Do you know what a rare privilege you've been given?"

"Believe me. It didn't feel like a privilege," Molly said. "What we're hoping, Harriet, is that you can fill us in on the mysterious Mr. Sherwin, the Institute and his family. Anything that you've got, history, fact or rumor, would all be welcome. But I'm afraid I can't explain why we need to know. Except that I almost married Michael Sherwin many years ago."

Molly had introduced me as a friend, not a detective, and an inquisitive squint narrowed Harriet Nilsson's eyes for a second, then her smile widened. A pixie's amusement with the world glowed from her face.

"Well, I love mysteries. Give me a minute to put my mental files in order."

She swiveled her desk chair from side to side and started rooting through old memories.

She looked like a Danish leprechaun. On the wee side of five feet and the far side of eighty, she had long ago captured and still held an impish fascination with life.

We were sitting in a small study in the corner of her home.

I had asked Molly where we could get some background on Sherwin and she had brought me here. Harriet Nilsson was the unofficial historian for the Monterey Peninsula and wrote a daily column for the area's papers. Molly guaranteed she knew everything that happened between Santa Cruz and Big Sur.

The room looked like a medieval philosopher's chamber, with books and papers stacked everywhere, from floor to ceiling. We were seated across the desk from her in two cracked and worn straight-back leather chairs, which were surprisingly comfortable.

Over her shoulder and through the piles of books on the window sill I could make out the tower of San Carlos Borromeo de Carmelo, the old Spanish mission at Carmel.

She stopped swiveling, leaned forward against the desk and said, "fire when ready, Gridley."

"If you give us a general history first, it will help me ask the right questions," I said.

She began in a relaxed manner with a soft smooth tone unbroken by age. I felt like a small boy again, listening to my grandmother weave stories out of fact, fable and fairy tales. I half expected her to start with "once upon a time."

"They came to the Peninsula about a year after the war. World War II, that is. I first saw them at the dedication of a war memorial they had funded, a few months after they arrived.

"They were a striking couple, Jonathan and Rebecca Sherwin. Very young, very rich and very handsome. He was tall, lean and elegant. And, even though he was in his early twenties, he commanded attention and respect. Rebecca was very glamorous and beautiful. A real standout.

"Monterey was a lot quieter and less sophisticated back then, and people thought she was a movie star. They had a son, about six months old, named Michael and were living in town while their huge house was being constructed on the coast just north of Carmel, on the Seventeen Mile Drive.

"They were a mystery couple and really livened up the gossip around here. Where they came from? Where they got their money? How much did they have?"

She paused and laughed. "I can tell you the local busybodies were in agony. Especially me. You see, we couldn't get any solid gossip on them. They were the biggest item on our menu and we kept serving them up, again and again, until they became leftovers."

She laughed again. "They were very private people. Open and friendly on a social level, they were very secretive about their personal life. It took almost a year before we got their story. And then we didn't get much.

"Jonathan Sherwin was from Bishop. Back then, before it became a recreation center, a very small town on the eastern side of the high Sierras. A god-awful isolated spot in those days.

"His parents were originally from Chicago and quite wealthy and had moved to Bishop because of its beauty and isolation. They were already well past forty and childless when Jonathan was born. Another child, a girl, came after him.

"Well, Jonathan, who was only seventeen, enlisted in the navy when the war started. He was stationed at Treasure Island in San Francisco Bay and met Rebecca there during the last year of the war. That same year, while he was on duty in the Philippines, his sister and parents were killed in a car accident on a mountain road near Bishop.

"So, in the spring of 1946, Jonathan and his new wife and

baby settled here and raised quite a large family for people with so much money. Five children total.

"And all the way into the late 60's they seemed to lead the ideal life. They attended social and political functions, donated liberally to charities and were charming to boot. Perfect, loving, caring citizens. Then something changed and for almost two decades I've tried to find out what happened."

She looked at us curiously. "I'd give my eyeteeth to know." She lingered over the words. "And they're still my own real teeth."

I grinned and Molly said, "well, if everything turns out right, Harriet, I think we'll be able to help you out. But we'll let you keep your teeth."

She smiled at us with the delight of four score and more successful years.

"Well, the 60's was a hard decade for a lot of us. Assassinations, riots, protests. Anyway, their family life changed dramatically.

"In 1967 two of their children, one boy and one girl, both in their mid-teens, were killed in separate accidents. Both in November. The boy in a car accident, the girl in a fall from the cliffs behind their home. Not long after, the oldest child, Michael, disappeared and hasn't been seen since. But I don't have to tell you that."

I interrupted. "Don't you think the two deaths and Michael's disappearance explain a lot?"

She made a silent, shrewd appraisal of me. "It should, but it doesn't satisfy me. I mean it does explain the change, but not all of it.

"You see, Jonathan Sherwin went from being the charming lord of the manor to the self-righteous son-of-a-bitch you saw today. He hardened and filled with hate. He built that damned

Institute on hate.

"Now, he has no compassion for the weak or downtrodden. He simply wants them purged. He has a vision of a purified America and he rails against public figures and programs he considers soft and unable to meet the challenge.

"Through his radio station he pours out hateful nonsense. Against immigrants and homosexuals. And many others. On and on. His views are unrealistic and simplistic. Unfeeling and uncaring. Nonsense! But dangerous nonsense.

"In bare terms he wants to put up the barriers to keep out all new elements he considers impure and abandon or imprison or deport all those already here.

"Now I can understand bitterness in a man after the senseless death of his children, but there's something else there. I can even understand his desire to build a better world, away from the one that let him down, and retreat to it. But there's still something else going on. Something else that explains the active campaign he's been waging against a sinful world."

She sighed in frustration.

"Maybe I should accept the obvious, the standard explanation for the change. Everyone else has."

Defiance crept back into her expression.

"But I can't. Put it down to an old woman's crankiness." Her mood brightened as she scrutinized us. "Judging by the looks of the two of you, though, I'll stick with my doubts. As I said, I do love a mystery.

"Well, to bring you up to date, Rebecca more and more retired from public life. Now she's almost a total recluse. And Jonathan entered public life on a grand scale. He built the Institute, he bought that radio station that pollutes our air waves and he has become a major political force. He's become an unhealthy influence. A bad neighbor and a mean citizen."

She sat back in her chair and began swiveling lightly.

"Now ask me questions."

She was quite a grand old lady. Feisty, as they used to say.

"Was there any doubt that the deaths of his children were accidental?" I asked.

She hadn't expected that. "Impossible. There were several witnesses to each accident. The girl fell while climbing with friends and the boy ploughed his car into a large truck on Highway 1 in the middle of rush hour traffic."

"What about the other two children?"

"Penelope's the youngest but she must be about thirty by now. She runs a sculpture gallery in San Francisco. Lives up there too. She's a staid, reserved girl. Doesn't have to be, though. If she'd let herself go, she'd be a real knockout. The spitting image of her mother thirty years ago.

"Diana's several years older. I've met her a few times. She's the most likable of the family. A real scholar. Teaches classical languages at Stanford. Lives in Palo Alto but visits here all the time. I think she's very close to Rebecca, her mother. As far as I know neither of the girls have ever married. Anything else I can help with?"

"How does Jonathan manage all the money for his activities? Is he still living off his inheritance?"

She grinned at us. "Ah, money. Money is always an interesting story. Now this is a real fairy tale. The stuff that dreams are made of. Of being in the right place at the right time.

"It seems Jonathan's parents were real nature lovers and they bought a great deal of land in the mountain areas north of Bishop.

A lot of that land was around Mammoth Lakes and Mammoth Mountain and is now one of the world's largest ski areas.

"On top of that Jonathan happened to buy up as much of the land as he could get along the south shore of Lake Tahoe. Now that was just after the War when land was still reasonably cheap.

"Well, you know what happened to that area. Gambling, skiing and resorts. He's still the largest private landowner in the Tahoe basin. And of course money gets money. He owns a lot of downtown Monterey and has agricultural holdings all over central California."

Molly glanced at me and I nodded. "You've been a big help, Harriet," she said. "Come by the restaurant soon and I'll make you a special dinner."

We both stood up. As I shook Harriet's hand I said, "maybe we can clear up that mystery for you."

TEN

The word for Carmel is quaint. The houses bear no numbers and everyone picks up his own mail. Its residential neighborhoods have no street lamps, sidewalks or curbs and cars make way for trees growing in the middle of the road.

At night, on a side street, with the trees arched over, you can feel like Hansel and Gretel lost in the forest.

I took Junipero up to Ocean, the main commercial street, turned left, and dropped Molly at Dolores near her restaurant.

After giving me directions to find the Sherwin house, she said she hoped to see me tomorrow evening after she finished scouting restaurant locations in San Francisco. She glided off down Dolores, flowing red hair and jaunty white feather.

I continued across Ocean, made a right onto San Antonio, heading for the Carmel gate of the Seventeen Mile Drive.

The Drive follows the coastline of the Monterey Peninsula between Carmel and Pacific Grove, a small community adjacent to Monterey. It passes the famed Pebble Beach golf course and provides views of the spectacular shoreline and some equally spectacular homes nestled along it. The largest and finest of which, Molly had warned me, was the Sherwin's.

I didn't want Rebecca Sherwin to know I was coming, so I paid the going rate for tourists at the toll booth. In California you can currently enter paradise for only four dollars. As long as you're just passing through. The man took my money and handed me a map. A salaried St. Peter in a dull gray uniform.

Amid such luxurious display I suddenly felt the need for spiritual uplifting, so I turned on Sherwin's three o'clock broadcast. I imagined him in his underground studio, like Hitler in his Berlin bunker, holding out against the advancing hordes.

But all was harmony and light. No ranting, but a sonorous voice of reason filled the compartment of my car. Explaining like a wise parent to neglectful children the dangers of a corrupt world.

Today's theme was nutrition and spiritual growth. He patiently described how the spirit is weakened by impurities let in through our polluted food chain, developing his ideas carefully and sensibly. The world began to seem a simple place.

Then I heard that faint flutter in his voice. His tone grew stronger and harsher. Now the protecting parent giving stern warning. Warning that impurities must be purged from our society, as well as our food chain. That impure elements are already polluting the body of our society and destroying its soul.

I turned off the radio after learning that two of the greatest polluters of American purity were the Asian and Mexican emigrants inundating our borders. And that we must begin an active campaign of deportation and restrictive immigration to eradicate their corrupting influence on American life.

I didn't wait for the commercial. Tune in tomorrow for more pollutants. Keep America 99 and 44/100 per cent pure. Use Ivory soap to wash away those troublesome Chinese and Mexican stains. Smoke Virginia Slims, you've come a long way baby and it'll seem twice as far when we send you back. So don't come to Marlboro country.

I passed the Pebble Beach golf links, rounded the northwest end of Carmel Bay and headed out the stretch of exotic coast between Pescadero Point and Lone Cypress.

In this relatively compressed area are the true grand houses of the Peninsula. Less than a dozen, all quite visible from the road and its stream of gawking tourists, jumbled side-by-side, all hugging the rugged cliffs and coves.

Some look like large fairy tale cottages. One out of large contoured stone blocks, even looks like a castle. None are new and all covet their limited space along the cliffs and their fabulous views. Only the last house had any real distance separating it from the road, lending an aura of seclusion to its other wonders.

I turned left into its driveway and stopped before a large wooden gate. A video camera, like a strange, silent one-eyed bird, watched me from its perch as I reached for the telephone hanging by the gate.

I spoke directly with Rebecca Sherwin. She was home alone but would see me. The gate opened and I drove through pines and cypresses down the short driveway to the house.

Another gate and another paradise I thought as I got out of my car and walked up to the front door. Well, I was getting used to my role as stranger in paradise.

I pushed the doorbell and a second later a woman's voice on the intercom said she was on the piazza and asked me if I'd walk around to the back of the house. Piazza? Well, when in Rome....

It was your standard forty room, two story, Roman villa. Except for the flowers, which were everywhere.

The walls seemed to be made of flowers. Trellises, matted with blossoms of all colors, stretched almost thirty feet to the roof. Roses, red, yellow, white and pink flanked the white seashell path I followed around the arch shaped curve of the villa and calla lilies raised their graceful heads as if listening to my footsteps. A fairy tale world.

At the far end of the curve, as I came near the back of the villa, I stopped.

The fragrance of the flowers was intoxicating. A kingdom of peace. The sea visible across forty yards of lawn, through a windbreak of pines and cypresses. Its distant white wall of fog motionless, like frosting on an aqua blue cake. No sound but the wind, spending its force in the trees, crossing the lawn as a soft breeze.

I closed my eyes, almost swaying in the perfumed air, under the warm sun. No sound except the breeze. So tranquil, I could almost hear the flowers. Ambrosia. Spellbinding. Spellbound. Bound in a spell.

Ulysses must have felt like this. When he fled the land of the Lotus-Eaters. The danger of being trapped in time, in a timeless tranquility, without memory of the outside world, stopped from completing his journey. Like an ancient insect frozen in amber. My weight shifted to the front of my feet almost as if I would fall.

The soft crunching of shells opened my eyes. I took a deep breath. Regained my balance and turned the back of the villa.

From the back the villa was a cupped curve open to the sea, which I could hear now surging against the base of the low cliffs.

On this side, the muted white walls were free of flowers, probably because of salt water and wind. A line of marble pillars connected the two ends of the concave curve, forming an enclosed semicircle out of the back of the villa. An incredible glass half-dome, resting on these pillars and connected to the back wall of the villa, provided a protective canopy for the open-air, semi-circular piazza.

I climbed five marble steps and passed between the columns, noticing with approval that no two of the pillars were close enough together for one man to reach. A building code regulation for temples ever since the days of Samson. The piazza was very spacious, about one hundred and twenty by forty feet at its widest.

The motif was ancient Rome, and carried out in marble. The floor was terrazzo, old and worn with a dolphin design pattern. It looked authentic, not reproduced. Plundered and brought over from an ancient villa, luxury transposed from another time.

A circular fountain with reflecting pool occupied the center space. The sound of its splashing water echoed off the hard marble surfaces, producing a softening effect. A massive marble table stood in front of the fountain. It must have weighed several tons. Scattered about the rest of the area were chairs and benches, lushly cushioned, all in marble. Lawn furniture for the super rich.

She sat in the middle of all this splendor, beside the fountain, like a Roman queen, on crimson velvet cushions, on a huge marble divan. She was smiling and gestured me forward.

As I approached her I said, "you look like a Roman queen. Do I bow?"

Her smile broke into a full laugh. "Please. If you will, an Egyptian queen. I much prefer that to Roman. Though the house is Roman in style, it has an Egyptian soul. As do I."

She asked me to sit beside her on the large divan. The velvet cushions were plush and kept the beautiful cold marble at a comfortable distance.

I had a good look at her in the bright sunlight filtering through the glass dome. She appeared a vibrant, handsome woman, a couple of years shy of sixty. Still holding together the last vestiges of great beauty through cosmetic artistry. Her fine red hair hung loosely about her shoulders and she still managed to radiate a waning sexual appeal.

She must have been a real heart stopper when she was younger. As Harriet Nilsson said, if Penelope would open up and brighten up, we'd see exactly what the mother looked like thirty years ago. Maybe that's what Penelope was hiding from. The pressure of her mother's famed beauty.

"I take this as a good omen," I said. "I've met four beautiful redheads today."

My compliment pleased her but also made her uncomfortable. Maybe she wasn't used to sharing her compliments.

"Who are the other three?" she asked coyly.

"My client, Mary Dugan, and her daughter. And your daughter, Penelope."

She managed to smile and frown at the same time. "All my children have had red hair. Except Michael. And it's about him that you're here, isn't it?"

"Yes. Would you mind talking about him?"

I watched her uncertainly. Wondering if she would show the same resistance as her husband. A flirtatious smile settled my doubts. She took my arm and we both stood up.

"Of course I wouldn't mind. Let's not talk here, though. My eldest daughter, Diana, is due any moment."

She looped her left arm through my right and we started off like secret collaborators. "We'll have more privacy if we walk about the grounds. And it's such a lovely day." It seemed I wouldn't need to coax her.

It seemed, from the light but firm hold she had on my arm, that I was a prize she had captured, a prize that she wasn't going to let get away.

First, she guided me over to the massive marble table that stood in front of the fountain. "Do you know what carrara marble is?" she asked me.

"I know that's what Michelangelo's Pieta is made of, that it comes from Carrara, Italy, and that it's highly valued."

She inspected the table, proudly, running her free right hand slowly across its top.

"Well, this table is carved from a single block of the finest carrara marble. From one twenty-metric-ton marble block." She let go of my arm so I could appreciate the feel of so much grandeur. "Of course it doesn't weigh nearly that much now, after all the carving."

"It's very nice," I said, trying to show enthusiasm. "Is it from the Renaissance period?"

She looked startled. "Why, no. It was personally commissioned by Mussolini in 1930." I was the one who looked startled now. "We bought it out of a catalogue after the War, when we built this place."

It seemed appropriate. The glory of the ancient Roman empire, reproduced by Mussolini's failed reincarnation, reincarnated again in another dream of Roman glory.

From the center of the table she picked up a golden statue of a woman, about sixteen inches high, Egyptian, and handed it to me. Very heavy, about eight or ten pounds. A figure of a woman, standing, legs pressed together, arms lifted, outstretched from her sides, palms slightly up, a cape over her shoulders, head turned a bit from center, wearing a headdress topped by a scorpion. I didn't need to be told it was real gold. I set it back down, carefully, in the center of the table. It was the only ornament decorating the piazza.

"That's Selket," she said. "She's a miniature of a half life-size statue, from King Tutankhamun's tomb. Guardian of his internal organs, a great and powerful healer. She wears the scorpion as proof her powers could cure even its sting."

All I could say was, "aren't you afraid someone will steal it?"

"Oh, I don't leave her out here alone. I always take her inside with me."

And with that she hooked her arm through mine and we strolled out onto the grounds.

"You're a very handsome man. Do you know that?" She looked me over carefully, her eyes reading mine for a reaction. "Of course you do. Women must tell you that all the time."

She kept her arm in mine but turned and reached up to my face with her right hand. We were stopped in the middle of the lawn.

"You're bigger and taller but you look a lot like William Holden. In the movie Picnic. Do you remember it? Especially there, the dark black hair, and there, about the forehead. And the blue eyes. And there, the same determined jaw."

She brushed my features as she described them, with her fingers, as if she were a sculptor.

"Then again, there's a certain cockiness about your eyes, more like the young Burt Lancaster."

I submitted to her movements of easy familiarity. Her full white silk skirt and loosely draped white silk top resembled a toga, and she reminded me of a fading Roman goddess. The same voluptuous figure and sensual face as her daughter. But now in decline.

I couldn't figure her out. She wasn't just flirting with me. She was certainly no aging beauty out to reassert and prove her charms. Something deeper was there.

We continued across the lawn to the line of cypress and pines that served as a windbreak. Two alternating rows of trees traced the winding indents of the small cliffs. We entered between them on a worn footpath, looking out at the rocky cove about fifty feet below. She finally let go of my arm and walked easily beside me. Maybe feeling I was secure between the walls of trees.

"Do you know the only thing about this beautiful spot that bothers me?" Before I could answer she said, "the wind. It can sound so doleful when I'm all alone. But right now it's nice." She looked up at the tree tops swaying in the breeze.

We stopped at a shallow promontory, occupied by a small, ornate wooden gazebo. Inside, a ring of benches around its perimeter formed an open circle about six feet across. We sat down with a comfortable space between us. Her manner was more serious now as the shadows on her face and her mood shifted in the latticed light

"I saw him a couple of weeks ago. It was quite a shock. After so many years."

"You mean Michael?" She nodded. "Where did you see him?"

"Right here, in the house. It was mid-morning and I was coming out of the kitchen. He was sneaking down the back stairs. He nearly scared me to death."

"What did he say?"

"Nothing. That's what made it so alarming. When he saw me he rushed out the door. I called after him but he wouldn't stop. I was so upset I had to sit down and rest. Ten minutes later it seemed like a dream. I began to think it hadn't really happened. But when I went upstairs I found my dresser drawer open and some papers scattered about."

"Did any of the servants see him?"

"We don't have any live-in servants. We value our privacy too much. I was home alone, like today."

"Do you know if he took anything?"

"He took some old letters. Letters from my husband to me. Letters he wrote me during the last year of the War. Also some he had written to his sister during the same period. Why he would want them so badly that he would break in and steal them after all this time, I can't even imagine."

She looked more subdued, less vibrant than before. Her eyes glistened with forming tears as she spoke.

"Why didn't he stop to talk with me? After all this time, to see my oldest child, like a burglar."

She wiped her eyes with her finger, careful not to smear her eye makeup.

"What did your husband say about all of this?"

She looked alarmed. "My God! You don't know my husband. I didn't tell him anything. Almost eighteen years ago my husband suffered a stroke while fighting with Michael. Michael ran off after that and my husband, Jonathan, hasn't mentioned him since. Yes sir! You obviously don't know my husband."

She was a strange combination. Ethereal and exotic. Then down-to-earth, ordinary and practical. I kept looking for the real behind-the-scenes drama.

When she had let me in at the gate I had said I represented Mary Dugan and wanted to speak with her about Michael. I decided now to keep my meeting with her husband secret a little longer. It would be more interesting to hear her explanation of things that way.

"Have you also seen Terry Rose lately?" I asked.

She didn't seem surprised by the question. "As a matter of fact he came here too. Let's see. That was three days ago. On Tuesday morning."

She seemed more in control again and laughed faintly. In explanation she said, "it was highly appropriate, you see. Where Michael is, Terry can't be far behind. And vice versa. At least, that's how it always used to be, and still is, it seems."

For some reason she found this amusing and laughed softly again. "Yes. I saw Terry. In fact, I fixed him breakfast. We talked for almost an hour. We always got on well together."

An image of the Roman goddess, a redheaded Delilah, preparing breakfast for the blond Samson, flashed through my mind.

"What did good old Terry have to say?"

"I take it from your tone that you've heard bad things about him." She shrugged. "Well, I guess they are probably true. He's a rough boy. Always was." Then a twinkle glinted in her eyes. "But the right woman can always handle men like that. Anyway, I never had any trouble getting along with him. I think Terry's more of a problem for men than for women."

She glanced at my plaster cast, and I wondered what she wondered. Again she watched me as if trying to read my mind.

"Was he here looking for Michael?"

"Yes. He said he and Michael were in business and Michael suddenly disappeared and it was critical that he find him."

"What kind of business?"

"Fruit orchards. Growing pears. Can you believe that!"

The mere idea of it entertained her.

"It seems that now through November is their growing time. Somewhere north of Santa Rosa. And Michael is the orchard specialist. Terry just markets the fruit. So he's lost without Michael and needs him back. Imagine them, tree farmers. I can hardly believe it."

"I can hardly believe it either," I said. "Do you think it's true?"

She paused and considered it.

"I don't know. I really haven't given it much thought. I was just so glad to see Michael and talk with Terry about him and old times." She was less amused now. "Of course it doesn't fit their characters. At least not their characters as I knew them. To tell the truth I would have been less surprised if Terry had said they were bank robbers."

"Did Terry explain what they've been doing all these years?"

"He made a stab at it when I asked. Said they got caught up in the Hippie movement for a few years. Drifted around the world for quite a few more years. Then finally settled down on this orchard Michael had bought during their Hippie period. Said it had been neglected and it took them a couple of years getting it in shape."

"Why didn't Michael get in touch with you during all those years?"

A tone of sadness crept into her voice, clouding the good old days.

"It wasn't all his fault. I was hardly a good mother to Michael. When he ran off I hardly cared that he was gone. It took a few years for the loss and my guilt to sink in."

I looked at her sympathetically. Surprised by her candor. She noticed.

"You see, I was a very spoiled and selfish woman in those days. I never had any real education or money before I met Jonathan. All I had was beauty."

For a moment she was lost in time. Remembering. She started to touch her face but pulled back instantly. Remembering. Her memories betrayed by the dried and wrinkled skin she would find there. She gave me a wistful gaze that spoke of former glories.

"I was a real Cinderella."

Then she sighed her lost dreams away and returned to the present.

"Unfortunately I took life very superficially then, and Michael was an especially demanding child. He was always troubled and moody. It was hard to reach him."

She looked at me shyly, apologetically, like a guilty little girl.

"You see, I still try to blame him. The problem also was that I didn't try very hard to help Michael with his troubles and moods. Then, when the problems between Michael and his father got bad, I let myself abandon Michael. Telling myself it was for the good of the family."

She took a long, deep breath.

"But I stopped being able to believe that many years ago. I eventually realized I didn't have the character, the courage required to save my own family."

She sat hunched over, weary, with her elbows buried in her skirt and her arms outstretched. Responsibility and guilt had come late in her life and taken their toll.

"The year that Michael ran off was a tragic time in our family.

Two of my other children died that year, nearly destroying my husband. He went through his suffering then but mine was delayed, and I feel all the worse for it now."

"What were the problems between Michael and his father? Why didn't Michael ever feel a part of the family?"

In the shadowed light of the gazebo she seemed younger. Maybe that's why she had brought me here.

She pulled back, into the bench, her red hair back-lighted against the wooden slats. A flash of feline rivalry flared in her blue eyes. Territorial rights. It was her turf and her story and she resented intruders.

"My, Mary Dugan certainly has a long memory. You know of course that she had a child but never married. Everyone gossiped that Michael was the father but I figured it was none of my business since she never said anything."

She raced along, marking the boundaries of her territory with sly quips, not wanting any interference from me.

"Is she still as lovely as always? I haven't seen her in ages. Do you know that Michael once flew into a rage because Penelope teased him that he liked Mary because she looked something like me?"

Her dominance reestablished she reposed with feline contentment.

I sat admiring the artistry of her different moods. A feeling that I was watching a virtuoso performance by a great actress.

She was preening, like a complacent cat, using the backs of her hands to lift and spread her hair, so the sunlight could filter through it.

"What was your question again? Oh yes, about Michael not feeling part of the family."

Her mood shifted once more.

"Did you know Michael saw his aunt die when he was less than one year old?"

She leaned forward, her hair falling thickly about her shoulders, blocking the light from the side of her face. She peered at me, like a great actress, making sure she had my complete attention.

"Oh yes. He saw her horrible mangled body. In a car accident. He was less than three months old. There was blood all over the snow and he cried and cried. For months he had trouble sleeping he carried on so. I think that was the start of his personality problems. I don't think that's too young to experience traumatic shock. Do you?"

Like a good critic I tried to preserve my distance.

"You said there was blood all over the snow. Where was this?"

"On the south shore of Lake Tahoe. In March, 1946." She put her hand over her lips, coquettishly, as if surprised the words came out. "Oops," she said poutingly. "Now you know how old I am."

I ignored her little girl coyness and tried to bring her back to the adult world.

"Can you tell me what happened?"

For a minute she just stared at me. I felt like I should be wearing a raincoat and offering her candy.

Finally she answered in her best grown-up voice.

"In the second half of 1945, while we waited for Jonathan to return from sea duty and be discharged from the navy, his sister, Gloria, and I shared an apartment in San Francisco. I was pregnant and housing was in short supply. We were both only eighteen and I was glad to have her company.

"She had come to San Francisco to find Jonathan after surviving a car accident that killed both her parents. She was surprised to find me. She didn't know Jonathan had married. When he was discharged at Christmas, the three of us lived together.

"Then I had Michael, in January, 1946. We all got along fine but I don't think Gloria ever fully recovered from the shock of her accident.

"In March we set off by car for their home in Bishop. That's when Gloria tried to steal Michael from us. She drove off with him while we were sleeping at a travel court. Wrecked the car. Ran right off an embankment and into a tree.

"They were both thrown from the car. Her head was split open against a rock. When we got there a few minutes later Michael was lying in her blood. In the snow. Bawling. She had tried to protect him from the cold with her body and had bled all over him."

I looked at her in disbelief. I thought she was putting me on. But she was very serious and seemed to have passed out of her coquettish mood.

I said, "you describe it so matter-of-factly. You don't show much motherly concern."

"But I am concerned! I had to be tranquilized for over a week," she said proudly. "And I still have bad dreams about it. Anyway, I admitted I wasn't a very good mother to Michael."

She leaned further forward, taking me into her confidence. Her tone was no longer girlish but bore the weight of all her years. She spoke in almost a whisper.

"I've never told anyone this before. Not even my husband. But I think I unconsciously rejected Michael because of that horrible experience." Her voice grew very hoarse and loud. She sounded almost like a howling wind. "Because of all that blood. All that blood."

She looked around, anxious that her secret was out. Then she straightened and continued in a more normal voice.

"I was so glad when our next child, Diana, came. It felt like a new beginning. I think my husband felt that way too. I think we both felt like we were raising a new family and we never totally let Michael into it."

I wasn't sure whether she was still giving her performance or whether she was finally the real person after the curtain call. Maybe all her displays were genuine. She had just made a rather shattering confession and seemed sincere in her admission of guilt.

"Does Michael know about the accident?"

"No. We never told him. Now I realize that was a terrible mistake. When two of our other children died in 1967 our happy family collapsed about us."

Her facade also seemed to have collapsed about her. She began speaking rapidly. Without any apparent contrivance. With a rising cry of frustration and anger.

"Two of our children died. Senselessly, without meaning. We alienated Michael, then drove him from us. Out of our home. Out of cowardice. And over these many years I've seen my husband grow bitter with the world. Rigid and hard with hate. Unforgiving."

She was nearly shouting again. Overflowing with anger. Suddenly she went quiet. Totally still. The calm after the explosion. She looked straight at me.

"It's a bitter pill to swallow when you're my age. To realize the guilt I bear for my family's tragedy."

She stood up and then I did. She looked up at me and said, "I know you're here to find Michael. If you do, tell him what I just said. Or better yet, bring him to me and I'll tell him myself. Like I should have in the beginning."

The Sherwin family was straight out of a Greek tragedy. I thought Harriet Nilsson would love to hear this grizzly story. She had been wrong about the sister and parents dying in the same accident.

I told Rebecca Sherwin why I was looking for Michael. I had wondered why she hadn't asked me. As if she had her own story to tell me but wasn't interested in mine. Or maybe she knew my story all along.

I also told her I had just come from seeing her husband, but she showed neither surprise or interest. She was a puzzle. And, despite her frankness, mystery still cloaked her true shape. Like my floating island this morning. All my senses told me something was there, but I could not be sure it wasn't just illusion.

We stepped out of the gazebo and back onto the footpath.

"I've always loved this place," she said. "Serene and beautiful right now. But it's also a place of great violence. Elemental clashes of nature, when the wind and seas come up and drive against the land. Now, in the bright sunlight, this place has great clarity. But it can also be muted and mysterious in the fog."

She raised her right arm and pointed to the rocks fifty feet below us.

"That's where they found my daughter's body. Fell from this cliff while playing with friends. She was only fifteen."

She seemed locked in that distant time. I didn't say anything.

"You'd think that would make me hate this place. But it doesn't."

She brightened up as we started back across the lawn, leaving her moodiness behind on the cliff, and she insisted on showing me her main garden, which was on the side opposite from where I had entered.

The garden on the other side of the curved villa extended further out from the wall and was protected from the wind and salt air by a thick row of Eucalyptus trees.

We walked through the trees and onto the yellow brick road, into the land of Oz. At least that's what it looked like.

This was her special private place, she explained. Her fuchsia and begonia garden. Her favorite flowers.

Once again I was amazed. The whole garden had gone to glory and was a riot of colors. Flowers crowded together in beds, clung to trellises, and hung down in baskets from overhead redwood stringers.

Hanging all about me, exquisite lavender and white ruffled flowers brushed my hair. Blush of Dawn she called them.

She seemed to come fully alive in her private garden. Proudly showing me her favorites. The brilliant crimson of the Red Spider. The dazzling cream and rose-red blooms of the Hula Girl. And her favorite, Voodoo, deep purple and dark red. Exotic names for an exotic place.

It was the first time since I met her that I was sure she was genuine. The rich thick atmosphere suited her. She was in her element, but I wasn't. The air was heavy and sweet with fragrance, the beauty too concentrated, for me.

I kept looking for the way back to Kansas, for Dorothy and the Tin Man, but I didn't find them.

I was glad when we stepped back out through the trees and made our way back to the piazza, feeling the contrast of the warm sun against the sharp, crisp air that signaled the fog would soon return.

My meeting with my fifth beautiful redhead of the day was not as auspicious as the others.

We saw her as we cleared the large marble table, floating on her back in the pool of the fountain. Her long red hair spreading out from her pale white face like the petals surrounding an ivory blossom on one of the flowers we had just seen.

A murky smear of blood was spreading out from her head like tendrils seeking an anchorage.

"Diana."

It was a gasp. Rebecca Sherwin stood paralyzed by the sight, her hand covering her mouth. Then she collapsed.

I carried her across the piazza and into the house. Away from the fountain and its evil looking flower.

I placed her on a couch and then called the police. I also called the Institute and told them it was an emergency and to send Sherwin and the family doctor home immediately. Rebecca was still unconscious so I went back out to the piazza.

On the ledge of the reflecting pool I found the golden statue of Selket. Her head and right arm were sheared off across the shoulder, revealing a hollow core. Thick, dark blood and some long red hairs were clotted on the jagged edge of the statue's cape. I didn't touch it.

Diana's body had drifted over to the other side of the pool. I followed the rim until I was about ten feet from her head. I shuddered. She had obviously been an attractive woman. Alive and breathing just minutes ago.

The entire left side of her face was caved in, and something golden shined from just beneath the water. I peered over the ledge. There, just above her left ear, was the golden scorpion, protruding from the broken bone and torn skin. It looked like the right arm and the head of the statue were still embedded in her skull.

I backed off. Horrified. Wondering what we had been doing when her head was smashed open and her life was draining out into the pool.

I made a quick search of the piazza and I circled the house but found nothing. I checked Rebecca. She was breathing steadily but still unconscious. Then I sat down on the steps leading to the lawn, away from the body, and waited for the police.

They and Jonathan and the doctor arrived with the first wisps of fog and the cold, damp, salty air.

The police kept me about two hours. I was questioned and re-questioned. Jonathan seemed in a trance and hardly spoke. And the doctor had immediately sedated Rebecca so I was their only witness.

Except for the flowers and the trees. Except for the warm summer day and the breeze that brought the incoming fog. All that peace. All that beauty saw more than I did. Bore witness to her violent end. I couldn't get away from that first image of her, floating in the fountain, as if she were just one more exotic flower.

At six o'clock they let me go and I drove back to San Francisco.

ELEVEN

Along the coast to Santa Cruz and half way up the Summit grade on Highway 17 the fog was wet and heavy. Isolating me in my small compartment as I drove through the nearly invisible landscape.

Fog is a great limiter of perception. But it can also open your imagination. Sharpen your senses. Make you aware of how much you can't see. Conversely, sunlight is the proper medium for illusion. Illusion works best in settings where you think you understand what you see.

I had just seen a murder, or more precisely, the result of a murder. In bright sunlight. In a place of peace and beauty. A woman who should have still been alive. Instead, a corpse, floating, like an evil flower, in a reflecting pool. In a setting that seemed all harmony and light.

What had we been doing at that exact second when her life ended so violently? Intoxicated by the perfumed scent in that lush, overripe garden?

Probably not. According to the coroner we were likely out in the gazebo when it happened.

Maybe her daughter was murdered at that very moment Rebecca Sherwin described the elemental violence possible in her lovely landscape.

No matter. Somehow, human evil had penetrated that perfect

setting, had intruded under that sunlit dome.

I guess when the surroundings remind you so much of paradise, of Eden, the appearance of the serpent is always more disturbing.

In New York evil is often projected into a threatening environment. It is just as disturbing, just as horrifying. But it's also more expected. Even prepared for.

In California, the environment seems benign. You feel at ease in its pristine clarity. Beauty and tranquility, not menace, are expected. Therefore, when evil enters, it sits more devastatingly in your soul. As if paradise had betrayed you.

The California myth is the reverse of the Biblical story of creation. Instead of being born innocent in the Garden of Eden and then expelled for sinning, you enter already corrupted, discovering to your horror that you have brought evil with you into such a wondrous place.

Many unstable people are attracted to California for this very reason. They come thinking they have left their problems behind, expecting to find peace in paradise. Instead they only find their old problems in a beautiful setting.

Yes, California is surely the end of the dream for some people. The end of the dream of natural innocence and perfection.

Right now the police were looking for Michael Sherwin, for bringing evil into paradise. Thanks to his father's wild accusation, he was now the main suspect in his sister's murder. There was an all-points-bulletin out for him which wasn't going to make my job of finding him any easier.

Molly thought such a suspicion absurd when I called her before leaving the Sherwin house. But she was very upset. It had been almost twenty years since she knew Michael, and she couldn't be sure of him.

A personal family matter and an ordinary search had turned ugly.

Disregarding Michael and Terry or the possibility of a random killer, I couldn't stop wondering about so many violent deaths in one family. And who had killed Diana Sherwin? And why? Did her death have anything to do with my search for Michael? And why so much tragedy in one family? In classical Greek tragedy there would be a fatal flaw behind it all that would explain everything.

Well, tomorrow I would start my search for Michael at his ranch. But tonight I wanted to see Penelope. The San Francisco police had tried her sculpture gallery and her home, but had not located her. That was a couple of hours ago now. I hoped I'd have better luck.

Her gallery on Union street in the Cow Hollow section of San Francisco was my first stop. It was open until nine and I could just make it.

I left the fog behind when I headed down 17 into the Santa Clara Valley. Ahead the lights of San Jose were bright and clear. I took Interstate 280 north and caught up with the fog again, thirty miles later, as I passed the Serramonte shopping center and entered the south end of San Francisco.

My wipers were busy clearing the wet fog from my windshield when I came over the back side of Pacific Heights and first heard the giant fog horns, booming their warning from the Golden Gate Bridge.

I took Steiner down past the mansions and turned right onto Union, a singles' and a yuppie haven nestled at the base of luxurious Pacific Heights and less than a mile in from the Bay.

In this Yuppie stronghold, on this part of Union, a parking space is as tough to find as a successful relationship. I parked in front of the Metro theater by a sign that said "No Parking During Performance" and walked directly across the street to the gallery.

It was recessed somewhat from the sidewalk, in a restored three story Victorian with all its wooden trim brightly painted in assorted colors. These Victorians, with their designer colors, are now the height of fashion but were torn down by the hundreds before the 1960's.

The gallery occupied the ground floor. I read the word "Metro" reflected backwards in colored lights from the marquee across the street. I peered inside, through the reflection.

A dozen or more Plexiglas pedestals topped with small sculptured objects filled the open room. Otherwise it was empty, except for a woman, sitting off to the side at a desk, looking bored. Her expression didn't change when she noticed me. "The Re-Formed Form" was stenciled across the glass door. I pushed it open and went inside.

She watched as I crossed the thick gray carpet to her desk. Not happy to see me. She had chipmunk cheeks like Sally Field. About thirty-five, plain but pleasant looking, designer jeans and a thick blue flannel man's shirt. Short and straight brown hair, freshly scrubbed healthy skin. No trace of makeup.

"May I help you?" she asked. "I'm about ready to close up."

"You're the first woman I've met today who doesn't have red hair."

Curiosity and a trace of irritation erased her bored expression. "If you're looking for Penelope, she's not here."

"Has she been in today?" My toothy smile made no impression.

Annoyance grew in her voice. "I haven't seen her all week. I might as well be just hired help."

I didn't know what she was mad at and figured I didn't have time to find out. I was just about to leave when she scrunched up her chipmunk cheeks and said, "you wouldn't happen to be Prince Charming, would you?"

"Gee, I bet you've got one swell personality and I wish I had time to discuss fairy tales with you but I've really got to run."

"Don't play cute with me. I'm not interested."

She said it with great finality and her message finally got through to me. She was suffering a lover's sulk, but wasn't susceptible to masculine charms.

She continued in her best defiant manner.

"Or would you rather be called Lover Boy?" I showed no reaction. "Or Superman?" I revealed my toothy charms again but that only upset her more. "All right, Mack. What do I have to do? Put on a dress to get you to answer me?"

If Penelope was the object of her sulk, maybe she was worth my time after all.

"Hold on a second. I'm not who you think I am. And I'm certainly not your rival for fair Penelope's affections. That is what were dealing with here, isn't it?"

She withdrew some of her hostility but still eyed me suspiciously.

"I hardly know anymore. I've barely seen her outside the gallery for the last three months."

As she talked her suspicion turned again to curiosity.

"If you're not Penelope's new friend, what was that crack for, about the women with red hair?"

"Why don't we start all over."

I sat down across from her, flashing my pearly whites again. Still no impression but at least she was listening.

"Weren't the police by here earlier this evening?"

"Yes. They said she was to call her parents as soon as she came in. But they wouldn't tell me why. Nobody's been telling me anything lately."

Her little ego was bruised and she was feeling neglected. Maybe information would bring more information out of her.

"I've just driven up from Monterey, from the Sherwin house. Penelope's sister has been murdered and her parents are anxious to have Penelope come home."

"Diana's been murdered?"

Her eyes changed from shock to anxiety.

"Where's Penny! I haven't seen her all week."

She rose partially from her chair and for a second I thought she would climb across the desk.

"My God! Is Penny in danger?"

"Calm down. She's okay. I saw her this morning with her father." She plopped back into her chair. "She's in no danger. But her parents need her with them."

The shock had broken down her defenses.

"It's just that things have been so strained between Penny and me lately. I've been so worried about her, and then to hear this, this horrible thing. How was Diana...." She hesitated to say the words. "Killed."

"Someone bashed her head in and left her floating in the fountain at the Sherwin house."

She made a grinding sound with her teeth and her cheeks stretched flat. She was quiet for a minute, then she reached over and shook my hand.

"I'm sorry I was unpleasant before, Mr. ?"

"Walker," I said.

"I'm Beth Benoit. Have you been by Penelope's house yet?"

"That's my next stop. But the police were by there earlier and she wasn't home."

"That doesn't prove anything," she said. "Not if they rang the front doorbell. Penelope spends most of her time in a room at the back of the house. There's no phone there and she can't hear the doorbell either. When she's in that room it means she's off limits to ordinary communication. So you'd better go around to the right side and knock at the door at the back end."

"Thanks for the advice." I wondered just how far I could push our new cooperation. "Would you mind telling me, are you and Penelope still lovers?"

Her temper flared again. "Hey, Mack. That's a pretty damn personal question."

She started to erect her defensive barriers again but stopped. Her mind raced through some secret decision making process. Calculating whether I was an enemy or a potential ally.

"What business is it of yours? Exactly who are you?"

"I'm a private detective trying to find Penelope's missing brother, Michael. I was with Rebecca Sherwin when the murder was discovered."

She still wasn't sure which way to go with me. She had been feeling ignored and left out of things so I decided to let her in.

"I've been hired by Michael's former fiancée who hasn't seen him in almost eighteen years."

"Ah, the trials of 'straight' love," she said, sarcastically.

"Aren't those the trials of any kind of love. Straight or otherwise?"

She gave me an approving nod. Score one point for me.

"So why the rush after all these years?"

"It seems Michael left something behind. An unclaimed part of himself. Species human, sex female. She's old enough now and wants to meet her father. Isn't that enough reason to help me?"

I had just about won her over. Just one more small shove.

"Besides, we New Yorkers ought to stick together."

That did it. Her first smile.

"Okay. Okay. So my Brooklyn accent is still pretty obvious. Yours isn't. That probably means you were a Manhattan brat. Exposed at an early age to the sights, smells and sounds of the whole wide world. Right?

"Born and bred on the Upper West Side." I smiled and got another one in return. "But I was no Manhattan snob. I always had a special spot in my heart for Brooklyn. For the Loew's Kings theater on Flatbush Avenue and White Castle hamburgers in Bensonhurst and Bay Ridge."

She laughed. "I've been out here almost twenty years and that's the one thing I miss most. White Castle hamburgers. They call San Francisco sophisticated and yet the nearest White Castle is in St. Louis." She smiled easily now. "But, of course, they're best in Brooklyn."

"Especially if you take a sack down by the Narrows and watch the ships come into the harbor."

"All right," she said. "We're not strangers anymore. Let's even say were expatriates, even soulmates. But, tell me, what does the state of affairs between Penny and me have to do with your finding her brother?"

"Honestly, and I would never lie to a Brooklyn girl, I don't know. But this morning I thought I had a simple case of finding a missing person, even though he's been missing damn near twenty years. But other players keep entering the game. And then there was the murder and the police are now also looking for Michael."

I decided to leave Trimbler's death and Terry out of it.

"So, my quest is pointing off in different directions and I can use all the help I can get. Penelope's connected to Michael and Michael's missing. Therefore, I'd appreciate any help you can give me understanding the key players in Michael's life."

That seemed to make sense to her.

"Okay. Penny and I were lovers, but don't seem to be anymore. We've never lived together, although we've been pretty much of a couple for over two years. And, to answer your next question, no, her parent's don't know about her. That's why she lives up here and not in Monterey. She has a secret life, so to speak.

"Penny's family is a little strange and so is she, I guess. Well, she had a nervous breakdown of sorts about four months ago. Nothing really major, she just sort of came apart at the seams. That's when our troubles began. She became more distant and mysterious and I couldn't get through to her. She was constantly agitated, moody and depressed. She couldn't sleep. About a month went by like that and then she was totally different."

She paused and waited for dramatic effect.

"Totally different?"

"I mean totally different. Literally. I thought the pod people from Invasion of the Body Snatchers had gotten ahold of her and replaced her with a look-alike. She had always been a pretty tense girl and all of a sudden she went California-mellow. She got on my nerves. She went from shy and quiet to outgoing and aggressive. She had always been plain in her appearance, so suddenly she starts buying expensive, colorful clothes. For Christsakes, she even started wearing makeup. Bright red lipstick even."

Her voice was cracking with frustration.

"I saw her this morning and she was very plain and reserved."

"That's because she was down there, with her father. She hides her new life from them just as she hid me. What's worst of all, she's cut me off. Doesn't explain anything and doesn't want to see me except here at the gallery. Well, she owns the place. So pretty soon I'm just hired help."

She stopped to catch her breath, almost snorting with indignation.

"It didn't take me long to read the messages she was sending."

"Prince Charming?" I suggested.

"Exactly. She's gone straight on me. Found true love."

The cracking left her voice and her tone was clear and smooth. She looked at me sheepishly.

"And do you know what bothers me most?"

I shook my head no.

"That she seems so much better since she's gone straight. Just like those goddamn fascist preachers are always screaming at us. Heterosexual love has made a new woman of her. Made her happier. More at one with herself. And I have to watch this shit from the sidelines. Benched. Out of the game."

She made a wry smile and expelled a puff of air.

"I tell you, it's enough to make a dyke wonder."

"As they say, at least you've still got your sense of humor."

"Yeah, but what else?"

"Do you have any idea who the man is?"

"Don't I wish. It's a strictly top secret affair."

"I don't know if this will help," I said, "but I appreciate your openness."

I stood up.

"You know you can order White Castle hamburgers from Columbus, Ohio." Her face brightened slightly. "They come frozen, packed in dry ice. Sometime I'll bring some by and we can reminisce about New York. Pretend we're roaring across the Manhattan Bridge on the 'D' train."

I reached over and shook her hand again, then walked out the door, leaving her with her unsolved puzzle.

I was lucky there was no ticket on my windshield. I drove another two blocks east on Union before turning around and heading for Penelope's house. On Union the crowd in Perry's was packed in like sardines, as usual. It's one of the city's unofficial headquarters for well-groomed, well-tailored young singles. Yuppies. Strictly heterosexual.

If you believe the jokes on television, San Francisco is all gays. As a former New Yorker this amuses me, coming from a city that has more homosexuals than San Francisco has people of any persuasion. Los Angeles has a bigger gay population by a multiple of over three but you seldom hear about them. And even Houston and Washington, D.C. have larger gay communities.

So what makes San Francisco so special it gets all the media attention? New York friends insist its because San Francisco gays are too blatant. These are the same people who never drove down Washington street in Greenwich Village on a hot summer night. Who never saw the slender young men climbing into the backs of semi-trailers for a quickie, by the dozens, just off busy Christopher street. The same people who never notice the "rough trade" bars on West street or the couples filing out onto the deserted Hudson River piers to do their business.

Of course the AIDS scare has now cut down on such open displays everywhere. Still the disparity in attention seems to be that New York is just too big to pay particular notice to any of its minorities. When the country needs a stereotype someplace has to fit the bill. God knows New York has suffered through enough of its own.

Not that the gay community in San Francisco doesn't have a strong presence and a loud voice. It does. But its presence and voice are just part of the total, though a significant and notice-able one.

I took the Lombard gate into the Presidio, past Letterman hospital, past the administrative buildings and the parade ground. I followed the drive along its big lazy loop around the small, neat headstones of the military cemetery and through a thick grove of Eucalyptus trees. The fog-laden trees filled the air with their spicy perfume.

I put down my window and breathed in their pungent aroma until the inside of my nose tickled. Tomcat smells, permeating the wet night air.

Just past the Golden Gate Bridge the fog was blowing up from Baker Beach and shooting across the road as I hugged the rim of the steep cliffs. My headlights reflected off spumes of mist as they shot into view, funneling up the cliffs and over the road so fast they looked like a waterfall flowing uphill. No other cars or lights in sight. A raw and untamed place right in the heart of the city.

I exited at the 25th Avenue gate and re-entered the regular residential area of the city.

The fog, like gray cotton candy, tumbled down the streets in wispy billows. The air was sea-fresh and sea-moist. The night quiet and dreamy. Cloaked in the muted yellow glow of the street lamps. The huge fog horns from the bridge, bellowing their doleful warnings, adding just the right touch of foreboding. I felt like I was entering the set of an old Sherlock Holmes movie.

I turned right into Seacliff, an expensive old-money enclave on the cliffs watching over the seaward entrance to the Golden Gate.

Penelope's house was on a dead end block, third last in a row that backed right onto the cliffs. Impressive but not overly large and intimidating like her parent's house. The front had a small, high-walled courtyard with two lonely looking palm trees, strangely out-of-place in this brooding setting.

I unlatched the gate and went in. No lights and no car. I made my way around the back of the house and found the door Beth Benoit had mentioned.

I could feel the vibrations of the music through the thick wooden door almost before I heard them. I concentrated, straining to separate the music from the breaking surf below. A sudden lull and the melody floated through the door and vanished in the night air. I smiled. The Beach Boys, singing "California Girls." This might be fun. Maybe Prince Charming was with her.

I knocked once, then again. She was singing along as she opened the door. "I wish they all could be California girls...." Her mouth hung open but no words came out. Dead silence with the Beach Boys as back up. "You...you! What are you doing here?"

If she was astonished, she had nothing on me. My own mouth was slack and open at the sight of her. She was wearing tight red silk lounge pants with a snug fitting matching blouse, unbuttoned almost to her waist. Standing on red high-heeled slippers, her beautiful red hair hanging loose and silky halfway down her back. Full sensual lips glistening bright red beneath her blue eyes and a golden bracelet dangling at each wrist.

She finally closed her mouth, pursing her moist painted lips. As she took several deep breaths her breasts swelled against the silken fabric like ripened fruit, ready to fall from the tree.

"How in the hell did you find me here?" she demanded.

She still blocked the doorway, with her hand on the knob. I brushed past her glaring eyes and entered her secret retreat.

"Now wait just a damn minute," she yelled, and I turned to watch as she jiggled across the room to catch up with me, her firm bottom swishing in its luxurious confinement.

"Ripeness is all," I said, and sat, uninvited on her couch in front of the fireplace.

She walked over to me, blocking out the fire. From my sit-down angle I had quite a view, looking up at her. If the ripe fruit falls this is the place to catch it, I thought. Standing so near, her perfume was very provocative. But the sweet musky fragrance reminded me of her mother's garden and spoiled the effect.

"What is this?" she demanded. "Why don't you say something?"

Her tone softened. Finally she sat across from me on the edge of a chair, her breasts ballooning together, half visible in the open "V" of her blouse.

"What do you want?" Then, "you can't stay here." She glanced nervously at the door. "I'm expecting someone any minute."

"Where's the demure, bashful girl I met this morning?"

"I left her behind in Monterey," she answered sarcastically. "What business is it of yours, anyway?"

"Your parents have been trying to get you since late afternoon. Where were you?"

"My parents?" She seemed confused. "Why, I just saw my father this morning. You were there. What have you got to do with my parents anyway? Did you go see my mother, too?"

"You answer my question first."

"All right. If it will get rid of you. I drove up the coast road from Monterey. I got here at exactly four o'clock, the hall clock was chiming when I came in. I ate a light dinner, took a long hot bath, got dressed and have been sitting here listening to music since seven."

"Waiting for someone?"

She glared at me again. "Yes. I already told you that."

"Tell me, why do you put on the repressed little girl act for your parents?"

"You answered it yourself. It's for my parents." Her tone and mood were shifting into sincerity and she reminded me of her mother again. "Anyway, it's not strictly an act."

She watched me. Observed me carefully, rather. Trying to read me. I felt I had been through all this with mom so I just smiled, encouraging her to go on.

"Until a few months ago, I really was the way you saw me earlier. But I've changed a lot recently. I feel much more sure of myself now." She checked to see if I were keeping up with her. "However, I don't feel comfortable around my parents. I mean, the new me doesn't know how to break with the old me. And you saw what my father's like. He's a very severe man. I haven't figured a way to let them see the new me yet. You could say I'm still kind of in the closet. At least around my parents in Monterey."

Another confession. They seemed to run in the female side

of her family.

"You wouldn't tell them, would you? I wouldn't like that. Not before I can prepare them better."

She had confided in me. Confessed to me. Let me into her secret life. Like her mother she seemed sincere.

But I was troubled by all this secrecy followed immediately by such openness. Something was very deliberately hidden away in all these luxurious compounds. I was beginning to gain some insight into Michael's disappearance. And some sympathy for him.

I had no idea if she was close to her sister, Diana, and I had no desire to torture her by keeping her death a secret. Not on the stray chance that I might learn something that probably wouldn't get me any closer to Michael anyway.

So I told her. Described what had happened and how the police had looked for her. How her father was accusing Michael.

She didn't cry or go into shock. Just went very still and quiet. All reaction internalized. Within a few minutes she said she would drive to her parent's house as soon as she could change her clothes.

A few moments later I was standing back outside her door.

I was still sitting in my car outside her house when she came out. I was mulling over the day's events. Wondering if I had really seen what I thought I had seen today. Or was it like my floating island? An illusion. A vision of reality without the proper perspective.

She drove out along the left side of the house, from a driveway I hadn't noticed. In a sedate four door sedan. I wondered if it were her Monterey car and she kept another flashier one for San Francisco.

She didn't notice me but I had a glimpse of her under the street lamp as she pulled out and disappeared up the quiet street.

She was wearing the same dowdy tweed suit I had seen this morning. All that bright red was gone. Her lips and face were scrubbed, her hair pulled back and up, and that voluptuous body re-packaged for a different market. Exotic behavior and exotic settings. But what did I really see?

I drove back through the Presidio, back to my home on Green Street, near the eastern edge of the Presidio, on the bottom bayward slope of Pacific Heights. The crisp, damp salty air revived my senses and the two fog horns on the bridge, alternating from a deep heavy bass to a resonant tenor, kept me company.

TWELVE

My headlights held her face for a second as I turned into my garage on Green Street.

Beautiful pale skin and animated eyes, watching me from her parked car as my garage door opened automatically on signal.

I pulled in, parked the car and hit the genie switch, scooting back out under the closing garage door just as Molly emerged from her car with a bright welcoming smile.

"I was too nervous to stay in Monterey after hearing about Diana's murder," she said.

"I packed Katie off to friends in Santa Barbara where she'll be safe. I thought I could relax after that but I still didn't know what to do. Couldn't keep my mind on anything. So I drove up here to see you. And so I can scout locations for my new restaurant tomorrow."

She shifted the weight of her large shoulder bag, which could double as an overnighter, and said, "but mainly to see you again."

She seemed a bit nervous but not quite embarrassed by her own bluntness. I was glad to see her and calmer than early in the day, during our previous intimacy.

"Fate seems to have taken a hand in arranging our relationship," I said. "And I don't believe in denying fate. Not when all the other signs feel right too."

She liked that. Her whole face lit up.

"I've always prided myself," she said, "that I wouldn't chicken out. That I wouldn't play meaningless games." She paused a second. "Not if I found someone worth the risk."

I was less calm now than I had been a minute before but I felt good.

The real thing is always a little frightening up close. Face to face. But the risk is always worth the taking, if reality and not fantasy is allowed to determine the outcome.

I took her hand and we climbed the outside flight of steps up to the front door.

She stood back and stared up at the front of the house.

"How did you ever get a place like this? It's fantastic. I love these ornate wooden Victorians. Especially with the bay windows and turrets."

"It's the ancestral home," I answered. "My great grandfather built it in 1882. My grandmother left it to me when she died a few years ago. That's when I moved out here from New York."

"It's huge. What do you do with all the room?"

"I've only got the top floor. I was forced to divide the house and rent out the other two. That's the only way I could afford to keep it and keep it in good shape."

"Have you got a view?"

"Of the Golden Gate Bridge, most of the Bay and of the Russian Consulate just a half block down, across the street."

She looked down the street at the bulky square building, out of place in the quiet residential neighborhood and almost lost in the fog.

I turned my key in the lock, we entered, and I closed the main door behind us.

"They might be listening to us right now," I said. "They supposedly have all kinds of electronic gear on the roof to eavesdrop on sensitive communications. Especially from Silicon Valley."

I led her up the carpeted central staircase, past the two lower floor tenants, to my third floor apartment. Inside, I took her bag and set it on a chair. Every time I looked at her I thought of a 40's movie.

"Where did you get that outfit? It's really got me going. I keep thinking I'm with Barbara Stanwyck."

"Don't you like it? I wore it especially because of your comment about Myrna Loy today. But it's not Barbara Stanwyck. It's Jean Arthur. I copied it last year from an old movie I saw her in with Cary Grant."

She moved into the middle of the living room and twirled once.

"See." The full black skirt spun and twisted around her legs.

She was wearing a black jumper over a white silk blouse, open two buttons at the neck, with long loose puffed sleeves. The wide black straps formed a "V" in front at her waist and flared up and out over her shoulders. Her nylons had black seams stitched up their back and on her feet she wore black, patent leather, low heeled shoes. The hanging part of her red hair was gathered in back into a silky contoured mass that seemed to float inside an intricately crocheted white net bag. Bright red lipstick defined the appealing shape of her lips and matching polish highlighted the fine tapered curve of her nails.

"I'll bet you don't think I know what that's called," I said, pointing at her hair net.

She lifted and patted her satiny confined hair with the backs of her hands and waited.

"It's a snood," I said proudly.

A mischievous smile re-shaped her lips. "You've been watching too many old movies."

I had seen traces of her special smile that morning, a preview of the main attraction I was seeing now. I watched in admiring wonder.

It was a misbehaving smile. Bewitching and capable of delivering its own messages. Independent and frisky like a bright school girl. Never tamed. Moving in stages, spreading asymmetrically up from the right corner of her mouth. Revealing her world to me. A lighthouse smile, inviting me in to a special place.

She said, "you have a nice nest here, gathered under your sloping roof beams." She walked around the perimeter of the large open living area. "Lots of beautiful natural wood. Ceilings, beams, floors." She ran her hand along the top of a teak table I had made myself. "All simple and strong and yet unusual. Comfortable padded chairs and couch."

She turned and faced me. "Very solid and very masculine. Also, reassuring." Her eyes sparkled at me. "I heartily approve. A fitting lair for a detective, filled with the fog horns' forlorn calls."

She noticed the glass doors and peered outside.

"You've got a wooden deck out there." A playful smile parted her lips and her jade eyes wrapped me in mischievous glances. Her full skirt twirled around her legs as she spun towards me and whispered excitedly, "let's go outside."

The fog was damp and thick so I got out an old color-patched quilt and wrapped it around her.

We sat along the rail on the padded bench, side by side in the chilly midnight air.

The street below was deserted and almost obscured by the swirling fog. Above us loomed the high western ridge of Pacific Heights, spotted with the dim yellow glow of random house lights. One block further west, at the dead end of Green Street, the rolling tree covered hills of the vast Presidio were now invisible. To the north and east the rest of the city was also lost to view, put to sleep under the soft gray blanket. Only the sonorous, melancholy resonance of the bridge's big horns penetrated our private little world.

She removed her shoes and drew her feet up in front of her. Then she took off the snood and shook her hair down freely about her face. She turned sideways, with her nylon-stockinged feet pressed through the quilt against the side of my leg. She was completely covered, with only her face and red hair showing.

"You look like an Indian madonna," I said.

"Madonna's feet are cold," she answered, and pushed her toes under the side of my leg. "Do you mind?"

"You can keep your feet there, safe and warm, if you show me that special smile again." It spread teasingly across her face. "I think I should change that description, though. It's not proper for a madonna to have red hair and such a naughty smile."

"And you are not what I expected of a private detective. At least not before I talked with your sister the other day."

"That's because I don't have a theme song yet. I was thinking maybe Henry Mancini could work one up for me. Then I could carry a boom box around and play it whenever I meet a new client. Give myself a recognizable identity."

I felt her toes wiggle under the side of my leg.

"That might help. But you still wouldn't fit the traditional mode. You're supposed to have a seedy office down on Mission and live in a run-down apartment somewhere, with a bottle of bourbon and a Colt .45 for your only comfort."

"Well, I've got the Colt .45. That makes me half a detective, anyway."

"And you're a property owner, a landlord no less."

She shoved her feet further under my leg and that incredible mischief-making smile remade her face.

"There appears to be no hope for you. Unless you're a mean landlord. Are you a mean landlord?"

"Afraid not. I guess I'm a big letdown for you. I even carry Detective's Blue Cross. Eighty per cent coverage on all bullet and stab wounds and a dental plan to cover any teeth I get knocked out."

"Well, maybe there's hope for you yet. If you're a real loner you might still pass the test. But then you've got family in the area. A real detective should be an orphan. Unconnected at all points. Or has the world just gotten too complicated for that?"

I decided to answer her question seriously.

"No. It's always been too complicated for that. And I'm still a loner where it counts. Inside. Despite the family connections.

"I'm just a variation on an old theme. The knight errant prowling the underside of life. That's what makes me a detective. A fascination, maybe even an obsession, with evil. With the banality of evil and how it grows. Like an everyday flower, unrecognized, in plain sight. If I'm not traditional in my obsession, it's because I reached the underside by falling in through the top."

Her hand came out of the quilt and she touched my face.

"I'm sorry," she said. "I didn't mean to force you to explain."

"That's okay. I want to explain how it happened.

"Exactly four years and six months ago tomorrow, my wife was murdered in New York."

She scooted closer to me, hugging her knees tightly against her chest, her face sympathetic and encouraging above them. She kept the front of her feet anchored beneath my leg, a fast hold on the intimacy growing between us.

"We had been married for fourteen years, since our junior year of college. We were both actors, doing commercials, parts on Broadway and even a few movies. The parts were getting bigger and things were really beginning to click.

"Then, two days after Christmas, she interrupted three drug addicts burglarizing our car. She was hit across the face with a gun and knocked out. It was dark, but two people witnessed it from down the street. They yelled, and the three men started to run off. But one of them stopped and shot her in the head. While she was unconscious. It seemed to make no sense at all."

Her face had grown sad as I talked. Watching me. Two big eyes and two big knees. The beginning of tears.

I reached over with both hands and wiped the moisture from her eyes, careful not to scratch her with my cast.

"It's a sad and distressing story," I said. "I know. But I don't want to go back. God! I don't ever want to feel that way again. So, don't take away that pretty smile."

She made a genuine try but managed only a weak approximation, and her voice was hoarse as she spoke.

"Your sister, Shirley, said you and your wife were the best couple she's ever seen together."

"We were. A long time ago, now. That's how I fell through the top of the world and ended up prowling its underside."

She waited, curious and concerned. Beautiful and positively

radiant. She was the first person I had ever wanted to tell.

"The two witnesses couldn't identify the three men, so the police never caught them." Her eyes widened with the question, and I answered. "But I did.

"It took me exactly thirty days. I would have gone insane if I hadn't kept after them. I used resources and energy I never knew I had. I was obsessed. Almost a madman.

"I finally found them in a chop shop up in the Bronx, a place where thieves break down stolen cars and equipment into parts for resale.

"I was in a cold rage when I confronted them. I wasn't interested in arresting them. I wanted revenge. One of them still had the gun he shot Janet with. In the fight that followed I took it away from him and killed all three of them."

She had almost stopped breathing.

"I learned a terrible secret during those thirty days. I discovered that evil isn't exotic. It does not cry out for recognition. It simply is.

"I also learned that the banality of evil doesn't make it any less dangerous or terrifying. Just harder to recognize and destroy."

Molly sat transfixed, watching, listening. Evil has its own hypnotic power, and it had enclosed her in its spell.

"You see," I said, "the man with the gun who shot my wife, the one I took the gun away from and killed first, was one of our closest friends."

The shock broke the spell. Her eyes narrowed and her lips parted but all that came out was, "what?"

A neutral tone, softly spoken, a little deeper than her normal voice.

"Yes. A close friend of ours. A struggling actor who had

gotten hooked on drugs and started ripping off tape decks to support his habit."

"My God!" she said. "How did you feel when you recognized him?"

"After the rage, after they were all dead, I felt unprepared for what the world had offered me. And that's why I eventually became a detective. My life had been shattered and I didn't want to ever be that unprepared again."

"That's why he turned back and shot your wife. Because she had recognized him."

"Yes. It had seemed senseless at the time. But evil always does make sense. In its own terms. If you can understand them.

"A few months after that my grandmother died out here. She had been worried about me since Janet's death and she left me her house. Even though I had no children and she had other grandchildren who did. I think she gave it to me as a kind of compensation. So I could start over again."

"And have you started over again?" she asked.

"If it's true that you can't go home again, then it's equally true that you can't start over again. Not completely. But I have changed.

"Through my uncle, Matt, and my sister, Shirley, I was allowed to take the training course for police officers at the academy. Unofficially, that is. Afterwards, I got my investigator's license. I guess you could say I'm all 'copped' up."

For some reason she smiled, the first real smile since I had begun my story.

"I guess you know Shirley is a lieutenant and special media liaison for the police department. Sets up all the arrangements for filming in the city." Her smile began misbehaving again. "For movies, television and commercials."

Her face was resting on her pulled up knees, her smile complete, spreading into her eyes. I began to wonder.

I said, "I sense a secret here. Some sort of female conspiracy. Just how well do you know Shirley?"

She laughed. "I've only met her twice, like I said. I'm not part of the conspiracy, I'm its object. Like you."

"Knowing Shirley, that means she set us both up."

"I think," Molly laughed, "she's been acting as our own personal liaison. When I told her my problems the other night and she recommended you, there was something concealed in her manner. Something unsaid but very definitely in the air."

I swung her feet out from under my leg and pulled her next to me. She opened the quilt and passed it over my shoulder.

In the half dim light reflected off the fog from the street lights below I could just make out a few faint freckles on her nose. Her lovely Irish pug nose.

I pulled her closer and kissed her, her soft long hair against my face, and the supple feel of her inside the loose silk blouse under my hand.

She kissed me back and pressed hard against me, then lowered her arms as I slid the straps of her jumper off her shoulders. Because of my cast she was better at undoing my buttons than I was at hers. But I managed. Taking my time, enjoying the slowness of my handicap.

For a long while we just sat there, under the old quilt, exploring the possibilities of each other, melting together, wrapped in our quilted cocoon.

Gradually, we shed the last of our clothes and stretched out, side by side, on the cushioned bench.

We both began laughing immediately.

"Is this damp vinyl as cold on your bare ass as it is on mine?" I asked.

"Yes, oh yes!" she cried out, half giggling.

"Do you want to go inside?"

"No. I like it here. Besides, I feel we can warm it up in just a few seconds."

And we did.

The quilt slid off to the floor, letting the chill damp air on my back, the soft hot press of her full, firm body under me. Straining against each other, coming together in a fast, eager ecstasy.

The second time she was on top. Straddling me. Slower this time, more relaxed with our pleasure. Her beautiful hair, hanging just short of her swaying breasts. Light, fiery hair on alabaster skin. Lovely to behold, she glistened in the damp night air. Curvaceous and enchanting.

Afterwards, she rested on top of me, breathless, her hair fanning out across my chest. The sweat of our bodies creating sharp tingles in the cool air.

"I sure hope the Russians weren't watching."

She started laughing again, uncontrollably, and said, "if they were, we sure gave them a lesson in a different kind of detente."

The third time was between the sheets of a proper bed. My bed, after the chill drove us inside. Sweet and unhurried, with as much talk and playfulness as passion.

My tragic past began to seem a long way off.

The next morning we were up and out by ten. A busy day for both of us. For her to scout restaurant locations, for me to find Michael's marijuana ranch and, hopefully, Michael.

We had breakfast at the Seal Rock Inn, at the western edge of the city, out near Land's End. One Sutro omelet each. The special of the house and the best omelet in town.

Afterward, I dropped Molly at my place to get her own car. We made plans to see each other as soon as I got back.

Then I drove downtown to the U.S. Customs House on Jackson and picked up the Geological Survey maps for the area around Clear Lake, where the marijuana orchard was supposed to be.

At noon I cleared the fog just north of the Golden Gate Bridge and headed up Highway 101.

I figured about two and one-half hours to cover the hundred and thirty miles to the north end of the lake. And I figured about a hundred degrees in the shade when I got there.

It was going to be a long hot day.

THIRTEEN

Clear Lake is about fifteen miles long by about two to six miles wide. Stuck in the middle of the dry Coastal Mountains, with rugged brown and golden ridges flanking its shallow waters and clusters of live oak and chaparral dotting its hills.

Near the lake, in the hot valleys between the ridges, grow walnuts and some of the finest pears in the country. And sometimes something else. I was looking for the something else.

That something else, marijuana, usually grown on a small scale by a few individuals on remote wooded plots of land, has become the biggest business in northern California. So common and so profitable that a reputed thirty thousand growers will soon need to celebrate their annual harvest with a regional fair and rodeo. Sponsored by a Northern Counties Pot Growing Association with a trimmers' competition and a search for the mythic twenty-five foot cannabis plant.

The center of this thriving cottage industry is the tiny, unimpressive town of Garberville, another hundred miles north of Clear Lake. A town unusual only for the huge quantities of plastic pipes, heavy gage Ziploc bags, black plastic tarps and Weiss clippers sold there. And for the hordes of buyers who descend on it every October. And for the incredible amounts of legally unaccounted-for cash circulating there.

Increased aerial surveillance and the legal threat of confiscating the growers' land favors the small operator and has put a crimp in the larger growers' harvests lately. But, according to Trimbler, Michael and Terry seemed to have found an ideal setup, removed from the more northern hot spots, with a legitimate orchard for a front.

As I drove into Lakeport and neared the lake I noticed that winter's solitude had ended with the summer's heat. Hundreds of vacationers and hundreds of boats had descended on the cool waters along with the hundred degree temperatures.

At Herb's Auto Shop a description of Terry and his red T-Bird, plus a little friendly conversation, led me to a small, isolated valley about eight miles northwest of the lake.

My four year old Mercedes was still in the downtown parking garage, accumulating fees, and I was driving my equally old Grand Wagoneer.

I figured the Jeep's four wheel drive and steel cable winch on the front might be useful. For the same reason I also packed a rifle and a pistol behind the back seat. In case I wanted to shoot a pear off Terry's head or a joint out of his mouth.

I parked on a ridge hidden by bushes from a turn off that wound down from the main road to a small enclosed valley. My windows were down and I was soaked with sweat.

A wooden sign read: Hidden Valley Pear Orchards in small black letters and Absolutely No Visitors in foot high light-reflective orange paint. I got the feeling they weren't going to be glad to see me.

I sat there baking in my steel and glass oven as long as I could stand it, going over the detailed Geological Survey map for the area.

A thin gray line of dashes traced a loop completely around

the valley, starting near the turn off and rejoining the main road a few miles further north. The legend on the map said the gray dashes were a trail. According to the squiggly brown elevation lines, it followed the ridge about six hundred feet above the valley floor.

It took me over three hours of on foot reconnaissance to check that my four wheel drive could handle the crude narrow trail and get me safely around the rim of the valley. I also checked out the lay of the orchard and ranch buildings and spotted the red T-Bird through my binoculars.

Before leaving San Francisco, a phone call to my uncle, Matt, had confirmed that Terry had the expected unshakable alibi for the time of Trimbler's murder.

I used my winch to drag a heavy log across the entrance road to the ranch, set the four wheel drive on the Jeep's hubs and drove about a mile down the ridge trail. No one saw or heard me and the temperature had dropped to a cool ninety.

The forest along the valley side of the ridge was quite dense, not scattered oaks and chaparral but tall pines and tangled underbrush. The high ridge around the inner side of the valley acted as a mini rain trap and caught more of the winter storms than the surrounding hills. It was perfect cover for my one man commando raid. Unfortunately, I had not had time to shop Giorgio Armani for the latest in black cashmere knit commando outfits.

At six-thirty I sat under a digger pine, braced against a rock, with my trusty old 30-30 Marlin by my side. I had finally found a clear shot of about three hundred yards down to Terry's red T-Bird, parked in front of a ranch style house.

The house was in a narrow bottle neck at the left end of the valley where the road came down. To the right were scattered a half dozen sheds and out buildings, and still farther to the right the valley fanned out into a broad arc.

About two square miles of flat orchard land, planted thick with rows of squat fruit trees, all in leafy bloom. Almost thirteen hundred acres. A lot of cannabis plants could be sheltering between those pear trees and no one would ever know it. At least not from the air where most of the detection is done.

I could see six or seven workers near the sheds, but Terry wasn't one of them. And no sign of anyone fitting Michael's description either. They were all dark-complexioned and wore coarse white pants and shirts like the Indian peasants in Mexico. Things were still relatively slow in late June. Another few months before the fruit would be harvested, forbidden and otherwise.

I decided to act quickly before someone discovered I had barricaded their entrance.

I've never hunted animals, just targets, but I'm an excellent shot, even without a scope, especially on a downward clear slope. I braced against the rock and sighted down the barrel across three hundred yards to the red convertible.

Miniature thunder echoing through the hillside trees and the sharp recoil against my right shoulder. Several workers stopped and looked up toward the ridge.

The bullet impacted two feet short, ploughing the dust against the side of the car. I levered another round into the chamber, corrected my aim, and fired. Then two more, in rapid order.

A 30-30 is very loud and very sharp. My ears were ringing and the workers below were running for cover.

Through my binoculars I could see three large gray marks on the red Thunderbird, where the paint had puckered off around the entrance holes, all in a row along the left front fender.

Above the car the door of the ranch house opened and filled with Terry Rose. Magnified he appeared startlingly close. He looked over at his car, then squinted up the slope under the palm of his hand. I could see him barking orders to the terrified workers before he turned back into the house.

All the men dashed for two pickup trucks and headed up the entrance road. Two of them had rifles.

A nice little diversion. Mission accomplished. I got in my Jeep and bounced and grunted along the rough trail.

Twenty grueling minutes later I was on the other side of the valley behind the house, gloating over my childish revenge on Terry's car.

I left the rifle on the seat and made my way down the steep hill with only my Smith and Wesson .22 long-barreled, automatic target pistol for protection.

A real desperado. Might scare Terry to death with it. But I can hit a six inch metal circle three out of five times with it at a hundred yards, freehanded. At ten yards I can plug a one inch circle every time. The male Annie Oakley of the tin can plinking set.

I angled down the steep ridge so that I came out just past the work sheds at the beginning of the orchard. With the gun in my right hand and the cast on my left, the angled descent made my climb down easier, and I wanted to see the forbidden fruit of this hidden valley.

Luckily, the first thing I saw were the trip wires. Three of them, stretched at different heights near the first row of pear trees. At night the fine black wires would be all but invisible. A different kind of scarecrow for a different kind of scavenger. Not birds but poachers gave growers paranoia.

The orchard was clear of all workers as was the work shed

area. They all seemed to be up on the ridge looking for me, and, for some reason, Terry was still preoccupied inside the house.

The first dozen rows of trees were just what they appeared. Pear trees, about a hundred equally spaced in each long line. A big legitimate operation screening from view the even larger number of trees that filled the dead end of the valley.

The thirteenth row back from the sheds marked the beginning of big money agriculture, northern California style.

Around every pear tree grew a ring of four coveted cannabis plants resembling bristly Christmas trees with long pointed leaves instead of needles. Each almost double my height, lovingly cared for with an irrigation system of plastic pipes and rubber hoses snaking across the orchard from tree to tree. Each pear tree also sheltered a sack of special fertilizer and an assortment of plant nutrients for the small colony of plants that surrounded it.

The arrangement was ingenious, allowing for a good amount of sunlight to filter down to the plants but still keeping visibility from the air to a near impossibility. But these pear trees were not as healthy or well cared for as those in front and I wondered if they even bothered to pick the fruit back here.

I made my way back toward the work sheds and was at the front row of trees when the door of the house banged opened and out came Terry and an older man. I took cover behind a pear tree in the second row and hoped its small trunk would hide me.

I needn't have worried. Terry was preoccupied, yelling at the man about ridiculous ideas and the business going to hell as they strode across the wide yard and entered a long narrow shed.

It would have been easy if it had been Michael but the other man was in his fifties with a long white beard and long white side hair flanking his bald head.

I didn't know what part the marijuana played in Michael's continuing disappearance, but it wasn't a good sign. But I had to find him first before I could determine if he was fit to meet his own daughter. To determine whether he was just illegal or dangerous over-the-edge whack-o. And there was no time like the present, before the workers cleared the log from the road and discovered I wasn't up on the ridge.

I left the security of the orchard and made for the shed, hoping that my .22 automatic would be enough of an edge to pry some useful information out of Terry.

I entered the long narrow shed at its opposite end, passing through a dimly lit maze of tools, boxes and farm implements.

At the far end was an open, brightly lit office area. I could see Terry behind a desk, cluttered with paper, facing my way, reclining in an old swivel chair with his long legs propped up on the desk.

He had exchanged his city duds for ranch wear. Jeans, long sleeve shirt and less fancy leather boots. His thin blond braid hung in place, behind his left ear. Altogether, a scary, sinister looking man. No matter how he dressed. No matter where he was.

The older man was facing him in a straight back chair with his back to me.

Except for a sharp cracking sound there was silence as I worked my way towards them. The noise came from Terry. He was shattering walnuts between his right thumb and forefinger and eating the meat.

Terry said, "we've got to work this problem out. We can't afford not to."

Terry saw me as I emerged from the shadows and entered the office area. He also saw my gun. He didn't move. Just kept snapping the walnuts between his fingers, sighting me down his long legs and over the top of his boots.

It took a few seconds for the other man to realize Terry wasn't looking at him.

He turned his head, saw me and the gun and bolted forward out of his chair. Straight out the door. Leaving me with a glimpse of white hair and beard framing an angelic face. It was either shoot, or let him go. I let him go.

I pulled his empty chair back several feet and sat down. Even though Terry was in an awkward position with his feet up, I wanted to keep a good distance between me and the Jolly Blond Chipmunk crunching nuts behind the desk.

"Well, if it isn't the Rag Doll man," he said.

His blond hair, pale skin and gray unblinking eyes reminded me of a large, sun-bleached lion biding his time for a kill. Although the shallow depth of his eyes revealed nothing, something behind them let me know that I had entered his private preserve. That despite the gun it was his territory and he was the hunter to be feared.

"I'm here to redefine the parameters of our interface," I said. "Keep your chair tilted back and your feet up on the desk."

He stared at the small bore of the automatic, contemplating the risk.

It unnerved me a little that he was so relaxed and unthreatened. Our last encounter had been too one-sided for my peace of mind. He had already reminded me that he had shaken me like a rag doll and I needed to disturb his sense of dominance.

I was a little less than the recommended ten feet from him, but the desk was between us.

"Toss me a walnut," I said.

His hand stretched toward the open bag on the desk.

"Lob it. Underhanded," I warned, waving the gun slightly.

He tossed it in a high arc. When my angle was clear I pulled the trigger once, exploding a shower of walnut across the room.

I flinched more than he did. He didn't even blink. Neither the noise nor the scattered fragments affected him. But something in that animal-like stare let go, conceding me the moment, letting me know he could wait till next time.

"Let's get this over with. I know what you've got growing under the pear trees and I saw the human greeting card you left for me stuffed in the laundromat. You're a big bad man and I'm impressed. Right now I'd rather shoot you than your little toy car, but that wouldn't do me much good, except make me feel better. So, if you want to get rid of me, answer a few simple questions."

He watched but said nothing.

"Where's Michael?"

Still nothing.

"Why were you so sure he'd return to Monterey?"

His indifferent expression changed.

"She hired you," he said. "You're working for Molly."

His manner was now animated and easy, as if he had just recognized an old friend.

"I couldn't figure you out, where you came from, who hired you." He paused and smiled. "What do you want to know?"

He was a lot more cunning than I had realized. He was going for the dominant position again. I was holding a gun on him and he was acting like I was doing him a favor.

"Why would Michael return to Monterey?" I repeated.

"He has this crazy notion that his parents aren't his real parents.

That they murdered his real mother when he was a baby." He watched me closely for the affect. "He went back to steal some letters that he thinks prove his case."

It was a lot more than I had expected. His responsiveness didn't set well.

"Why did you use Katherine to find Michael? He doesn't even know about her."

He locked his thick fingers together behind his head.

"Because you can't go home again, and, when you try, you usually find out more than you want to know."

I let that pass. Pretty soon he'd be speaking in parables and instructing me in the ways of the world.

"Do you know any reason for Diana's murder? You notice I'm not accusing you. I know it's not your style. You like to use your hands."

"I read about it," he said. "That family's nuts." I agreed but it sounded funny coming from him. "The only good person in the entire family is Michael."

A human weakness, a little personal affection and sincerity. Maybe Michael was Terry's Fay Wray and I could use him to knock the big blond ape down from his lofty perch.

"But Michael's run out on you too, hasn't he? Deserted you, in your hour of need."

The hands came down from behind his head and he almost started from the chair. I waved him back with the gun. He wanted the upper hand again.

"Molly's quite a little piece, isn't she? Does she let you call her Molly yet?"

He watched for some sign. I didn't let him see one.

"I confess I never had her myself." His smile returned.

"Never understood how Michael could let such a sweet thing go. I can imagine the special perks that go with your employment." His tongue wet his incongruously delicate lips and he whispered, "Have you been down in the furry meadows for a little tongue-and-groove yet?"

I've gone a long way past locker room baiting. When he saw no reaction he gave up and his mood changed. I figured I had little time before the men in the trucks returned or the guy who ran out set off an alarm.

I threw a pair of handcuffs onto the desk and backed up a few feet.

He laughed. "Won't work chief. Not unless they're making them bigger these days. Can't get them around my wrists."

He held both hands up showing me. His wrists were almost as big as my forearms.

I spotted a two foot length of chain hanging on the wall. I got it and tossed it to him.

"Wrap that tightly around your ankle and close one of the cuffs through the links so it can't come off your foot."

He did as I said. When I heard the ratcheting sound of the cuff closing I had him get up and fasten the other cuff to the beaded desk leg. If he was going to move, the desk would have to come with him. Not an impossibility considering who I was dealing with. He stood there, chained at the right ankle, like a blond King Kong.

I had him chained up just in time. All hell broke loose. Out the window I saw the two pickup trucks return in a roar of dust and shouts. The men piled out and ran past our shed shouting in Spanish.

Then both Terry and I noticed the pungent, bitter smell. One of the workers burst through the door babbling in Spanish. I understood only one word. "Immigration." He stopped when he saw me and the gun.

Outside two official looking cars and a truck squealed to a stop. Several men in uniforms jumped out. My God, it was a raid by the Department of Immigration. And a fire.

Terry spoke quickly in Spanish with the worker then turned to me.

"It's that cocksucker, Jonathan Sherwin. He threatened he'd get even." Then, "you want Michael! That was him. The one who ran out when you got here. He's set fire to the drying shed and he's out in the orchard cutting down the plants."

Desperation was building in him and I figured I had to get out or shoot him. He was close to making a break, desk or no desk. Then a look of betrayal washed across him, stemming the rising tide of fury.

"Get him out of here before I kill him," he yelled.

I turned and ran out the way I had entered.

I made my way through the chaos outside. Most of the workers had scattered and the Immigration officers were trying to put out the fire in the large high shed with the help of a couple who hadn't. They must have had their green cards.

I held my breath so I wouldn't succumb to an instant high and ran back into the orchard. I found the white-haired old man merrily whacking down plants with a scythe in the fourteenth row. He'd already gotten through over a hundred of the little darlings.

I couldn't believe it was Michael, but, when I yelled his name, he turned in surprise, mine as well as his.

He was slender and about five feet ten, reminding me of a

sentimentalized painting of one of the apostles. A bald circle crowned the top of his head and long shoulder length silky white hair draped down on each side, flanking the white beard that hung six inches from his chin. He looked like a bleached friar. Or a lost mendicant searching for his guru.

Even though I knew he was almost forty, the shock was that up close his face didn't look old at all. His bald spot, long white hair and long white beard were misleading, for his thirty-nine years had left no trace on his face. He seemed to be both child and old man.

In the twilight his skin was unlined, his face untroubled. Yet some harsh realities had marked him with the contradiction of innocent youth and premature age.

"Who are you?" he said, confused, as if I were a visitor from another world.

"Molly sent me."

The simple words could find no anchorage in his memory at first.

"Molly sent you?" he repeated. Then, "Molly!" as his eyes widened with recognition and amazement.

I said, "you have to come with me. There's little time. Terry's coming and the police are after you."

"I can't come," he shouted. "I've got to get over the mountains to Bishop. Tonight. Across the High Sierras."

There seemed to be a little of his father in him after all. He was impassioned, like a prophet set on doing God's work.

The crackle and roar of the fire in the shed grew louder behind us. Time was running out.

"I'll take you," I said. "I have a car waiting on the ridge."

The look of reality came back into his wild eyes. He dropped his scythe and followed me on the steep climb out of the valley.

From the Jeep the fire in the darkening valley was a harsh red counterpoint to the soft glow of the sun as it slipped behind the opposite ridge.

FOURTEEN

Even though it was going to be a hard night, I was lucky. The long drive to Bishop, over four hundred miles, would allow me to take the measure of the strange man sitting next to me, and maybe clear up some mysteries.

I didn't want to tell him more than I had to, which wasn't much of a problem. I got by with Molly hiring me to find him.

He wasn't curious as to why, especially after all this time, and he didn't seem to know about his daughter, Katie. So, I let it pass. He was preoccupied with his own problems and seemed to be on some sort of a mission to Bishop. Well, that suited my purposes fine. I just wanted to start him talking.

We passed the fire engines coming up from Lakeport as we headed over to Highway 20.

"That was some little trick you played on Terry back there." He didn't answer. "Sort of burned your bridges, or sheds, behind you. The end of a beautiful partnership."

He laughed. It was now dark and his white hair and beard glowed like a spectral presence.

"It was a symbolic act," he said. "Also very real. That shed contained over a hundred thousand dollars of prime leaf. Up in smoke."

He laughed again. His voice was pleasant and smooth without the tension I had expected.

"I thought the harvest was still a few months off."

"It is. That was part of last year's crop. Stored for the high prices of summer. The unnerving doldrums on the trip to the great Pacific High. Before the new supply arrives." He chuckled softly.

"You seem very happy with yourself, but I'm sure Terry isn't."

"There was no other way." His tone was colored with regret. "I tried to get out before. I even disappeared for a couple of weeks, but that wasn't going to work, so I came back."

"Why did you want out?"

His voice was tired with resignation.

"It was getting out of hand. Terry wanted to make the jump to the big time, I didn't.

"We started off simple four years ago. Each year we planted more. This year's crop would be well over ten times as big as last year's, and I didn't want any part of it. I never wanted to be Smokey the Bear, watching over the whole forest."

His breath came out slowly. "So I went back this afternoon, just before you showed up."

"Why?"

"Terry needed me for the harvest so I knew he wouldn't leave me alone, and I wanted to end it all at once. Our business and our whole crazy friendship."

I didn't say anything. For a long time he was silent. When he started again it was half pride, half confession.

"Terry and I drifted around the country for over a dozen years before we found our place in the sun. In Mexico, five years ago. That's where we learned about sinsemilla.

"We were pretty bummed out by then." He let out a soft laugh. "Ironically, we both gave up using drugs when we started growing them.

"After our apprenticeship in Mexico to the miracle weed, we came back to the ranch, the one sensible result of my Hippie days. I bought it for a commune in '67, but it never worked out that way.

"Anyway, it was in terrible shape. We used our Mexican profits to fix it up, and started small four years ago. Last year was our first big harvest. We made over a half million profit on sinsemilla and fifty thousand on pears."

He chuckled again. "Terry insisted on putting almost all of it back into a gigantic harvest for this year. A gigantic harvest of the magical sinsemilla. Enough high for the whole fucking state. That's when everything got out of hand."

He stopped chuckling to himself and asked, "do you know what sinsemilla is?"

"You're the expert. Educate me."

"It's somewhere over the rainbow time for all believers in the perfect high. It's five to ten times more potent than regular marijuana. It comes from just the female plants and the word means 'without seeds' in Spanish.

"Sinsemilla isn't a plant really. It's a technique of culling the male plants from the female plants, so they can't pollinate them. That makes the female plant horny, and she produces more gummy resin. It's that special sex starved resin that makes sinsemilla so potent."

"You make it sound erotic."

"It is for a lot of people. A real high. But it's a lot of work. That's where I came in."

There was a lingering trace of pride and excitement in his description.

"I had almost four thousand plants in that orchard. With my special skills and our near perfect growing setup we could expect almost two pounds per plant. Even with a twenty-five per cent unforeseen loss factor knocked off that's about five thousand pounds, top quality.

"Terry can hustle that at between a thousand and two thousand dollars a pound, wholesale to retail. We're talking over six million dollars in sales, over five million in profits. Do you know what that means?"

"A lot of money and a chance for Terry to climb the next rung to the big time," I answered.

"Exactly! I've got a giant green thumb and Terry's a master at marketing the stuff. I couldn't see an end to it, and he didn't want to. He spends all of his time now down in the city, hustling. And I spend all my time at the ranch."

A short, poignant silence produced a wistful inflection.

"Growing pears is the only thing I've ever liked and been good at at the same time."

The almost lilting pitch of his voice sank back into troubled dark silence.

We descended from the hills onto the agricultural flats of the vast Central Valley. My headlights reflected off the sign for Interstate 5. We joined its light flow of traffic, gliding through the balmy night, down the giant, flat fertile valley, just freed from the oppressive heat of day. Sweet night smells of fresh cut grasses and hay permeated the car.

Michael seemed to be growing moody and I didn't want to lose him to the pervasive dark night.

"What about the magic of sinsemilla and all that money?"

"I don't care about the money. That's Terry's dream. My

family had too much of it to start with. I know too well what often comes with it. I wanted to cut down all those gummy little plants and be free of them forever."

"What happens to them now?" I asked.

"I don't know. Terry will nurse them along without me. I'll let him finish this year, I guess. But then I'll want my orchard back."

I said, "I don't think it will work that way. Immigration pulled a raid while you were hacking away in the orchard. All that bitter, pungent smoke will give the operation away. Terry will be lucky if he escapes jail, although they usually just confiscate the plants."

"Immigration?" He was shocked. "That was our achilles' heel. That's how we kept the operation secret. We always brought our workers in straight from Mexico for both the pear and plant harvests. But they won't arrive for over a month. And only a few of the regular workers are unregistered. Who would know about that?"

"Terry says it's your father."

"My father?"

The word's meaning seemed lost in his distant past. Finally, it found its way up to the present.

"He's not my father! He's the Big Bad Wolf!"

It came out as an anguished shout. He was an uneven blend of the nice boy next door and a refugee from the buzzed out drug culture of the late 60's.

He sat quietly for a while before he spoke.

"It would be just like Father Sherwin to get his revenge by acting indirectly. Siccing the immigration people on us. Saintly Father Sherwin, preaching long and loud, piercing the night air so everyone will know the right. A real gangster of the air waves."

He simmered with indignation awhile before saying, "I don't know how much you know about me."

The anguish was gone, replaced by something softer and sadder.

"Terry's been my only friend all my life. But it hasn't been a healthy friendship. Together we've formed a strange unit, feeding off each other's strengths and weaknesses.

"In a way Terry's a pure child of nature. In the unnatural way of things he grew up with a bad attitude to match his huge size and special physical gifts. He's also very shrewd, one of nature's sinister children.

"But I see from your cast that you know that first hand, no pun intended."

He continued. "I used to get off on Terry's violence. I couldn't face the real evil in me and in the world so I became its secret sharer. Through Terry."

A bitter, hissing sound escaped through his teeth.

"I've avoided my problems and responsibilities that way. I...I..I've wasted my life hiding from what I couldn't face."

He stopped. "Hell, it's too complicated to explain. I've never understood it, really. It would take ten shrinks ten years."

He seemed to have lost the thread. I interrupted.

"Why are we going to Bishop?"

His tone was hard and cold. Determined.

"To do what I should have done eighteen years ago."

"When you disappeared after your fight with your father on the pier in Monterey?"

"You know about that?"

It was more a question of who I was than mere surprise. He was finally wondering why I was there.

"Why did Molly hire a detective after all these years?"

"I'll make a deal with you. I'll take you to Bishop, if you clear up your mysterious disappearance. And, when we come back, I'll answer your question."

"It's a deal."

He sat thoughtfully for a while.

"I'm going to Bishop to clear up a lot of my own mysteries. With a little luck I plan to finally unmask the evil that started there. The evil that's rotted out the heart of our family and destroyed its soul."

He said it calmly, with grim determination.

"I thought you said you weren't part of the family. Why do you care?"

A bitter, self-deprecating laugh came from his darkened corner of the car.

"That's been the dilemma of my life, man. The solution and resolution of which I've been running from all my life."

I could almost taste the scorn he felt for himself.

"I hope to prove I'm not their son by blood. But, yes or no, their blood has corrupted me. In spirit I've been as soulless as my would-be/might-be parents."

"What's all this got to do with Bishop?"

"Why Bishop's Sherwin Hometown, U.S.A. It's where the bad blood first came gurgling up out of the ground, like a corrupt mountain stream."

I began to worry that he was a hard nut about to crack, but he started to calm down.

"I'm looking for the old family doctor. I checked, and he's still alive, though he's retired. He used to treat Jonathan's sister, Gloria. My supposed aunt."

"Your aunt?"

"Yeah. I think she was my real mother. I suspect her dear brother, once my uncle, now my Dear Father Jonathan Sherwin, and his then new bride, once my new aunt-in-law, now my Dear Mother Rebecca Sherwin, killed her near Lake Tahoe in 1946. And I think they then adopted me, Dear Baby Michael, into their cheery, bloodstained new family."

I looked quickly over at him, the lights and shadows passing across his troubled face. Was his the reflected face of the long hidden evil that had plagued the Sherwin family?

"That's an incredible accusation. Are you sure you're not confusing the Sherwins with the Hamlet clan in Denmark?"

"You mean like in, "it hath made me mad" and "we will have no more marriages"? Something like that? Well, the answer is no. I'm not using my background in literature to give class to a neurotic obsession.

"Neurotic I admit. Obsessed I might be. But I am also right. I just need the proof."

He sank back into the shadows, brooding like Hamlet over his fate.

"Just what do you hope this aging doctor will do?"

It popped out of him with unexpected force.

"Give me an identity." He paused. "Let a little light through this cloud I've lived under all my life." He hesitated. "Maybe even set me free."

I began to think maybe he wasn't crazy.

"I know Jonathan's sister was pregnant the year before she died. I need the doctor to confirm the date, to prove that it coincides with my birthday."

"But why would they kill her, if she was your mother? Why

murder, and not just an accident? Rebecca claims Gloria died in a car accident after stealing you from them, and they found you lying in the snow, covered with her blood. She thinks that was the trauma that has plagued you."

"Bullshit!" he yelled.

"Well, Rebecca's story fits in other ways. If Gloria was pregnant and lost her baby in the earlier accident that killed both her parents, she might have tried to get another one by stealing you. She could have died just as Rebecca said."

"Bullshit, again. There's a lot more wrong in my family than just a couple of accidents. And, half the family fortune my mother would have inherited, is motive enough for killing her. Especially in my family. And I remember what my father yelled at me that day on the pier. About divine punishment and rivers of blood following him down from the mountains to the sea. And that I wasn't a member of the family. Let's see what the doctor says. If the date of Gloria Sherwin's pregnancy fits my birth, I'll have my proof."

He was calm again, and I began to think he might be right.

"I went there once before, you know. To Bishop. Terry and I. From San Francisco, about a month after we left Monterey. I was going to find the truth then, too. I was going to set myself free.

"But we had already gotten heavily into drugs that first month, and we got stoned on the way over, and I made an ass of myself, questioning everyone I could find with wild accusations. I wish I had done it right then, but the truth was more than I could bear. And I've been running ever since.

"All my wanderings with Terry, the drug business we've gotten ourselves into, have just been a deviation, an inability to face this fundamental problem with my family.

"When I remember all the murky horrors I've slogged through, eyes only half open, these last nearly twenty years, I shudder."

I was beginning to like him. He was carrying the grief of all his unaccepted responsibilities and, somewhere through his labyrinth of memories, a new man was struggling to emerge.

"If you find what you want in Bishop, what then?"

"I plan to go back and confront Mother Sherwin with the past. I've always sensed that she is the real source of our family tragedy.

"And I'd like to confront Father Sherwin too. I don't want to deny him his share of responsibility. Until I face both of them, I'll never have any peace."

He snickered softly to himself.

"I'd like to have it out with the self-righteous old coot on the pier in Monterey. Just like last time. But this time I wouldn't run away."

"What did happen between you and Jonathan on that pier so many years ago?"

"What happened is that my manhood collapsed like a house of cards. I went there full of hope. That was before I really suspected he wasn't my father.

"I was just engaged to Molly and wanted to tell him. I also wanted to share in the family grief about the then recent deaths of my sister and brother. It was to be my first 'adult' conversation with him. A new attempt to be part of the family that had always rejected me."

He rolled his window down and stuck his head out into the dark night air. His long white hair and beard blew wildly, like a demon riding the wind. After a minute he pulled himself back and closed the window.

Bitterness cut his voice like sharp knives.

"Well it didn't work. Little Boy Michael didn't grow up that day on the pier. Father Sherwin wouldn't even let him talk.

"Father Sherwin was in the strangest mood. I remember his face to this day.

"His eyes couldn't focus on anything and his usual elegance was drawn long and tight. His arms stiff at his sides, his fists clenched. He seemed to be holding himself together by sheer willpower. The only movement was on the right side of his face, especially under his eye, which began to twitch as we talked."

I thought of Jonathan's similar reaction during our lunch at the Institute and remembered Rebecca saying he had a stroke after fighting with Michael on the pier.

"He suffered a mild stroke on the pier after you left," I said.

"That doesn't surprise me. He was under great pressure and he wouldn't let go. Something had to give. He was being forced to accept an imperfect and impure world. But he wouldn't give in. He denied the world and just screwed the lid on tighter.

"I had always been afraid of him, so tall and dignified, and when I approached him that day I was very nervous."

"What happened?"

"He started preaching at me. Ranting about rivers of blood that had followed him from the mountains down to the sea. Carrying on about divine punishment. Screamed that I wasn't a member of the family and that I had better escape before it was too late."

"Did you know what he meant by that?"

"No. Not then. All the while he was ranting, I was like a miniature version of him, building up tremendous pressure inside, about to explode myself.

"I was so mad because once again he was rejecting me, wouldn't listen to me. I had piled all my hopes for the future on that one conversation and he denied me.

"Well, I exploded before he did. He's almost a half foot taller than I am, and I began beating him on the chest with my fists, like a small child. Then I punched him in the face with all my might. Blood squirted from his nose and ran freely down his face and covered his clean white shirt.

"I was almost hysterical and was about to hit him again when I heard horrible screaming. At first I thought it was my father and then I thought I was screaming. But it wouldn't stop.

"Finally, I snapped out of my violent trance and became worried that people were watching me. But they weren't.

"About ten yards past us, at the very end of the pier, were a bunch of kids and a few adults. All of them were shrieking, especially the kids. It was the most horrible sound I've ever heard. Then I noticed the terrified barking of the sea lions.

"I ran up to the railing by the kids, who had been feeding fish to the sea lions. Some of the kids were still holding fish in their hands while they were screaming.

"I looked over the railing and saw a half dozen sea lions escaping in panic, their alarmed barking filling the air.

"Then I looked down into the water. It was like staring into your worst nightmare.

"The water was stained thick with blood. And thrashing in that blood was a huge white shape, still tearing at the one remaining sea lion, whose eyes were frozen, locked in a shocked glare. The white form was a great white shark, ripping apart in great chunks the captured sea lion.

"I'll never forget the look of startled disbelief in the sea lion's eyes or that fixed, unmoving, unfeeling glare in the eyes of the white shark as it rolled over and finally swallowed the head and eyes of that sea lion, putting an end to its misery.

"But not mine. My misery was just beginning.

"It was then, after the shark disappeared under the bloody water, that I realized the children had stopped screaming and everyone was staring at me.

"Then I heard the moaning and realized it was me.

"I was holding my hands in front of me, staring at the blood on them. My father's blood. I kept moaning, staring back and forth between the bloodstained water and the blood on my hands.

"Then I turned and saw with revulsion what else everyone was staring at.

"My father, standing behind me, blood streaking down his face from his nose. Deathly calm. His eyes frozen in the same shocked glare as the sea lion's. He was like a collapsed man with his insides taken out of him, staring blankly at the scene.

"I turned and ran in panic back down the pier and disappeared, like one of the escaping sea lions."

"Then you and Terry went to San Francisco and just disappeared for eighteen years?"

"Yeah. What happened on that pier really fucked up my head. Over and over the words--'the horror'--echoed through my mind. Not just at what I saw, but at what I began to realize about my family and myself.

"All my new resolutions and all my moral courage melted away and I started on an orgy of self-pity.

"I got Terry and we went to San Francisco that same night and just lost ourselves. In every way imaginable."

"How could you leave Molly without any explanation except

that one note?"

"It was easy."

He had the sound of a soldier familiar with defeat.

"She was an embarrassment for me. A sign of hope in a world without hope. An uneasy reminder of a time when I still thought I could be saved."

"And what about now?" I asked. "Can you be saved now? Aren't you trying to save yourself by finally clearing up this family mess?"

His voice was weary but carried the steady note of grim determination.

"What I want now, for the first time in my life, is to know what I'm doing and like what I'm doing. And that means clearing up my family identity, quitting the drug business and sticking with my pear trees."

He was quiet for a few seconds and then asked, "should that be so impossible?"

"No. That isn't too much to want. And I think I can help you get it."

We were both quiet for awhile. I took the Manteca exit and started east across the Valley floor on 120, heading for 108 and the High Sierras. On the state highway there was little traffic and the night seemed much darker.

"Why did you return to Monterey to see your mother and father?" He started to protest but I said, "I've got to call them something."

"I didn't go to see Rebecca. I went to steal some letters she had. I only saw her by accident when I was leaving."

"I saw Rebecca the other day. She tells a different story than you do, but she admits they drove you from the family. She told me to tell you she bears all the guilt."

"It's a little too late now," he said sarcastically. "She fucked with my head for years and I won't ever let her again. So I'm not listening. I know what I have to do and for once I'm going to do it."

"Why did you go see Jonathan, then?"

He snorted, then snickered, gleefully.

"For revenge. Pure revenge."

He turned sideways and became excited.

"I laid a real head trip on the old man. I got in to see him at that monstrous place he built, and then wouldn't say anything. I sat across the table from him and just smiled.

"I really fucked up his head. He went into a rage. Then I stood up and simply said I'd be back when I got the proof. I left him stammering like an old idiot. It was fucking fantastic. Perfect revenge."

He reached into his back pocket and pulled out a crumpled letter.

He was still excited and said, "turn on the dome light and I'll read you what I found."

"It's a letter from Jonathan to my mother, his sister, Gloria, in Bishop. He was still in the navy and the letter is postmarked, Honolulu, July 25, 1945. Just before the War ended. It says:

Dear Sweet Gloria,

I just got your letter and am terribly upset. My God! How could you have let such a thing happen? My God! How could you let yourself get pregnant? Good God! What will mother and father do when they find out? Do they know who the father is? If I had

EVIL AT ITS EASE

thought this could happen, I would have put an end to your immoral behavior on my last trip home. How can you ever marry and have a proper father for the baby? Since that is impossible you must tell everyone that he was a stranger passing through town. The War is hard on all of us and maybe they will forgive you. I will do everything I can and promise to stand by you.

"He was a real charmer even then, don't you think?"

"Who was the father? Do any of the other letters say?"

"No. This was the only interesting one. But, in a small, isolated town, it could have been any supposedly respectable citizen.

"I even saw this letter once before, when I was about eighteen. But it didn't mean anything to me. Ironically, its significance only dawned on me during my first acid trip, in San Francisco, the week after the fight on the pier. That's why we went to Bishop the first time. But I didn't have the guts or sense to follow through and it's been haunting me ever since.

"Now, if I can get the proof I need from the doctor, I want to confront Jonathan and find out just who my real father was. I don't even care about the murder after all this time. I only want my own identity and to be free from them."

"Unfortunately, it's become a little more messy since you disappeared again two weeks ago. Where were you yesterday afternoon?"

"I was tide pooling near Bodega Bay. I've been camped out on the beach near there most of the week. Trying to clear my head and get my courage up."

"Can you prove it? Any witnesses?"

"Not that I could find again. Why?"

"Because Diana was murdered then. I found her floating in

Rebecca's fountain with her head smashed in."

"Jesus Christ! Isn't it ever going to stop. Diana. She was the best of the family."

"And the police are looking for you right now, thanks to some pretty wild accusations Jonathan made."

"It's like a curse following me. Maybe Jonathan was right. Rivers of blood have followed him down to the sea. Do you have any idea who did it?"

"The most obvious is you or Terry. You've both been seen in Monterey and you've both been stirring up old troubles."

"Christ, I didn't do it!"

"I believe you. And I don't think Terry did it either. Even though he was in Monterey yesterday. It's not his style. He would have used his hands, and she was killed with a heavy statue."

"You're right. Terry always uses his hands. He won't even carry a gun."

"That leaves me with no good suspects. Unless you're right and there was a previous murder. Murder has a way of breeding more murder, even forty years apart."

Then I told him about Terry's contribution to all the confusion. How the police found Trimbler with almost all his bones broken after I had questioned him.

"I've never seen Terry kill anyone," he said. "Never even knew he killed anyone, for sure. But I've had some suspicions. He's gotten worse since he got his big dream. But murder. I've had my eyes closed too long. It's definitely time to get out."

Then he said, "eyes closed or not, I've got to get some sleep, if I'm going to be any good tomorrow. Can you handle the driving?"

In a few minutes he was asleep. Snoring like Rip Van Winkle

with his long white hair and beard.

It was exactly midnight. I continued up the western slope of the Sierras on Highway 108. A long, gradual climb that takes you from the floor of the Valley at near sea level to almost ten thousand feet at Sonora Pass.

Highway 108 is always closed all winter because of heavy snow but it had just been cleared by Caltrans. The road surface was dry but at eight thousand feet we reached the snowpack.

There was no traffic. I drove on the cleared road, between high walls of last winter's snow, with Father Time snoring away beside me.

An eerie sensation. Isolated in all that whiteness, with star-pocked darkness on top. Shapes and shadows forming and dissolving around every white bend as my lights followed the curves.

At Sonora Pass the snow walls were even now over twenty feet high. Stillness. Absolute. No other lights or sounds but our own.

Then over the top, down the precipitous eastern escarpment, a violent contrast to the gradual western approach. Out of the snow again, back into the past and a possible murder.

After turning south the tiny town of Bridgeport on U.S. Highway 395 jarred my memory. The late 40's Robert Mitchum film noir movie, Out of the Past, was set there.

The film's brooding, shadowy images of undiscovered murder and deception floated before me. Haunting me. Palpable. Like my unseen strawberry fields and my floating island.

Images, lingering in the night air. After almost forty years. Like the smell of murder we were pursuing.

What had I got hold of that wouldn't come to light? Or what

past evil had been in the light so long it wasn't recognized anymore? What had been breeding and growing through all those forty years that so troubled Michael's soul?

It had seemed at first a difficult but uncomplicated missing person case. Except for the letters. They were the first signpost to trouble.

Then came a regular parade of strange events and even stranger people that brought me to where I was now. Screening memories of murder from old movies on my mind's eye and looking down the road for the real thing.

Two very real, very violent murders already and the prospect of one more.

At just past four I pulled into Bishop. I woke Michael and we turned into the Vagabond Motel at the north end of town.

FIFTEEN

In the morning I talked him into shaving off his beard and cutting his long white hair after I had been out earlier, getting gas and buying scissors and a razor and other supplies.

I convinced him he'd have less trouble getting serious answers from the doctor that way, and it was time he made a new beginning. I also had his daughter, Katie, in mind and wanted to reduce the shock for her.

The change was incredible, revealing a sensitive chin and mouth. He now looked his own age and less like a wild man escaped from an ashram, although the pale skin beneath his missing beard lent a peculiar cast to his expressions.

After breakfast we were in front of the retired doctor's house by ten, two blocks west of the only busy street in town, Highway 395.

It was a quiet residential block, totally removed from the traffic and businesses just two streets away. A white, two story frame house surrounded by a wide expanse of green lawn and many large shade trees. Reminding me that the afternoon heat would soon be up to near a hundred again.

We knocked on the door and were greeted by a pleasant woman in her late fifties. She was the housekeeper and told us Doctor Kline was up at Lake Sabrina, fishing.

We took 168 west of town, beginning the eighteen-mile drive

and five-thousand-foot climb to Lake Sabrina.

The eastern side of the Sierras is nothing like the western. No gentle rolling grassy hills. No old gold rush towns in the foothills swarming with tourists. No orange groves, vineyards or nut and fruit trees nestled against the first hillocks. No people, hardly.

Less than twenty thousand live permanently in a two hundred mile north-south stretch down from the crowds at Lake Tahoe. And, for all two hundred of those miles, the only three highways that connect to the main body of California, across the high wall of mountains to the west, are all closed by thirty to forty feet of snow for six to eight months a year.

Bishop rests in isolated splendor in the middle of those two hundred miles. A town of three thousand residents, at four thousand feet elevation. Supply center for the entire eastern slope, rampant with motels and stores that cater to vacationers. Straddling its lifeline to the outside world, the all-weather, north-south highway, U.S. 395.

We followed Bishop Creek up into the high mountains, leaving the small town behind. Sprawled on the arid floor of ten mile wide Owens Valley. Cradled between the jagged granite peaks of the Sierras to the west and the towering dry ridges of the White Mountains to the east.

An awesome place. One of the world's deepest valleys, with two miles of sheer vertical climb to the mountain walls on both sides.

Even the nature freaks and skiers from L.A. can't spoil it, although their minions long ago stole its lushness. Diverting its clear mountain water to quench the thirst of their great southland metropolis, transforming the once green valley into high sagebrush desert.

We made the ascent up long slanting grades, sliced into the mountainside. Out of the arid valley, out of its rising heat, into cool mountain air, pine trees and crystal alpine lakes.

As the housekeeper promised, we found Dr. Kline on his favorite rock outcropping along the north shore of the small lake. We recognized him by his eighty-one years and the large orange sun hat he wore.

Snow still covered the mountainside just above us and, in the immediate background, gray granite spires provided a storybook setting for the liquid crystal lake.

We walked out onto the flat granite outcropping which projected about ten feet above the water's surface.

Michael was nervous and blurted out the doctor's name while his back was still to us.

"Dr. Kline?" he said, in a loud voice resonant with hopes and fears.

"Yes," the old man answered, and slowly turned to face us.

A kindly face and smile greeted us. His eyes were bright and as steady as his hands, which held the fishing rod, and contentment, as well as age, was written on his face with every wrinkle.

The dry mountain air had preserved him well and the Sherwin name brought instant recognition.

It was important that this remained Michael's show, so I stood off to the side while he talked. Listening to the conversation, but absorbed by three young boys in a small rowboat.

Doctor Kline patiently reeled in his line as they approached the spot beneath us.

I watched them awkwardly manipulate the wooden oars, moving erratically in half circles, splashing the water and carrying on in a noisy manner.

Only youth or a focused indifference to the world's troubles can produce such simple pleasures, I thought. There were only a dozen people scattered around the lake and the three boys were the only ones out on its surface.

All was quiet. All sound except the three boys and the steady murmur of conversation behind me absorbed by nature's grand indifference. I breathed deeply the clear fresh air, just warming from its morning sharpness to pleasant shirt sleeve levels.

Crisp, pure smells filled my lungs. The scent of pine trees. The tang of air moving down from the raw granite peaks. Over slopes of melting snow, across pristine groves of pine, skimming the green crystal lake. Nature's elemental breath.

I breathed it in again, deeply. Absorbing the high thin atmosphere, until I felt light-headed.

I looked down at the boys in the boat.

The snow fed waters were icy cold and kept them confined to their safe, floating island. Tucked securely into their bright orange life jackets, their energies channeled into splashing handfuls of frigid water at each other.

I peered past them into the translucent, green-tinted waters surrounding the small boat, seeking its bottom.

None could be found.

The water's great purity and depth produced the illusion of total clarity. Of vision so unclouded that no object appeared to mark its limits. Until transparency itself seemed the proper medium of perception. Like looking into a fortune teller's crystal ball, waiting for some recognizable shape to come into view.

"Murder?"

From over my shoulder that all too discernible word pierced my reverie, blew across my hearing and out over the lake like a deadly pollutant. Conjured up the one recognizable shape I didn't want to remember, until a monstrous white figure seemed to form just beneath the boys' rowboat.

I stared, half-hypnotized. Waited. Half-believing and half-expecting to see the huge glassy eyes, unblinking, and the rows of large, triangular teeth. And all the blood, staining the water red. Half-feared for the innocence of the three boys playing below.

"Murder!" I heard the doctor repeat it again. Louder. Its meaning rising to consciousness.

I blinked and watched the water below. Uneasily. Until memory and imagination disentangled themselves. Grateful, nonetheless, when the three boys rowed back to the safety of shore. Reassured again by the perfect beauty and peace of the day.

Either my tuning apparatus needs checking, I thought, or I'm picking up the same signal Michael has. In either case, I figured I needed a week in Vegas to put me back in touch with normal unreality.

Michael had handled his part of the conversation well and Doctor Kline agreed to check his records for us, if we would follow him back to town.

As we started the long grade back, down into the intense heat of the valley floor, Michael looked at me and smiled. Then a full-blown grin, and said, "Foul deeds will rise, Though all the earth o'erwhelm them, to men's eyes."

Seven hours later, after leaving the doctor's office, we finally escaped the searing heat of California's interior valleys and came down into the cool Pajaro Valley, on the coast, just north of Monterey.

If rivers of blood had followed the Sherwin family down from the mountains to the sea, we did not see them. But, as everything else on this case proved, that didn't mean they weren't there.

The doctor's old record books seemed to confirm Michael's suspicions. Or at least didn't disprove them.

He had diagnosed Jonathan's sister, Gloria, as three months pregnant on July 10, 1945. That coincided almost exactly with Michael's January 8th birthday in 1946.

Dr. Kline also assumed that her injuries from the accident that killed her parents were not serious enough to have adversely affected her pregnancy, though he couldn't be sure.

When her parent's car ran off the road on their drive to Reno, on July 14th, she had been thrown clear and had only suffered a gash on the back of her neck. He felt reasonably sure that, given her youth and excellent good health and the early period of her pregnancy, the baby would have been unaffected.

He said Gloria had left Bishop shortly after that, in August, 1945, to wait for Jonathan in San Francisco, and he had never examined her again.

But he remembered the strange Sherwin family well. The richest family ever to live in the valley.

He said the parents were too old and should have known better than to start a family so late in life. That they ended up uncomfortable with their own children and frequently travelled, leaving Jonathan and Gloria alone in the care of a nurse, a cook and a maid.

He said they were forced to rely too much on themselves and never adapted socially. Blamed the parents for all their problems. Remembered clearly Jonathan's shock after the death of his sister at Lake Tahoe, when he returned to Bishop. Had sent his new wife and baby back to San Francisco first and came on alone, to attend to his sister's burial and settle the family's finances.

No matter how odd the Sherwin family seemed to him, though, Dr. Kline was incredulous at Michael's allegation of possible murder. But Michael had remained calm and got the necessary information from him.

He even showed us the coroner's report from the accident that killed Jonathan and Gloria's parents. Also, a copy of the coroner's report on her own death at Lake Tahoe.

Both reports and all the information he gave us seemed to confirm the facts as generally known. Nothing in the Lake Tahoe accident report to suggest murder. No unusual marks on Gloria's body that couldn't have been caused by an accident.

Only the coincidence of Michael's birth and Gloria's pregnancy and the wild statements that Jonathan had made on the pier eighteen years ago pointed in the direction of Michael's suspicions.

And, possibly, the unexplained death of Diana and all the other tragedies that had so plagued the Sherwin family.

Then, there was the uneasy feeling that had been creeping over me ever since our visit to Bishop.

It was as if I had picked up a disturbing scent through some ancestral, animal level of smell and was following it down to the sea. Out of the glaring, stark heat, into the cool fog air.

That all too familiar scent of evil. Still unrecognized.

SIXTEEN

As we passed through Monterey I fulfilled my bargain with Michael and told him why Molly had hired me. And about his daughter, Katie. Our trip and his determined behavior had convinced me he would be more of an asset than a liability in her life.

Too much had happened to him lately for the information to shock him. He just sat there, quietly absorbing the news.

Finally, he said he was happy he had a daughter. Then he thanked me for my help and said he was glad I had found him, but he wouldn't be any use to anybody until he resolved his problems with his family.

Then he settled back into a grim silence until his agitation level increased as we approached Rebecca's house.

She admitted us through the electronic gate after scanning us on the video monitor and met us herself at the front door. Jonathan wasn't there and, as she had mentioned before, there were no live-in servants.

It was just seven-thirty and the fog was in, thick and wet, as we entered the large living room of the crypto-Roman villa.

I was surprised to find it furnished in a comfortable, modern style. We all stood around awkwardly for a minute, glancing nervously back and forth, before we sat down across a wooden coffee table from each other. Rebecca in a wing back brocade chair,

Michael and I side by side on a crimson velvet couch.

The three of us all alone in that huge room, carefully studying each other, as the sun lost itself behind the fog outside.

Rebecca started.

"I'm very pleased to see you, Michael. I'm delighted Mr. Walker brought you here."

"He didn't bring me. I was coming anyway."

She seemed distracted. Kept clasping her hands together.

"Well, no matter. You'll have to excuse my nervousness. It has nothing to do with you. I'm worried about your father. I haven't seen him in almost two days. Not since the night we found Diana.....dead."

Michael's hands were trembling and his voice quivered as he spoke.

"I'm sorry about Diana's death. But she wasn't my sister and Jonathan isn't my father." The shaking spread to his voice. "And you are not my mother!"

Her full attention turned to Michael and then me.

"Why Mr. Walker, how ever did he get such a silly notion?"

It was the little girl act I had seen the day before.

"He thinks he has proof," I said. "And it will save time if you don't treat us to three acts of beautifully played drama. As much as I enjoyed the show the other day."

She glared right at me. Then she threw back her head and let out one loud, harsh laugh.

She startled both of us. Her long red hair whipped forward as she snapped her head back towards us. A strong willed young woman was now staring at us.

The cosmetic artistry, the partially hidden wrinkles, the almost sixty years were still there. But inside, in her predator's eyes and in her commanding voice, was a self-willed young woman. Vital and alert, and taunting she was more than a match for both of us.

Was this the real Rebecca Sherwin or another great performance?

"All right, boys. Unbuckle your pants and show me what you've got."

"Now there's a mother a boy can relate to," I said.

She ignored me.

"Whatever happened to the guilt ridden old woman who wanted her son back?"

"Stay out of this. If he thinks he's a man, he can speak for himself."

I saw Michael wince as he pulled the old letter from his back pocket.

"Oh, this is strictly family business," I agreed. "But you've got to have a referee to watch out for fouls in the clinches."

"Show me what you think you've got, boy!"

Her tone lifted the word "boy" onto a double level of derision.

"I've got this old letter I took from here the other week." He handed her the letter.

Her tone became less abrasive.

"I know what this letter is. And it doesn't prove what you think it does."

"I think it proves you're not my mother. That I was that baby mentioned in the letter. That I was born in San Francisco while you and Gloria waited for Jonathan to return home. And that you and Jonathan killed my real mother at Lake Tahoe, for her share of the inheritance, and adopted me as one of your own. Which is why I've been so screwed up my entire life."

She gave a wicked little twist to her lips. An evil smile.

"You know that letter doesn't prove anything like that. And I warn you not to push me. You really don't want to know the real truth."

"That's not all my proof. Before I had my fight with Jonathan on the pier, he warned me to get out of the family. That I wasn't a real member. And he said rivers of blood had followed him down from the mountains."

Bull's-eye! Michael scored his first point. She was very upset and knocked off balance by what he said about Jonathan. For a few seconds some very disturbing thoughts clouded her face.

"For chrissakes!" Michael pleaded. "You know this family is a mess. I don't care about the past in any legal sense. Nothing will happen to you, if you confess. I just want you to set me free. Do this one thing for me and I'll just walk away. I have to know why I've always felt guilty. Why I've always felt I was evil."

"All right," she said. "You really don't want to know what I'm going to tell you. But I'll help set you free."

I started to worry for Michael's sake. He was very vulnerable, wide open, in fact. And there was something troubling about her offer to confess.

Her mind seemed to be in two places as she spoke.

"Your father...." She stopped. "Jonathan never should have told you that. His mind was unbalanced then by the death of our two children.

"You are right on one thing. I am not your mother and Jonathan is not your father. If I were you, I'd be content to leave it at that."

She leaned forward from the edge of her chair and waited. I didn't trust her but I wasn't sure she wasn't being sincere.

JAMES E. COYLE

Maybe she was trying to save Michael from some hidden knowledge.

Her tongue wet her lips and I thought of the serpent in the Garden. Maybe it was an apt comparison. Maybe it was her nature to tempt and Michael's task to decide what he would do with the forbidden knowledge.

A curious, stunned expression occupied Michael's face. As if he couldn't believe he had really got it right for once.

"Then, Jonathan is my uncle and his sister, Gloria, was my real mother." His stunned expression changed to excitement. "Then, by blood, you're no part of me," he exclaimed in triumph.

"Good boy! That's correct. That's the easy part."

She said it like a schoolmarm instructing a backward student.

"But we didn't kill your mother. Oh, no!"

Rebecca called out her denial in a high, thin singsong pitch. Animal-like. Like a coyote baying at the moon. Her body hunched forward, totally alert, rocking forward ever so slightly. Her eyes bright, twinkling. Dancing to some secret, unheard tune, staring at Michael. Challenging him.

"Jonathan met and married me in San Francisco during the War, several months before Gloria arrived from Bishop. He was first attracted to me because I looked like her, looked like your mother, his dear sister, Gloria. The dear, long lost mother you've yearned for. But we didn't kill her."

The taunting, tempting sound of her next words chilled my blood. A siren's hoarse calling. They slipped out over her painted, aging lips in a haunting gasp, as if whispered by an imprisoned child.

"Do you want me to show you where you've been afraid to go? Michael?"

His eyes were glossy, transfixed. She had him under a spell.

"I've always known what you were afraid to know and you have always known I knew you were afraid. Haven't you?"

Michael said nothing. Gazed, fascinated.

"Well, here's the knowledge that will set you free and make you whole."

She leaned way forward across the table. Seductively. Her head between mine and Michael's. And she whispered clearly in his left ear, loud enough for both of us to hear.

"Your real mother, Gloria Sherwin, murdered her own parents. Both of them. Killed them on purpose in a car wreck on the way to Reno. That's what she told Jonathan and me that night at Lake Tahoe, when she went totally mad and killed herself in another car wreck. Almost killed you, too."

Her head swiveled my way till her face was inches from mine. All the advancing marks of time were clearly visible beneath her powder and paint. She smiled at me and swiveled her head back to Michael, who hadn't moved.

"Your mother was insane long before she was pregnant with you. Jonathan knew it for years and tried to protect her, though he never did discover who your real father was."

She made a shrill, deformed sound as close to an actual "tee-hee" as I've ever heard, and kept her mouth close to Michael's ear.

"Michael? Are you listening? Now listen carefully. This is the knowledge that will set you free. Do you know why your mother killed her parents? She murdered them for you! They were taking her to Reno to have an abortion. So she murdered them for you!"

She pulled her head out from between us and sat back in her

chair, laughing hysterically. Repeating, "she murdered them for you," over and over through her half-demonic howls.

Suddenly, she stopped. Totally composed herself and looked at Michael with great concern.

I reached over for Michael but he shrugged off my hand and stood up. He was totally dazed. Collapsed within like he had seen Jonathan on the pier many years before.

He stared at Rebecca blankly. Then he walked across the room and out the front door.

I was tempted to kill her myself, but left her sitting quietly in her wing back chair, and followed Michael out into the fog's misting night air.

His voice was drained. Hollow.

"I've got to be alone," he said.

"You can't run away again like last time. You can't let her do that to you."

"Immm...I'm not going to run away," he stammered. "But I can't see my daughter now. Not until tomorrow, at least. Tomorrow," he repeated, as if it were a safe place to be.

I shook him by the shoulders.

"Michael! There's been enough horror in your life. You've got to stop it now. If you can't handle this, you'll never make it back to your orchards. And you won't ever be fit to meet your daughter."

He came slowly out of his deep shock but was still groggy.

"You set up a meeting with my daughter for tomorrow evening and I'll call you tomorrow morning at eight," he said firmly. "But I've got to be alone tonight. I need to take a long walk somewhere by myself."

I gave him Molly's phone number and he started to leave

but turned, slow and heavy under the burden of his unexpected enlightenment.

"Don't worry. I'll call. I'm more afraid of running than I am of my past."

SEVENTEEN

I went to Molly's Carmel restaurant minus Michael. I had phoned from Bishop telling her I'd be bringing him with me.

I was greeted at the door by a hostess who guided me past an unexpectedly noisy Sunday night crowd at the bar, down a carpeted hallway, and through a large, elegant dining area, crowded but not noisy. A sure sign that the food was taken seriously.

Molly was waiting in a semi-private dining alcove at the very back of the room with three place settings on the table. She was wearing a bright green wool knit dress and had a fresh white rose in her hair. And she was nervous. Both disappointed and relieved when I sat down beside her, alone.

She leaned over and kissed me as the hostess departed with a curious backward glance and an amused twinkle in her eyes.

"Where's Michael? Has something happened?"

So, I told her the bad news first.

"But I think he's going to be okay. He's really trying hard to free himself from his lunatic family, which isn't really quite his family after all."

"I've been anxious all day. After you phoned this morning I called Katie and told her to take the first plane home from Santa Barbara tomorrow.

"It feels so strange trying to fit a twenty year old piece of my past into the present. All day I tried to imagine what I'd say to

Michael when I finally saw him. He's the father of my daughter and yet he's worse than a total stranger.

"The only feelings I have for him anymore are apprehension about the past and a nervous hope that he can play some normal role in Katie's life, even if it's a small one."

"He was really shocked tonight," I said. "He had hoped to be born again, clean, out of an evil family. He wanted to rid himself of one mother and lay claim to another. To exchange a murderess for a murder victim. He was desperate to prove a lost inheritance of innocence instead of guilt. But now he's inherited insanity and murder as his birthright."

Molly said, "if Rebecca is telling the truth."

"Yeah. I've been thinking about that. We could tangle spiders in the web she weaves. And she's certainly at least half-mad herself. But then, madness, like innocence, speaks its own truth. And she was frightfully convincing tonight."

"Despite all Michael's sins since he left home," she said, "I still believe he's an innocent victim. There was always an integrity about him that put him at war with his family, and that's got to be a healthy sign. Given what that family's like."

"That is the one certainty we have," I agreed. "Five accidental deaths and one murder are too damned many for any one family. They've taken more than their fair share. Like gluttons, they have a real appetite for tragedy. And there has to be a reason for it."

The "reason" itched somewhere in the back shadows of my mind, just out of reach. As if somewhere, deep down, at the bottom of memory's dark well, a forgotten piece of information broke loose and started its slow rise to consciousness. Not yet visible in form or content, its steady ascent drew my imagination.

"I'm pretty sure that Rebecca wrote those letters to Katie," I said.

"How do you know?" Molly asked eagerly.

"It's just a strong hunch, but I'm almost certain anyway. Do you remember how upset Jonathan was when I mentioned the letters sent to Katie the other day at the Institute?"

"Sure. He was just about to throw us out when you mentioned them. Then he seemed to go into a daze and he became hostile and nasty."

"Well, I think he knew who wrote them and it scared him. I saw a similar reaction tonight when Michael told Rebecca what Jonathan had said on the pier."

"So?"

"So, Katie began receiving the letters just after Michael showed up at Rebecca's house after an eighteen year absence."

"But why would that make Rebecca write such obscene, demented letters to Katie?"

"Because she also saw Terry just after that, and she had a long talk with him. I think Terry told her about Michael's fight with Jonathan. I think Terry told her something Jonathan had said to Michael that she didn't know. Something that greatly disturbed her."

"What?"

"That Michael wasn't part of the family. The same thing she told him tonight. And Jonathan's comment about rivers of blood following him."

Molly looked confused.

"None of this is logical," I said. "Logic doesn't work when you're dealing with crazy people. The letters were meant to bring Michael out into the open. And Jonathan already knew where

Michael was. So, it was Rebecca who wanted to find him. Nothing else makes sense. She even asked me to bring him to her when I first met her."

"But why would she be upset if what Michael repeated about Jonathan was what Terry had already told her?"

"Because it's a sore spot between her and Jonathan. She even said tonight that Jonathan never should have told Michael that he wasn't a member of the family."

"Then something is going on behind the scenes between Jonathan and Rebecca that we don't know about."

"That's right. Michael is just a side show in the family drama. It's like a magic show. We've been watching Michael while the real trick is being done just out of sight."

We were both tiring of all the past's problems and decided to leave them for the morning. We loosened up and enjoyed a good dinner, and then went back to her house for the night.

EIGHTEEN

The next morning at eight it wasn't Michael who called. It was the police.

At five a.m. Michael had been found shot on the pier in Monterey. The only identifying mark on him was the scrap of paper I had given him containing Molly's phone number, and a nurse had only just noticed it on the floor of the operating room.

Molly and I hurried over to the hospital where we were met by the police.

Michael had just been taken off the critical list and was still unconscious. The .38 caliber bullet had barely missed his heart, but he was going to pull through, although he would probably not be conscious until tomorrow.

Molly had trouble recognizing him with all the tubes in him and after all the years, so I made the identification for the police and answered their questions.

When they were finished with us, we hustled out to the Sherwin house.

I had omitted any suspicions about which unbalanced family member might have tried to add another number to the family scoreboard. And I was anxious to talk with Rebecca before the police did. And Jonathan and Penelope, if I could find them.

I liked Michael and felt partially responsible for what had

happened. All the runs in his family had been scored against him, and I was determined to even up the game.

The electronic gate stood wide open so we drove straight in, unannounced.

The front door to the house was also open and we heard a sharp, commanding woman's voice inside as we entered.

They were all there. Rebecca, Penelope and Jonathan, without his usual bodyguards. Jonathan was sitting on the couch where Michael and I had sat and Rebecca was in her wing back chair. The commanding voice was Penelope's, who held the floor, standing between her parents.

The image of Michael, almost dead in his hospital bed, contrasted with their overindulged and underconcerned manner and brought a bitter taste to my mouth.

"Well, if it isn't a goddamned Sherwin family reunion," I said, as Molly and I walked down into the sunken living area.

All heads turned. Rebecca sat strangely listless and Jonathan stood and sniffed the air like a society matron seeking the owner of a fat fart.

He looked me over disdainfully and said, "Walker. Don't you ever wear a suit?"

"With your family's bloody background you're lucky we didn't come wearing hip boots and plastic gloves."

He didn't like that, but I was in no mood to humor him. His eye began to twitch and he was fuming inwardly, clenching his fists and trying to remain in control. But that suited me fine. I was anxious to provoke an explosion.

"You know, I used to think I knew what the term 'blood clan' meant. That is, before I ran across your sanguinary tribe." I looked straight at Jonathan, who seemed to need only a little more shaking. "You know what I mean, don't you, Pop?"

Just in time he was rescued by Penelope. She whispered a few calming words to him and sat him down on the couch where he continued to simmer on slow burn. Then she turned on me.

She took three forceful steps across to us. Inspected us, slowly, up and down, then frowned. She was no longer the timid little Monterey mouse she had pretended for her parents. She was now the bold cat from big, bad San Francisco. Both her manner and her clothes had changed. She was out of her closet, arrogant and dressed to kill.

"Get out!" she almost yelled. "How dare you speak to my father that way."

Molly answered. "Does anyone care to know that Michael was shot this morning and almost died?"

Not a blink among them. Not only had Penelope changed. Rebecca seemed a different woman. Worried and tired. Defeated. As if her age had caught up with her overnight, and she had lost her hold on the world. Only Jonathan remained his usual charming self.

Penelope broke the brief silence.

"No! No one cares about Michael here."

She laughed obscenely and strutted around the room in a little war dance.

Obviously, she was running the family show now and enjoying herself immensely.

Molly whispered in my ear to look carefully at Penelope's dress.

Penelope noticed and stopped her self-pleased strut long enough to scream, "what are you whispering about?"

"I was just admiring your dress," Molly replied. "But I'm an old-fashioned, modest girl and was too embarrassed to say so openly."

"Modest, my ass! You just wouldn't have the nerve." And she continued her high-heeled parade around the room, laughing as she completed the circuit back to us.

She was truly a knockout, like her mother must have been. A one-hundred-and-eighty-degree turnaround.

She was wearing a flowing peach-colored dress composed of several layers of diaphanous material. High at the neck, loose at the sleeves and full at the hem, it was both sophisticated and elegant.

Except that she wasn't wearing anything beneath the dress.

She stopped several feet in front of us, smiling wickedly at us, holding the full circle of her dress out from her sides.

I was staring for a full half minute, through several layers of gauzy, peach-colored fabric, before I was sure that the shadowy patch between her legs was what I thought it was. Higher up, beneath the sheer material, the full, upturned curve of her breasts and her pink nipples were also clearly visible, plump and stiff with the excitement of showing off for us.

Nothing overly obvious at first glance. You had to have both your eyes open and look at her for more than a second to notice.

She certainly had taken her treasures out from under the proverbial bushel. Flaunt it, if you've got it, seemed to be her new motto. So much luscious fruit with something rotten growing inside, I thought.

Mom and Pop Sherwin sat respectfully through her performance, like well disciplined house guests.

I looked at Molly and watched her sarcastic smile break into a brittle laugh at the absurdity of our situation.

Immediate rage flared across Penelope's face. She responded like an immature child showing off her new dress, only to be ridiculed. I saw cold hate well up in her eyes and knew she was capable of murder.

She turned quickly to conceal her anger and flopped down on the couch at the opposite end from her father. There they sat, all three of them, like three sulking children. Two, actually. Rebecca looked too tired and demoralized to sulk.

I wondered what had happened to Rebecca since last night, when she had so cruelly tortured Michael. And what had so blatantly brought Penelope out into the open, without fear of her parents. She seemed to have blossomed and grown strong while Rebecca had withered and faded .

Penelope had usurped Rebecca's role as the top woman of the family. Maybe, that's why Rebecca was so listless.

Direct questions would get me nowhere. Illusion and misdirection were the family bulwarks. My only chance was to keep them off balance, so I made an oblique approach.

"Penny?"

Penelope glowered at me, sullenly. She didn't like the nickname. I went for her sore spot, trying to get her to talk.

"Penny? You should really call Beth at your gallery. She misses you."

Contempt mixed with uneasy curiosity stared back at me. I sallied forth again.

"Penny? Are you still there? Where are you hiding your Prince Charming?"

"A good man is hard to find," she blurted out, and smirked as she said it.

"So is a good woman." I returned her smirk.

Short of pulling her hair and making her say "uncle," I wasn't going to get anything else out of her.

Jonathan was fidgeting uneasily at the other end of the couch so I turned to him.

"Did you shoot Michael out on that pier this morning?" No reaction. "I know it's one of your favorite spots." Still nothing. "Mind telling me where you've been the last two days?" He wasn't even looking at me. "Did you arrange that surprise immigration raid to get even with Terry?" Finally, a sinister smile.

I wasn't going to get much from him, either. I had no authority to question him and he knew it.

"You'd better keep your two bodyguards close by and hope that Terry doesn't catch up with you," I warned.

Molly couldn't take the Mexican standoff anymore.

"What the hell is the matter with you people."

She made the rounds, looking carefully at Rebecca, Jonathan and Penelope.

"Don't you know what's been going on? You've lost one daughter already this week and now Michael has been shot."

Blank expressions all around.

Molly took my hand and said, "let's get out of here."

"Just a minute," I said. "I figure one of you three shot Michael this morning."

I might as well have said it looked like a nice day. So I threw out the clinker.

"And I figure you, Penelope, or you, Jonathan, murdered Diana. I know how you folks so love to keep things in the family."

That accusation didn't go over so well. Jonathan and Penelope jumped to their feet.

As Molly and I walked out the door, Penelope was screaming obscenities at us while Jonathan turned to the phone. Probably calling for his bodyguards, Dryden and Shadow.

Rebecca, who hadn't said a word, sat in her chair, rocking back and forth, moaning to herself.

NINETEEN

The sky was a clear turquoise blue, the color of old Navaho and Zuni Indian jewelry, and the surf broke like liquid emeralds as we drove back along the coast. Toward Monterey, to check again on Michael's condition.

The air was refreshing after the Sherwin house. Warm, and tangy with the scent of salt water. No trace of fog, not even on the distant horizon. The sea, the sand dunes and the tree covered hills were all etched sharply on the landscape by the noonday sun. I wished for some of that same clarity in the Sherwin family landscape.

"I've got to go back later and talk with Rebecca alone," I said. "I think she's coming apart and might be ready to help clear up this whole mess."

"Back to that madhouse? Please, be careful. That family's dangerous. But it would be great if you finally get the truth out of her. Maybe even find something positive in Michael's past for him to hold onto."

"I need to know why Rebecca wanted to find Michael so badly. Why what Jonathan said to him on the pier was so troubling to her. Michael seems to be caught in some hidden conflict between Jonathan and Rebecca that probably resulted in his being shot."

Molly said, "their whole family history doesn't make sense the way they tell it. If Michael was wrong about them killing his real mother, why would one of them shoot him now. What would they have to fear? If his mother really started all the family tragedy by killing her own parents, why is it still going on? Why didn't it end with her death at Lake Tahoe?"

"Unless...." I shuddered. That forgotten piece of information that had been working its way up to consciousness finally breached the surface.

It came up out of the black waters of memory like a drowned corpse. The sickly white and bloated form of a long submerged crime, rising from out of the past to haunt the present with its mute testimony.

"No distinguishing marks or scars," I mumbled.

"What? What does that mean?" Molly asked.

"The coroner's report from the accident at Lake Tahoe stated Gloria Sherwin had no distinguishing marks or scars."

"So?"

For the first time in nearly a week I knew I had found the reality behind the illusion.

"Well, she should have."

I hurried on to the hospital where we learned Michael was still unconscious but doing well. Then I dropped Molly off so she could get her car and pick up Katie at the airport.

It was only eleven-thirty when I drove back through the still open gate and parked in front of Rebecca's house.

My mind was racing, back through the week's events, back through forty years, struggling to pull all the puzzle pieces together.

Everything depended on Rebecca being alone.

I rang the doorbell, then again, and waited several minutes, but there was no answer. So I retraced my steps of the previous day, around the left curve of the villa.

Along the seashell path the same sweet fragrances, the same seductive flowers, the same perfect stillness awaited me, but held no spell for me today.

A stronger, more urgent stimulus to my senses drew me quickly on, around to the back of the villa. A stimulus, not carried sweet upon the air, but a corruption, spreading contagion through the heart and soul.

I found her as I had the first time. Near her fountain. All alone on her luxurious, marble divan. Seated on a plush, crimson velvet cushion. An anachronistic Roman queen, dreaming again of vanished splendors, amid the chilly marble beauty of her palace.

Her languid eyes followed me as I drew close, and I saw that, now, she was no longer a vibrant Roman queen. The corruption she had so long hidden inside had broken out and withered her.

She was wrapped up tight in a large white shawl. Like an old pensioner out in the sun to warm her blood. Or a mummy waiting transport to the next life.

"I'm back," I said. "To finish what Michael started."

I sat down on a heavy marble bench across from her. Facing her, settling into the soft, velvet cushion.

Her eyes were still alert but had borne a bitter defeat since we had last sat here.

"You think you've got it figured out, do you?"

"Most of it. Michael was halfway there. He just didn't have the imagination for evil to go all the way."

"Evil, is it? I'd call it beauty and purity on a level higher than the ordinary mind can imagine. Or accept."

"Is it beauty and purity that you have now?"

The languid gloss dropped from her eyes and voice and was

replaced by something sharper, frightening in its intensity.

"Enough shadow boxing, Mr. Walker. Tell me what you think you know. I might even steer you in the right direction. Due to certain circumstances, you'll find I'm in a much more receptive mood today."

"Like I said, Michael had half of it right. But you sandbagged him. You're good, really good, at deceiving. You're half great actress and half magician rolled into one. You suckered Michael. And me.

"You gave us a little bit of truth. Shocked us with it. And, like an expert magician, you kept us watching that little bit of truth about Michael not being your son. Then, with your other hand, you pulled the rabbit out of the hat. Only it wasn't a rabbit. It was a club. And you beat Michael's brains out with it.

"We were so focused on the revealed truth about Michael not being your son, so startled by your willingness to admit it, that we forgot to watch you carefully.

"That's when you clobbered Michael with the big lie about his real mother murdering her parents for his sake."

She was enjoying herself. Accepting my accusations as compliments.

"But something kept bothering me since I saw a copy of the coroner's report on the accidental death of Gloria Sherwin at Lake Tahoe.

"There was no mention of a deep scar on the back of her neck. And there should have been one from the previous accident that killed her parents.

"Dr. Kline said it was the only injury Gloria suffered from the car wreck that killed her parents. Remembered treating her for it himself."

Her lips formed the faint upward curve of a smile.

"And what does that prove?" she asked, almost coyly.

"That you've got the scar."

She turned her head and slowly lifted up her thick red hair. A broad white scar zigzagged three inches across her neck. She dropped her hair and faced me again. Smiling.

A nauseous spasm twisted my gut and I felt my heart pumping blood at an incredible rate. Images flashed through my mind of the horror I felt when I tracked down the killer of my wife only to recognize him as a friend.

The same shock and horror came over me again. Even though I knew it was coming this time.

More images flooded in. Of the white shark tearing at the sea lions, shattering the children's innocent day. Of its final roll over in the bloody water as it swallowed the head and frightened eyes of its victim. Of Michael moaning, his hands stained with his father's blood.

I looked up. She was still smiling. Her eyes were testing me, I think. Testing if I had the courage to look her straight in the face and know what she was.

Her voice came out all soothing, as if she were calming a frightened child.

"Go ahead. You're doing fine. Don't be afraid. So many are, you know. Put it all together."

"You're Gloria Sherwin. And that means you're Jonathan's sister as well as his wife."

Life and fire seemed to come back to her as she egged me on, proudly instructing me in the ways of evil.

"Don't stop now. You've got hold of something. Bring it up into the light."

"The accident that killed your parents didn't happen on the drive to Reno. It happened on the drive back."

"How do you figure that?"

"Because you are not Michael's mother. Because Jonathan's letter said you were pregnant and yet you have no child to show for it. Because your story about abortion and murder had the chilling ring of truth, but with the wrong mother. So, you lost the baby somehow, and Dr. Kline doesn't think the accident would have done it. It figures best if you had already had the abortion in Reno and were returning to Bishop when your parents died."

"My, but you have been busy lately, haven't you? Do go on."

"You were diabolically clever changing the sequence to increase the horror for Michael. With the accident happening on the way to the abortion, you created a strong motive for murder for his supposed mother.

"But it didn't happen that way. You really ripped Michael apart, convincing him that this supposed mother murdered for his sake. But it had nothing to do with Michael, since it wasn't his mother who committed murder.

"The wreck happened after Reno, on the way back, after your parents forced you to have an abortion. That's when you killed them."

"Do you know why I killed them?"

She was living proof that evil exists with no special warning sign, that it can be such a comfortable part of human nature. The banality of the evil in her was devastating.

"I killed our parents because they destroyed my baby. Jonathan's baby. The first issue of our sacred love making. I became pregnant from the first time we ever made love, during his first visit home from the navy. It was a sacred child, and they destroyed it."

I was unnerved by her ordinary manner. She talked as if she were remembering a pleasant family picnic.

"Then the body at Lake Tahoe was Michael's real mother. Who was she? Was it an accident or did she have to be sacrificed to your sacred love?"

"Don't get nasty," she scolded. "If you expect mommy to help you with your detective work, you've got to be nice."

She was right. I didn't know if I had the courage to look her in the face and know her for what she was. But I held my rising disgust down and forced my tone into the same banal mold as hers.

"Who was Michael's real mother?" I repeated, calmly this time.

"She was a profane cow that he picked up in San Francisco after his visit home and our first sacred love making.

"I was always stronger than Jonathan. Even when we were children, I was stronger. Without me he is weak.

"When we first made love during his visit home in April, 1945, we both experienced an overwhelming surge of freedom. A thrill and a power. Our great sin, our great bond, removed us from the ordinary level of existence. Gave us special importance and special privileges.

"But Jonathan was weak away from me. Afraid of his new special status. When he returned to San Francisco, he married a woman who did typing on the base. He did it to escape from his new responsibilities. Because, without me, he couldn't face the higher moral and spiritual plane of our love.

"After I destroyed our parents for taking our sacred child from us, I left Bishop and went to San Francisco to wait for Jonathan to return from sea duty. I was horrified to learn from base personnel that he was married. Her name was Rebecca Barry and she even looked something like me.

"I arranged it so she and I lived together for several months, while we waited for Jonathan. It almost destroyed me when I saw she was pregnant.

"Well, Jonathan returned to San Francisco in December and, in January, 1946, the cow gave birth to Michael. Two months later, on our trip home to Bishop, I was forced to kill her.

"I struck her down like the common animal she was. Outside our cabin at Lake Tahoe. Beat her across the head with a piece of firewood. Until the deep snow was red with her blood.

"I did it there because she caught Jonathan and me making love. I did it there to free Jonathan from an ordinary, petty life with her and to purify him of her corrupt blood. I did it so we could share our sacred love."

"So Michael was never found lying in his mother's blood like you claimed."

"Oh, but he was. His mother was carrying him, trying to escape from us, when I caught up with her in the deep snow. When I hit her she dropped Michael. Her blood was all over him. Like I said, I always felt that's why Michael grew up so disturbed. Because of his mother's blood."

She sat there enumerating her grisly crimes, proudly. Like a matriarch passing down the wisdom of the generations.

I could almost smell the foul scent of corruption and unspeakable crimes. The scent of evil, stronger than all her flowers. Permeating the house for forty years. Forty years of unspoken horror. Neglected sounds, crying out like lost echoes.

As she sat there, so disdainful of human life, I kept thinking of the quote Michael had sent to Molly: "...the horror of finding evil seated, all at its ease, where she had only dreamed of good...." No wonder Michael had grown up such a mess.

"After we faked the accident, I assumed Rebecca's identity. I never went back to Bishop because someone would have recognized me."

"Then, who is Michael's real father? Jonathan?"

"No!"

It was the first note of uncontrolled anger that broke her calm.

"No. I now know for certain Jonathan isn't Michael's father. His marriage to Rebecca Barry was never a real union. He admitted today that he never even slept with her. He married her only because he was weak. As a final protest against the demands of our special love. I doubt if even he knows who Michael's father was. But you'll have to ask him.

"I lived all these almost forty years thinking Jonathan was Michael's father. Until a couple of weeks ago."

"When Michael stole the letter and you talked with Terry?" I asked.

"My, you are a good detective, aren't you?"

"Yes. Terry was so anxious to find Michael that he told me he was looking for him in Monterey because Michael was obsessed with the idea that he wasn't part of our family.

"Terry told me what Jonathan had screamed at Michael during their fight on the pier. At first, I couldn't accept it. The realization that Jonathan had violated our special bond, our unique union. That he had lied to me all these years, nearly destroyed me. And now his deception will destroy all of us. Everything."

"Is that why you wrote the letters to Katherine Dugan?

Because you were in a rage and needed to find Michael to confirm your fears?"

"Yes."

"Then you shot Michael this morning?"

"Yes. Michael phoned here at four this morning, trying to locate Jonathan. But Jonathan wasn't here. Michael told me to tell Jonathan he'd be waiting for him on the pier. So, I went instead and shot him."

It was said totally matter-of-fact. No remorse.

"Why?"

"Because Michael was living proof of the lie between us. Proof that Jonathan lied to me when he said Michael was his son and kept me from killing Michael along with his cow of a mother. When Jonathan violated our sacred trust, he created the flaw that is destroying us."

"Michael is going to live," I said.

"It doesn't matter anymore."

She was turning listless again. I was afraid I'd lose her to her brooding insanity before she answered my last questions.

"Who killed Diana?" I asked. "I know it wasn't you this time because I was with you."

My sarcasm was lost on her.

"Ask Jonathan. Ask my bitch-daughter, Penelope."

"The seed of your sacred union? Where is she?"

She didn't notice or wouldn't react to the disgust in my voice.

"She's with her father at the Institute."

"Can you get me in so they don't know I'm coming? Past the guards?"

Slowly, as if she were being pulled out of this world by inner forces, she wrote out a pass for me on the note tablet beside her.

As I stood up to go, I asked her, "why tell me all of this? Why confess your secrets when they were hidden safely away?"

"Because nothing matters anymore. Because five hundred thousand dollars can resolve a lot of family problems."

She giggled.

"Because you're the detective and all the secrets aren't out yet."

She began laughing convulsively.

"Because confession is good for the soul."

Her convulsive laughter approached hysterics as she glanced at a locked, leather attaché case on the table beside her. Then, abruptly, she was still again.

I left feeling disgusted and uneasy.

What had happened today that had so devastatingly brought old age upon her? Why had her attempted murder of Michael failed to bring relief as murder had so often done for her before? What had happened during that grotesque family reunion between her and Jonathan and Penelope? And why had Jonathan been missing the previous two days?

Too many problems still unresolved. And too much horror I didn't know what to do with. The police would have to be called in sooner or later. But somehow that didn't seem to matter. The sheer scope and horror of the crimes seemed to go beyond legal considerations. I felt like we needed an exorcist.

One thing I knew for certain. Even though the case was over for all practical purposes, I had no choice of letting go. The horror had a hold on me and I was in for the whole nightmarish ride.

I drove off toward the Sherwin Institute. To see Jonathan and Penelope and, hopefully, fit the last missing pieces into the puzzle. But, for every piece of the puzzle that fit, another seemed to be missing.

My mouth was dry and my gut was tight as I drove down Highway 1. Wondering why Rebecca had been so willing to confess. Worried that she had not yet read all the names on the role call of the Sherwin family's dishonored dead. Wondering what she hoped to buy with five hundred thousand dollars that could resolve her family problems.

TWENTY

Rebecca's pass got me safely into the Sherwin Institute grounds. Even got me a friendly smile from the two armed guards who didn't phone ahead or log my entry time into their big ledger book.

I drove up to the crest of the hill and stopped, looking down onto the broad marine terrace. The noon sea air was pristine in its clarity and every manicured bush and tree and building stood out sharply.

I gazed across the rolling expanse to the Institute's cottages and administrative buildings, huddled together at the base of their headland, and I contemplated Jonathan's luxurious, little "cottage," perched out at the tip. Surrounded by its wall of protective trees, silhouetted against the calm aqua sea, it seemed to be waiting for me.

As I started down the long slope I began to feel like the lone gunfighter entering the enemy's town for the final showdown. Or a motorized Adam, returning to paradise with a new vision, born of the tree of knowledge and tainted with original sin.

I avoided the main building and Elliott Russell's scrupulous attentions and took the pebbled driveway directly out to Sherwin's cottage.

I had barely gotten out of my car when Sherwin's two body-guards came out.

The cut above Dryden's left eye was healing nicely and his dark facial bruises were now just patches of slightly discolored skin.

The other half of the act was obviously the previously missing William Johnson. Or "Shadow," as Dryden so cutely called him.

The name was strangely well suited. He was a deep brown version of Dryden. Coffee bean colored. Like Dryden, he was a two hundred and twenty pound hunk of heavy muscle, aged thirty years and stuffed into the standard turtleneck sweater and cashmere jacket.

The only real difference between them besides color was Shadow's gleaming brown head. He combed his hair every morning with a straight razor and then gave it a thorough buffing.

Like me, Shadow also sported a Terry Rose special. But, judging from the stiff crook of his right arm, he had the deluxe model, extending from his wrist to well above his elbow.

"Well, if it isn't Dryden and Shadow, that famous song and dance team."

Shadow gave me a mean, hard stare. A don't-mess-with-me-or-I'll-stomp-your-eyeballs look.

"Is this that dumbo private dickhead you been telling me about, Dryden?"

"He's the one. The one that thinks he's cute. Let's show him just how cute we can be."

They both started towards me.

I reached into the back of the Jeep and pulled out a four foot shovel caked with dried mud. They stopped and eyed the shovel.

I said, "tell your boss I've got the body in the back and want to know where to bury it."

"Body!" escaped from Dryden's lips. He hesitated, confused.

"Get in there and tell him I need to see him," I demanded. "Tell him I know where all the bodies are, including the one at Lake Tahoe."

Reluctantly, he went inside while Shadow eyed the shovel suspiciously and made a wide circle around to the back of the Jeep.

"There's no damned body in there."

"It must have bounced out when I turned in from the main highway."

Dryden reappeared at the door and motioned me inside. I passed through the small anteroom and opened the large wooden door into the main room. Dryden and Shadow remained behind, sullenly. Planning unpleasant surprises and anticipating my departure.

The long rectangular room was flooded with bright afternoon sunlight. I walked along the wall of floor-to-ceiling windows to the other back wall of glass, to the same table where Molly and I had lunched with the Mad Hatter.

As before Sherwin was sitting at the back of the table, in the corner where the two glass walls came together. An array of papers and documents were spread out before him. Behind him was the same spectacular and dizzying view of cliffs with their four-hundred-foot plunge straight down to the sea.

Only one thing was different. Jonathan had exchanged his regular chair for a huge, hand-carved throne. A wide, high-backed, massive piece of tropical wood, covered all over with intricate and exotic carvings.

Sherwin was leaning back in this throne, king-like, his hands extended out along the broad chair arms.

I was sick of all his grand gestures and the rotten world he hid behind them.

"Where's Penelope? This concerns her too."

"She's upstairs." He smiled annoyingly. "Getting dressed for our departure."

"I wouldn't make any definite plans," I said. "The police might want to see you."

"Oh?" He was feeling very smug. "I don't think anything you've got to say will stop us."

But I was going to stop him.

"I've just come from Rebecca. She was in a very strange mood. Like she had just lost her entire family. And she was very talkative. Confessional, even."

His relaxed, smug manner vanished. He drew back his extended arms and then leaned forward against the table.

"Don't get careless, Walker. I've never liked your manners. So don't forget the two men in the waiting room."

"Rebecca said you were a weak man away from her."

He seemed to have found a new source of strength. I hardly made a dent in his composure.

I decided to try another tack.

"As you say, I can't really hurt you with anything I know. So, why not help me out?"

Playing superior lord to my supplicating, inferior detective appealed to him. He sat back in his grand throne, extended his hands out along the arms in a benevolent manner and waited for my humble petition.

"Rebecca told me about the murder of your parents and your wife."

"Her murders, not mine," he insisted. "I wasn't even there for the first killings."

There wasn't even a pretense of morality. Despite his high-toned radio sermons, murder, even the family kind, didn't disturb his principles.

"She also told me she shot Michael this morning."

His heart overflowed with concern.

"So? Her actions have nothing to do with me anymore. We are no longer connected."

"Ah, but you are. Husbands and wives may go their separate ways. But a brother and a sister are connected for life. She told me to ask you who Michael's real father was."

He didn't like my comment about being connected for life, but he recovered quickly and began to chuckle to himself.

"Yes, dear old sis had quite a shock lately, when she found out I wasn't Michael's father. That's why I was upset when you mentioned those letters the other day. I figured she had written them and that meant she suspected my long kept secret. Well, I don't care what she suspects anymore. I cleared up all her doubts this morning. In no uncertain terms."

"Who is Michael's real father and why did you pretend you were?"

"I have no idea who Michael's real father is," he said blandly. "Some sailor his mother met while she worked on the base, I guess. It really doesn't matter. I only married the woman and pretended I was the father of her child to protect myself. To keep some part of myself secret and safe from my sister."

He lifted his arms and pressed the tips of his fingers and thumbs together in a prayerful pyramid. A quizzical smile parted his lips.

"My sister's quite mad, you see. What she calls weakness in

me was merely sanity. I had to hold on to Michael to keep my integrity."

His simplistic explanation satisfied him completely. With such indecipherable, childlike logic he washed away his sins of forty years. Wriggled out from under four decades of incest and murder. Denied the two score years of his own insanity.

But the admission of his sister's insanity opened the floodgates that held back his own dammed up black pool of madness. His prayerful pyramid collapsed into his lap and a meek, small boy stared out at me from his oversized chair. In some insane, regressive way he seemed to be pleading for understanding.

I was still standing across the table from him with my back to the main part of the room. I felt that sitting down would contaminate me.

He continued to watch me. Like a small boy who had admitted to tearing the wings off a butterfly, he sought some sign of understanding from me. But the most understanding I could muster would be to get a large green garbage bag and stuff him in it.

"Why did you murder your own daughter, Diana?"

From over my shoulder came a rustling sound, and the light came back into Jonathan's eyes as he peered around me. It was Penelope as she made her way around the table and stood beside her father.

The rustling sound came from her white silk dress. It was exquisite and expensive, shimmering in the sunlit air. Both innocent and provocative. Trimmed with lace and ruffles, it summoned lost, innocent days. Fitted onto her voluptuous body, its slinky contour promised not so innocent nights. Crowned with a mass of red curls and school girl bangs, it conjured a high class hooker making her first communion.

Half little girl and half grown woman, her sensuous face and full, blood red lips advertised carnal delights.

Jonathan seemed to draw energy from her presence and regained some of his strength.

"Daddy's tired. Ask me your stupid questions."

She said it teasingly, even seductively, as I had seen her mother do. Her petulant challenge unsettled me and with memory's eye I saw again the white shark roll over in its bloody water.

"All right. Why did your father...."

I stopped. Her smile was mocking me. Goading me, like her mother had, to go further.

My gut tightened again as I began to realize what was waiting for me.

"Why did you murder your sister?"

"That's better," she smirked. "A detective has to get his information straight."

"The fathers have eaten sour grapes, and the children's teeth are set on edge," I remembered. A child of madness and incest. The pollution and impurity Jonathan so feared was living inside him. Passed down to the next generation, coursing through his daughter's blood.

"You've been quite a naughty little girl, haven't you?" I said.

She batted her eyes at me, shamelessly.

"Would you like a lollipop?"

"Yes I would. Like all good little girls I love lollipops."

She was daddy's little darling.

"Trouble is, most lollipops get smaller when you lick them. And pretty soon they're all gone."

She was the apple of his eye.

"But not daddy's lollipop."

She was sugar and spice and everything nice.

"Daddy's lollipop gets bigger when I lick it. Doesn't it daddy?"

She was a lollipop whore.

She reached down and began stroking Jonathan's crotch.

"And do you know what I like best about daddy's lollipop? He lets me have it whenever I want. As often as I want."

Jonathan sat there in a semi-daze while his daughter fondled him. Clearly, she was dominant in their unnatural relationship.

She inhabited a world where the unacceptable had become acceptable. Like Rebecca, she seemed to be drawing energy from the thrill of her forbidden sin. It had run amok with her and she felt no restraints.

Finally, when she was sure she had shocked me, she stood up.

"I killed Diana," she said proudly. "Daddy and I agreed it was necessary. Diana found out that I was pregnant and suspected that daddy was the father. She told me she was going to tell mother about it. So I stopped her."

She stroked the smooth curve of her belly, sensuously.

"I'm carrying daddy's baby right now. Inside me. Almost three months now."

She kept rubbing her belly as if she could feel the corrupt seed growing there. Almost purring in her contentment.

Now I knew what had devastated Rebecca this morning. She had lost her Prince Charming, forever, at the moment Penelope had revealed hers.

"And nobody is going to take my baby from me." Her voice became shrill as she stared at me. "You can't prove anything, anyway. And, if you try to stop us, you'll never make it out that door."

At that instant a loud noise came from the anteroom where she was pointing.

For a half a minute we listened to the crashing and smashing sounds coming through the thick door. Then we heard a single gunshot and all was quiet.

Jonathan sat bolt upright in his chair with the look of fear across his face. And Penelope started angrily down the long room towards the door.

The door exploded in a thunder of cracking wood. Blew off its hinges from the impact of the heavy object hurled against it.

It was Shadow. Landing a good six feet into the large room. Dead. His gleaming brown head was smashed in. Oozing blood and shattered fragments of skull from the impact against the door.

We stared at the open doorway. In came Terry Rose. Dressed in sneakers, white sailor's duck cloth pants and a white T-shirt stretched tight across his enormous torso. He was as calm as a weekend sailor fresh off a passing yacht.

I figured he was the five hundred thousand dollar surprise Rebecca had promised.

He was nonchalantly dragging Dryden behind him. They were back to back. Terry facing forward, Dryden backwards as he was hauled forcibly into the room.

Terry had his gigantic right arm crooked up over his own shoulder, wrapped tightly, vise-like, around Dryden's neck, which was cradled violently in the wedge between Terry's shoulder and arm.

Dragged backwards, Dryden was gagging and sputtering for

breath as his eyes bulged up toward the ceiling and the tips of his dangling feet barely kept contact with the floor. Both his arms hung uselessly at his sides. Broken.

Terry came across the room with his damaged cargo, paying no attention to Dryden's gurgling noises at his ear, and stopped ten feet in front of Penelope. Slowly, his eyes examined the room. Like a gunfighter asserting his dominance. Except that there was no gun in the room.

For a second I considered running for mine in my car or looking for Dryden's or Shadow's. But then Terry's delicate, almost pouting, female lips parted into that disturbing smile of his, and I knew I didn't have time.

"I've come to chastise you," he announced, looking straight at Jonathan. "The missus sent me. To clear up a little family misunderstanding."

For the first time I saw his smile break clear across his face and reveal a flash of teeth. He was grinning at Jonathan.

"And you shouldn't have pulled that immigration stunt up north. It's going to cost you."

Then he scared the hell out of all of us. Before our unbelieving eyes, he dipped his right shoulder to get a better hold on Dryden's neck, then slowly straightened up to his full height, until Dryden's feet completely left the floor. Dryden's body shook with violent convulsions and his retching filled the room.

Before I could move, Terry heaved the back of Dryden's head further up onto his shoulder. Used his shoulder as a fulcrum for all Dryden's hanging weight, until Dryden's neck snapped. Loudly. Terrifyingly.

The retching and the convulsions stopped instantly, and Terry dropped him to the floor, like so much unwanted trash.

We had just witnessed a hanging.

There was no tension in Terry's manner. No tough guy poses like Dryden would have made. Just disciplined, ruthless efficiency.

Penelope was nearest to Terry and she was trembling. Abruptly, she made a dash for the safety of the door. But Terry stepped into her swing around him and slammed the full strength of his right hand against the side of her head.

Her head twisted grotesquely as she went flying against the inside wall. She landed with a lifeless thud. A silk and lace sack of dead dreams and twisted fantasies.

Jonathan's eyes widened. Panicked eyes watching the horror unfold before him. He tried to get up but his body shook with spasms and he collapsed back into his oversized chair. His hands clutched the chair arms in desperation as he lost control of his muscles.

He had had another stroke. He sat there, paralyzed. All the tension had left him and he looked, with his arms outstretched, like a kindly grandparent. Only his eyes betrayed him. Straining. Swelled with all the horror and fear his body could no longer escape.

Terry headed straight for Jonathan, but I was in his way. I grabbed the back of the wooden chair beside me and charged at him.

It was like hitting a wall. He took hold of two of the chair legs and pushed back at me. The force was irresistible. The chair back punched my stomach, knocking the wind out of me, doubling me up.

Terry rammed the chair further into me, using the hard back to scoop me up like a bulldozer. He lifted me on the chair and threw me across the room.

I landed just short of the glass wall, groggy and winded. I staggered up and saw Terry standing behind Jonathan's huge throne-chair.

With incredible strength Terry raised the entire massive chair with Jonathan helplessly imprisoned in it. Lifted it chest high, holding it there for just a second as he whispered something into Jonathan's ear.

Then Terry laughed, triumphantly, and turned, heaving Jonathan, chair and all, out through the thick wall of glass.

The glass wall shattered, falling with a loud roar, like the cascade of a brittle waterfall.

Somehow, during that first second on that long plunge down to the sea, Jonathan recovered the use of his vocal chords and managed an eerie, ear piercing scream.

The unnerving scream ended abruptly, leaving only the image of Jonathan, paralyzed in his executive chair, the symbol of his lost power. His imagination failing him in the end, like his muscles. Failing to believe the final reality of his life.

I rushed toward Terry while he was still enjoying Jonathan's long plummet to the sea. I leaped onto the table and jumped feet first at Terry's back, trying to topple the big blond ten pin out the window.

But he turned just in time, just enough so I didn't hit him squarely. I caught him on the left arm and he stumbled back toward the window.

I landed hard on my right hip and bounced along the floor. Before I could get back up, those monstrous hands were at me, groping to get a hold on me.

I struggled with all my might, desperate to keep his fingers from my hands or arms. Remembering Trimbler and all those mangled bones and that goofy surprised stare that he died with.

I managed to pull my right knee up to my chest and as Terry bent down I kicked him in the stomach with every ounce of strength I could summon.

He staggered back and grunted. Holy shit! Was that the best I could do against this ape. I felt like Bruce Cabot going up against King Kong, but without the gas bombs. I needed an equalizer, quick. Something like a .44 magnum or an elephant gun.

I rolled over with more agility than I thought I had and surfaced on the opposite side of the table from him.

"You're not as strong as I thought you were, Terry," I yelled. "I didn't even need both my feet to make you grunt."

He studied me serenely, and I considered making a dash for my gun, but didn't think I'd make it. Better to stay and wear him down. Float like a butterfly, sting like a bee. That's me. Kept looking around for something useful. Like a chainsaw.

Terry tipped the table on edge and came at me with it like a snow plow clearing the road. He drove me back until I lost my balance and fell.

Before I knew it, he had one big fist tightened around the front of my shirt and the other on my crotch. Up I went, over his head, as he made for the window, determined to launch me in Jonathan's wake.

Three feet short of my bon voyage, I hit him hard across the eyes with my cast. The cast cracked wide open and plaster dust filled the air.

The impact probably only gave him a temporary headache, but the dust blinded him. He dropped me, and I hit the floor with a loud thud. I was bruised all over and my wrist was broken again.

The pain was intense but I knew I was still alive. And I was tired of Terry using me as a bowling ball.

I left the all too familiar comfort of the floor and got up on two feet again. A little wobbly, but standing.

Terry was still rubbing and scraping at his eyes with his back towards me. I hit him a hard right into the small of his back and another in his right kidney before he even took notice of me.

I was positioning myself for a good kick to his groin when he flailed out wildly with his right arm and caught me along the side of my head.

I went sailing down the room, smack into the wall, down to my usual place on the floor. I turned my neck slowly, hoping it wasn't broken, my cheek against the polished wooden floor.

From my low level vantage point I saw Terry stumble over to the stand holding Jonathan's precious glacier water. He doused his eyes with it several times until his vision cleared and he spotted me.

I grabbed the base of a heavy brass floor lamp and used it to stand up. Terry was watching, blinking away the remaining plaster dust. I leaned against the wall to brace myself and held the lamp like a club.

Terry was just about to start for me again when we heard a car horn blaring outside.

He looked at me another second, weighing the delay and the risk, and then he smiled.

"You'll always be the one who got away," he said, as he headed for the door.

He had decided I was no longer worth the extra effort, since, even if he killed me, the guards would still know he killed Jonathan.

I made it outside just in time to see Clementine drive him away in his little red T-Bird, unhindered by my three bullet holes in its side.

Despite the overwhelming size and strength of him, despite his unflinching brutality, despite the hot pain of my twice broken wrist, I felt strangely let down that he didn't come for me. Felt all my hot, pumped up blood and all my surging adrenaline reluctantly ebbing away.

That's when I knew I had to go after him. Knew I couldn't just leave it to the police. On some subliminal level pride had mixed with blood, and I no longer had a choice. Terry's great pale form and unfeeling eyes beckoned me on, like half-mad Ahab pursuing his great white whale.

At the main gate on the way out I acknowledged the civilized world long enough to tell the guards what had happened. Terry had also had a special pass from Rebecca and they had just seen the red T-Bird screech past them.

I stomped the accelerator to the floor and shot out onto Highway 1, thankful, with my one good arm, for the automatic transmission. I was hoping that Terry was smart enough to evade the police and that I was just smart enough to catch him.

I figured Terry had a second, less conspicuous car stashed somewhere and would change to it as soon as possible. And my old Jeep, even with its big V-8, was no match for his T-Bird. So, my only hope was to get to Rebecca. She had set Terry on his killing spree and maybe she knew where he was.

I found her just as I had left her, only the leather attache case was gone, replaced by an ornate, golden goblet. Its ominous presence told me she was merely waiting for the final word before she played out her last Egyptian-Roman fantasy.

"Are they dead?" Her voice was hoarse and hollow, the light in her eyes fading.

"Yes. Both of them."

She took the golden goblet and clasped it tightly to her breast, as if it promised life instead of death.

"I need to know where Terry is."

"He's gone to San Francisco to pick up the rest of the money I promised him. I already gave him one hundred thousand. He's to meet my banker at the foot of Hyde Street at five o'clock this evening to get the other four hundred thousand."

Her tone was as flat and lifeless as the world she saw inside her goblet.

"There's no need to hurry, though. You can catch him easily. His Nubian Princess is driving him to a marina at the south end of the city and they are going on by boat to the Hyde Street Pier. I think they're going to Mexico after that."

She raised the goblet to her lips and took one last look at me.

"I tell you this freely because Terry killed my beloved Jonathan and he must pay for his crime."

Then she drank her magic potion. I watched until the last light in her eyes was extinguished and the goblet dropped from her hand.

I felt neither pity nor sorrow. Her last act had finally set Michael free.

She had also set herself free. Free from her disturbed child-hood innocence. Where something first went wrong. Where, in-stead of pure crisp high-desert fragrances, she breathed in the foul scent of troubled dreams, and expelled nightmares instead of air.

TWENTY-ONE

I stood for almost an hour at the foot of Hyde Street. Waiting. Watching the crowds at the cable car turnaround waiting for a cable car to take them up the steep rise of Russian Hill, back to their hotels downtown. Watching them shiver in their summer anywhere-else-but-San-Francisco clothes, as the fog rolled back in through the Golden Gate.

Ice cream fog. Thick, white and fluffy. Making its evening onslaught on the city as if the sea had gathered up its forces and come to claim the land.

The waiting didn't bother me. Not even the pain in my wrist. I felt exhilarated. Alive to the changing patterns of landscape and weather.

Like Ahab, unwavering in my quest for the great blond brute. Unlike Ahab, I had no intention of going down with him. Inside a brown paper bag, so as not to upset the tourists, my right hand was comfortably wrapped around my Smith and Wesson .22 automatic.

Not the right caliber, I know, for stalking such large prey, but comforting nonetheless. A highly accurate and controllable weapon. Not likely to punch a hole through Terry and take out a couple of innocent bystanders. Although, by all proper standards, I should give it up for a harpoon.

I paced expectantly along the street, fending off the suspicious stares of passing tourists, who noticed my bruised and battered appearance and suspected I had something liquid inside my brown bag. But I was keeping my eyes clear for a sign of Terry's approaching boat.

At ten minutes to five, I spotted Rebecca's banker. He got out of a cab carrying a medium sized leather satchel. A proper man of the proper age wearing a proper blue suit, who stood near the cable car turntable. Nervously. The crowds, the large sum of money he was carrying and the unusual nature of his mission all made him apprehensive.

Ten minutes later a sixty foot sailing boat, running on its auxiliary power, tied up at the end of the pier.

I kept my eye on the banker and positioned myself so that Terry would pass me but not see me as he came off the pier.

A few minutes later Terry and Clementine strolled by, bigger than life. Terry had added a white jacket to his wardrobe and Clementine matched him exactly. Except she was all in black. Cute. They drew appreciative stares as they passed me.

I also noticed Terry's gold peace symbol back in place around his neck. Highly appropriate. He had had the sensitivity to remove it during his not so peaceful visit with Jonathan and Penelope.

I crossed Jefferson and kept about twenty feet behind them. Terry spoke a few words to Rebecca's banker, who gave up his satchel and eagerly trotted off to the bar across the street.

Terry was holding the satchel when they turned and saw me. I smiled and lifted the automatic slightly into view, letting them see it, and then lowered it back into its hiding place.

Terry whispered something to Clementine and passed the satchel to her. She started to walk away.

"Leave the satchel, Clem," I shouted. "Give it back to Terry."

She did as ordered. They exchanged a few more whispers and she walked off, around the corner and out of sight.

As soon as he saw she was safely away, Terry turned and walked over to a cable car that was just pulling out. Without a word he lifted a man off from the front side of the car and took his place, standing on the outside running board. He did it quickly, even gently, and no one dared question his right to do it.

As the cable car crossed Beach and started up the long hill, I caught up with the open left side of the car and bought myself a young boy's place, about four passengers back from Terry, for twenty dollars. I had to fumble for the money and shove the bag and gun under my left arm to do it, but the boy was delighted with my offer. The rest of the passengers weren't.

They eyed my unkempt appearance and my many facial bruises and my shattered cast, intact only around my thumb and fingers. Then they saw my brown paper bag, assumed it contained a bottle, and, somehow, found the extra room to leave a small circle of open space around me.

All for the best. I had to crook my right arm around a pole just to hold on as we crossed Bay and climbed the steepest part of the hill, and I banged my broken wrist in the process. The throbbing set my teeth to grinding.

The cable pulled our overloaded car up the hill at its steady nine mile per hour pace. Me on the left side, about midway back, with my right arm crooked around a pole for balance and my right hand hidden inside my paper bag. Terry about eight feet in front of me, at the front, on the same left side, standing on the outside running board with the leather satchel in his right hand. The Incredible Hulk was also drawing his share of uncertain glances.

We were facing each other, measuring each other's threat, and planning our next moves. He had called this one, with his unexpected hop on the cable car. But I'd be damned if he would call the last one.

"How do you know you've really got four hundred thousand dollars in that satchel? You didn't even look."

Several people near me looked at me incredulously, then stole quick peeks at Terry's bag.

"Oh, I trust Rebecca completely. The money didn't mean anything to her. See."

He unsnapped the top of the satchel and held it out for my inspection. Rows of neatly banded and stacked bills were piled almost to the top. Fresh and crisp. All twenties. Exactly two hundred banded stacks of a hundred bills each, if the count was right.

Every passenger on our side of the car immediately went bug-eyed, and excited murmurs followed when Terry closed the satchel. For a second I thought they were going to give him a round of applause.

Terry was amusing himself, again. Playing double jeopardy, flirting with the hazards of exposure. Like he had that first day I saw him. When he strutted his drug buy in front of the sailors.

But he was also showing me he wasn't afraid. And I believed him. Something in his makeup fed on the thrill of violence and danger, and I was caught up in his primitive game of pursuit and capture. More than caught up. Eager to prevail. To outwit, outmaneuver and outmaster my dangerous opponent.

"Are you really planning to shoot me with the gun you've got hidden in that bag?" he asked, almost politely.

"I'm going to stop you. Whatever it takes."

Psychological banter, establishing our relative positions. Like two dogs circling before a fight.

I got several more incredulous stares and an alarmed buzz went through the car. Passengers began stepping unobtrusively off the slow moving vehicle. We were alone on the car by the time we made the turn onto Washington and started across the saddle between Russian and Nob Hill.

The gripman, cornered in his center position between the benches, studiously ignored us, hoping we would go away, while the fare collector hid at the back end of the car.

"What now?" Terry asked, inquisitively, as he looked restlessly down the street at the old cable car barn.

I nodded toward the intimidated gripman, who was hanging onto his three large metal levers as if they were lifelines.

"We stop the car and have this gentleman go for the cops. Or I shoot you."

I thought the gripman was going to faint as he ratcheted the grip lever forward and stopped the car at Mason Street, just in front of the cable car barn.

Terry looked around and I realized he was searching for something. Maybe Clementine.

"Or I shoot you," I repeated.

"I don't think so," Terry answered, flatly, and quickly jumped off into a crowd of tourists, who swarmed delightedly onto the empty car.

I told the relieved gripman to phone the police and went after Terry.

I felt calm and unhurried, certain that Terry wouldn't get away.

The conviction spread through me on some instinctual, primitive, blood level. The stillness of the hunter as he becomes certain of his prey. I knew I had him. Like a great fish running loose on the end of a long line, thinking it's free.

I forced my way through a group that was entering the cable car barn at the corner entrance for visitors. Just down the block I saw Terry turn into the service entrance of the same building. A half minute later I carefully made the same turn.

Terry was midway across the large open work floor, pushing those long, powerful legs of his in determined strides.

He was heading straight for a catwalk, raised about four feet off the ground, right next to the huge, spinning grooved pulleys that wind the thick metal cable that powers all the city's cable cars. Giant, thick-spoked, spinning steel wheels, ten feet in diameter. Four sets of two each, humming their metallic song as they endlessly wind in and wind out the cable under several miles of city streets.

It seemed it wasn't just fate or chance that brought us to this spot. Right above the catwalk, just above two of the revolving wheels and one of the winding cables, was the mezzanine-level visitors' gallery. And there, among the tourists, was Clementine, standing at the rail, calling down to her great blond giant.

Their whispers when I had first confronted them had been about meeting here. Clementine probably went to get a car or a cab, and Terry was to lose me through the work area, use the catwalk's railing to climb up to the gallery, and escape by the other entrance.

I was just about to run back to the visitors' entrance when Terry was stopped by three workman, just twenty feet short of the catwalk and his climb to the gallery.

Terry faked a turn as if leaving and then swept his right arm around and sent two of the workers sprawling. Then he made a long, underhanded swing of his left arm and heaved the leather satchel up to the gallery. The startled visitors scrambled out of its way, and Clementine retrieved it.

I ran back up the street to the visitors' entrance and up the flight of stairs to the gallery, where I had to force my way through the crowd to reach the railing.

It was now a three ring circus, below on the work floor. Six or seven mechanics in blue coveralls were circling wide around Terry. One of them had a three foot long metal pipe. Just out of the human circle's ring were three men, stretched out on the floor, each in totally different directions, obviously injured. They had already tried their luck in the center of the ring. And lost.

Twenty feet down the railing from me was Clementine with the satchel at her feet. She hadn't seen me yet and was jumping up and down like an excited fan at the Saturday night fights. Screaming encouragement down to her defiant champion.

"Com'on, baby! Come to mama! Those shooflies can't stop you. No...no..no! Nobody can stop you, baby!"

And the tourists kept gawking, half revulsion, half fascination. And the workers below kept circling, building their courage for an assault.

The scene reminded me of King Kong on the Empire State building, with all the airplanes buzzing around him. But this blond giant was no sympathetic victim. He was a killer.

I made my way down to Clementine with my gun out of the paper bag. She saw it and me when some woman screamed, "he's got a gun," and half the crowd raced for the exit. Terry looked up at the commotion, and that's when they rushed him.

He sent the first two who reached him flying. Picked another up and used him as a battering ram to break out of the circle. But the man with the pipe got a good swing with it across Terry's back. Clementine saw it hit him and screamed, "Terrrrry!"

He had almost gone down, but, within a second, the man who hit him was crumpled on the floor and Terry had the pipe. And he was looking up, right into my eyes.

Clementine pounced on me, feline-like, just as I saw Terry drop the pipe and sprint for the catwalk and the railing.

Her attack spun me around and she got hold of my broken wrist and held on with all her strength as I tried to shake her off. White light began seeping behind my eyes, into my brain, and I almost passed out. My right hand opened and the gun clattered to the floor. My vision was blurring as I saw Terry's huge hands come up from the catwalk below and grab onto the railing in front of me.

Once again Trimbler's ghastly stare of death passed before my eyes and I could almost hear the soon-to-be sounds of my bones cracking. That great fish at the end of my line had turned back into a shark, turned round on me, and was gobbling up the line, heading straight for me.

I got my right hand into Clementine's thick, long hair and yanked back hard enough to break her neck. But it didn't. She was hanging on demonically, screaming a high pitched shriek like a banshee. And Terry almost had one leg over the railing.

Desperately, I jerked Clementine's head forward and butted her smack in the face with my head. With her high heels she was about six-four, and, ramming my head down, I caught her full on the bridge of her nose. Warm blood spurted onto my face as she lost consciousness and let go of my wrist.

Paralyzed tourists were screaming all around me and I could hear sirens and the screech of tires outside.

But Terry was still coming. He was just clearing the railing as I swung Clementine violently by her hair and pitched her right at him. The stumbling weight of her caught Terry chest high, just before he had his feet firmly on the floor, and he tumbled backwards over the railing. Clementine caught on the railing and toppled to the floor.

The screaming intensified until I couldn't distinguish it from all the sirens, and I saw cops running in through the service entrance.

My entire left arm felt like I was holding it in a fire, but my vision was clearing. I stumbled up to the railing and looked down.

The great humming wheels were silent. Stopped. Terry had landed on the cable and flipped under it into the massive steel spokes.

He lay there now. Wedged in the slot where the lower half of the great wheel dips down into its sunken concrete well. He was broken. Mangled. Far worse than Trimbler stuffed in the dryer. Like a heap of rags and discarded garbage. Beyond recognition.

Except for all the blood. Only the blood spoke of his human form. It covered the white paint of the giant spokes. Was still dripping from the parts of the silent wheel. Splattered for ten feet around.

I bent down and checked Clementine's pulse. She was still breathing. I straightened up and wiped her blood from my own face. Looked at it on my hands, and thought of Michael. And wondered if he would finally be free.

TWENTY-TWO

After some initial confusion with the police, when they tried to arrest me for assaulting Clementine with a gun, I managed to clear things up.

Tied Terry into Trimbler's murder, and had them contact the Monterey County Sheriff's Department about Terry's more recent crimes. Then, pleading extreme pain, I had them take me back to Children's Hospital where they reset my wrist and kept me overnight.

The next morning I awoke to Molly's smiling face. Also, a heavy, white plaster cast that covered my arm from my wrist to just below my shoulder. My new compound fracture required absolute rigidity to heal, and they weren't taking any chances.

After hearing about the carnage at the Sherwin Institute last night, Molly said she drove up to San Francisco in a panic, her imagination running wild with fears that I'd actually catch up with Terry and she'd lose me.

Said she heard about me on the evening news when the entire cable car system came to a grinding halt. Said she got to the hospital last night, but they wouldn't let her see me. Said she was grateful that I was only slightly mangled. Said it smiling, as she signed my cast: If lost, return to Molly Dugan.

After two more hours of police questioning and almost another hour answering questions from an unruly group of reporters,

I checked out of the hospital at noon. Despite my handicap, I insisted we pick up both my cars. The Jeep at the Hyde Street Pier had the expected ticket on the windshield and the Mercedes had accumulated seventy-five dollars in parking fees.

Molly insisted I wasn't fully recovered and that we spend the night in town and start for Monterey the next day. Anyway, she claimed I had promised she could soothe my bruised brow after every fight, and she was going to hold me to it.

So we went back to my place where she made me feel that every bruise on my body was a badge of honor and deserved special attention.

We got into Monterey at noon the next day and went straight to Michael's hospital. My cast was awkward but I was feeling really good, despite the preponderance of hospitals in my life lately. It seemed all the killings and all the recent horror had not produced new nightmares, but purged the air of the past's troubled dreams.

One look inside Michael's room made it all worthwhile. He was sitting up in bed listening to his new daughter. Katie was going a mile a minute, filling him in on the important experiences of her life, allowing no hesitation or embarrassment to interfere, as she finally claimed the lost father she had so long been missing.

Michael was listening to her and watching her with bemused amazement. And, for the first time since I had seen him, and probably for the first time ever, he looked completely contented to be exactly where he was.

When Katie saw us enter the room, she ran over and threw her arms around my neck and whispered in my ear, "thank you."

I saw in her bright, youthful eyes that strong light of forming character that would successfully lead her in her passage from girl to woman. And I saw it reflected in Molly's eyes, too, when I looked over at her. A family strength safely passed down to the next generation.

Katie stood back from me, positively glowing, and winked at me.

"You look like you could use a vacation," she said, conspiratorially. Then she turned to her mother. "And I'm almost eighteen and old enough to look after the restaurants. At least for a week or so," she added, mischievously, as she left the room.

When she was gone, we went through the entire messy story. Told Michael about Terry's death after killing Jonathan and Penelope. Told him about Rebecca taking poison and about his real mother and her violent death, and that no one else knew who his real father was.

I looked carefully at Michael, wondering how he felt. He had lost two entire families and found a daughter he didn't even know he had. He had also lost his once potential wife and was seeing her again for the first time in eighteen years.

So, I stared at him. Like I was peering into a crystal ball, searching for future problems. But I could find no ill-omened signs. He had looked horror in the face for so long that he was now calm.

Unbelievably, his troubled life finally seemed to have been blessed, and he had emerged from his bloody, thirty-nine year nightmare, washed clean.

He realized what I was thinking.

"I want to thank both of you," he said, his voice filled with gratitude. "When I get out of here in a few days, I'm going back up to my orchards. But I promise not to disappear again. And I've promised Katie that she can come up and see me, if that's okay with you?"

I looked at Molly and then I went out into the hall and left them alone. Five minutes later she came out.

"He apologized and I didn't know what to say. Katie can talk with him for hours, but I feel like I never knew him. For her, he's an exciting new person. For me, he's the lost past. Does that make sense?"

"I don't think it could be any other way."

"Well, I'm very happy that he's finally free from that evil cloud he lived in. And I think he's going to be good for Katie. He gave me this."

She handed me a folded sheet of note paper.

"He said it was appropriate that he give me a new quote to replace the one he sent me after he disappeared."

I unfolded the paper.

"He said the quote was from Job, from the end of Moby Dick, when the ship is sunk by the great white whale and only Ishmael survives, saved by a floating wooden coffin."

It read: "And I only am escaped...."

We spent the rest of the afternoon at the Monterey County Sheriff's office answering more questions. At least this time I knew the answers. Then I went another round with yet another group of eager reporters who were especially interested in the more sensational aspects of the case. Their altruistic hearts showed unusual concern about who had a legal right to the vast Sherwin fortune. That was one question I couldn't answer, except I knew Michael wanted no part of it.

I finally freed myself, and, after Molly and I reached the quiet and safety of my car, I said, "Let's run over to Harriet Nilsson's house. She said she loves mysteries and we promised her the rest of the Sherwin story, and I'd like to wrap up all the loose ends before we leave town."

"Leave town? Where are we going?"

"Down into the desert. Into the purifying, searing heat of its long days and the rejuvenating vigor of its starry nights."

"Are we going to be hermits and deprive ourselves of all earthly pleasures?"

"Hell, no! I'm talking Las Vegas. I'm going to show you its hot bright days and the balmy, colored-light nights of its beautiful neon heart."

AFTERWARD

THE ART OF THE DETECTIVE NOVEL
BY JIM COYLE

August 7, 1986

American detective fiction is existential, as opposed to the British mystery which is more cerebral. The American detective hero does not think things out. He gets involved, has and suffers various experiences and gradually pieces together random elements until he can see the entire picture, usually just before the novel ends.

With almost no exceptions, he is not married. At the best he had a happy marriage but his wife died. Usually, he is unhappily, even bitterly divorced, or often he has never been married. Anyway it's done, the woman has to be disposed of on a meaningful day-to-day level.

The woman exists in his world as a victim, a client and, sometimes, as a bed playmate. The relationship is valued but usually doesn't last long. Sometimes the woman is elevated to a regular helpmate and love-mate but he still does not marry her or even live with her regularly.

This brings us to the soul of the detective. He is the modern wounded male who preserves and practices the vanishing code of male ethics and integrity. Like Lancelot he has glimpsed a vision

— 273 —

of purity and true love, but he can never find it in the real world. And since the real world he moves in is dark and dangerous, the detective's mode of perception is never the same as the society he inhabits. Irony and even cynicism are the result. This allows endless opportunities for the detective to function as an actual *"eye"* that sees and comments on the world, and is a lot of fun.

So, what are the traits of the American detective novel? Go for the lurid and sensational since it's a deceptive and sinister world out there. Ulysses' epic voyage home would have been no fun at all if he had just encountered wine merchants and shepherds. So, go the whole nine yards, join the great romantic American tradition of the fantastic (like Moby Dick) but make it fun and believable according to its own exaggerated forms.

Character development is purely functional and our detective hero can never be fully rounded or developed. He must remain a partial blank. It is his experiences in the dark world you create for him and his integrity under pressure that hints at a depth of character we never see. He is an eye for the reader to see through and it is that act of perceiving which is the center of the detective novel. Not the character of the detective, but the character of the detective as he perceives is the center. If you want to develop character more you would have to write a different form of novel.

Now this is just the way I see the form when it is used at its best. Most detective writers seem to embody much of the same view but many get bogged down along the way. One of the elements I get very bored with but is very popular with most readers(judging by sales)is the endless discussion of what I call "macho" ethics. Which simply translates into endless prose about how a man should act. Such things should remain unexplained and only be shown through actions.

So, here are some of the standard traits I had to deal with. I am tired of the American hero who can't deal with women. He wants to but can only manage a very limited and frequently maudlin and self-pitying success. Again, this is a tremendous feature of these books and obviously appeals to most readers. Endless prose is penned positioning the detective vis-à-vis the female. The strong male might be able to deal unflinchingly with almost any horror but he needs a quart of scotch to cope with his unsatisfying love life.

And yet the form does demand (unless you go for The Thin Man) a male domain free from a permanent intruding female. So, my solution was to have Walker come from a very successful relationship that ended tragically. This way Walker is not a total failure at love but love doesn't have to get in the way (you would have to read a lot of these books to realize how often this comes up).

Molly will be Walker's running helpmate. I'm going to try to make her more positive as a woman (again you can't realize how badly women usually fare in these books) and yet I have to keep their relationship like the characters on the Grecian Urn. It's like a comic strip, if you plan to run them through a series of novels. You can never complete the original picture of your characters, just add new elements. You can't do anything drastically different here, you just try for a coloring of originality.

To sum up, the hero is obviously wounded and not fully functioning with a woman, but I prefer to keep this problem on a limited level. Many books make speculation about this a main part of the book and many readers seem to get off on it so I might be in trouble. However, I still find the wounded male hero honorable, if he isn't always wallowing in his agony.

Another major concern for me was plot. I like a complicated plot. Most of these books have very little mystery or tension in them. They're like a television show that just takes you through the basic elements of the genre. But I wanted that deceptive world out there and its interaction with the normal world that's "seen" to hint at the very nature of perception. That's why Walker says bright sunlight, not fog, is the proper medium for illusion because you think you know what you are seeing. Hence, the illusion of the floating island in bright sunlight which seems real but is not and the strawberry field in the fog which can't even be seen but is perceived, nonetheless, as palpably real.

Also there is frequently a conflict between descriptive prose and dialogue. Many writers shun description and opt for dialogue to carry all the weight. Description can slow the movement down unless it's done well and many writers keep things moving with dialogue. Also, dialogue produces a less dense look in print and doesn't intimidate many potential readers(such mundane things must be considered).

Again, I wanted both. And I went for both. I feel that it's great to carry the plot forward through dialogue but description can add a lot of substance and offers many opportunities to externalize and project character traits, motivation and plot. So my goal is to use both. Most writers come down mainly on dialogue. The novel Fletch (Chevy Chase made a very successful movie of it last year that I enjoyed) has almost no description at all. It's 98% dialogue. Also the use of the detective's private narration(his own musings) is a great device that's fun to work with.

Another major concern of mine was place. Many writers are very sloppy about the place of action. They sometimes create imaginary towns or even if they use real cities (which they usually do) they are not that accurate and do not make the location a real part of the novel. At least not for my taste. So I went all out and plan to capitalize on my sense of California and New York and any other place I take Walker.

Detective fiction has created a thriving sense of regionalism. There are San Francisco and New York detectives and Los Angeles is still the preferred choice. But there are two detectives set in Seattle, one in Boston, one in Indianapolis, one in Cincinnati. There is even a series with an openly homosexual claims investigator (insurance) working out of Los Angeles.

And then there's the most successful character of all who's not really a detective but a "salvage" operator who takes on cases just like detectives but claims half of what's at stake. This is Travis McGee who operates out of a houseboat in a marina in Ft. Lauderdale. John Macdonald (the author) is the best writer of them all but his plots are never totally satisfying and Travis McGee is an example of too much speculating about women. He's always redeeming one, then losing her. Anyway, I admire John Macdonald's writing most of all but not his plots or his main character, although I enjoy them, nevertheless.

Another issue is that the hero is usually an ex-cop(I chose an actor for literary opportunity) who doesn't get along with the police. It's definitely a tense relationship with the police always pissed that the detective is messing with their affairs. I chose to avoid that just to be different and even gave Walker relatives on the force. You see, you have to give him some access to the police because he will need to use their vast organization at times. Frequently, this is resolved by giving him one cop friend who's always giving the detective a hard time but secretly is in love with him and does him favors. I chose to make Walker's conflicts more personal and less societal and organizational and political.

Which brings up another choice of mine. It is fashionable today to make the source of evil external. Either big business, big government, the military, politicians etc. I chose to keep evil a personal affair even if the villain is in one of the above. It personally scares me that people seem to get off on blaming large organizations and thereby absolving themselves. So, in Walker's world, evil is definitely a personal issue.

Which brings up the problem of why Walker does what he does. The detective feeds to some extent off of other peoples' problems. That's a given. He's a moralistic voyeur.

But why? Usually it's because of personal problems. That's why the detective can't deal with women more successfully. If he could he would be more integrated into society and less willing to risk the danger of his job. Think of how many movies have the conflict between the cop or detective's dangerous job and the wife's complaints, Madigan, for just one. That's also why the detective lives on the fringes of society. He's an outsider who feeds off his job and leaves the social amenities behind. Remember in the movie how Harper has to force himself awake in the morning and uses coffee grounds from yesterday's garbage.

So usually the detective has a seedy apartment and a seedy office and a rundown car. And he drinks and womanizes and lives for his case where he comes alive focusing on other people's problems. Making his small contribution by helping heal the wounds of the world around him. But remember, "physician heal thyself!" The detective is the wounded physician. That's why he understands the ills around him. But he never really fully heals himself. He keeps trying by solving other people's problems.

That's his real motivation and his integrity.

Well, I opted for Walker to be psychologically hooked, more than economically or sociologically. I wanted Walker to be in the business for pure personal reasons. He found himself in the underside of life by falling in through the top, as he says. Because of the violent death of his wife the hook in him--his never healing wound--is being prepared for evil. Always looking for what isn't seen.

I've generally tried to keep within the expected conventions but I varied some for personal taste. I wanted mainly to emphasize the element of choice for Walker. He was forced in not by being down and out but by life itself. In other words he has the means to do other things but chooses not to.

LaVergne, TN USA
15 December 2009

167003LV00002B/8/P